# WHEN DEATH PARTS US

## KATHRYN KNAPP

Published by Kathryn Knapp LLC in Nashville, TN

ISBN 979-8-9941071-0-2
Preassigned Control Number application on file with Library of Congress

**Warning:** This story was written for adult readers and includes mature
language, bloody violence, explicit sexual acts, captivity, human
trafficking, and assault.

Dearest Reader,

   *Thank you* for picking up my debut novel. Know that you are making my day by reading it. Whether it's over a cup of tea or a glass of wine, in your favorite coffee shop, nestled in front of a fire, or sunning on a beach. Or with a rotisserie chicken in your car because it's *that* kind of day. I'm honored you chose my book and truly hope you enjoy this story.

   Welcome to the first installment of *The Curse of the Vampire Series: When Death Parts Us.* This is a prelude and introduces a found family and love stories you will be eager to open Book 2 for.

   Please note: This book has a sprinkling of spice and the start of a slow-burn storyline, setting the stage for the series.

   All good things taste better when they're earned.
   Let's sink our teeth in slowly, shall we?

   Happy reading, my darlings!

For my parents,
who sharpened my blades
and sent me into battle with everything I need to survive

# CARAVIA

GOREON KINGDOM

GOREON CASTLE

BROADBANK

NORTHERN WALL

*SEREIA SEA*

THE SANCTUARY

CASTLE PROSPERITY

MORTIFER FORTRESS

GOREON CITY

SOUTHEND

CASTLE DEATH

OLD TRITAN TERRITORY

CASTLE RUTHLESSNESS

MEADOWBROOK

NIGHT KINGDOM

ARMY ESTATE

LILYGATE

SICARIUS CHANNEL

# CHAPTER 1

## VEYA

Present Day

IT'S BEEN CENTURIES, and I still haven't killed him.

I crumple the correspondence from my scouts in my fist and shove it into my gown's hidden pocket, pacing the turret I've stashed myself in.

We know so little about King Nerian of Goreon's defenses, and I can't convince myself to jeopardize my warriors and attack blindly. Nerian should have an army, but my scouts can't fucking find them anywhere. They can't get eyes on numbers, skill, location—none of it.

All they've found is the squalor and the suffering.

This king has forced his humans to scrap for survival as he consumes the land with his wealth, spreading vampire estates and leaving few options left for the remaining humans. And he feeds with no limits, allowing his vampire population to drink from the vein, fueling bloodlust that can lead to a dangerous addiction. Not to mention the killing of humans at an alarming pace. And when his human population dwindled, he began stealing lives from his neighboring territories.

Including ours.

So we locked our borders down tight as soon as we finished the construction of the Northern Wall eighty years ago. No vampire has been allowed to pass into the Night Kingdom from Goreon. It is a risk we will not take, and crossing our wall is now a death sentence.

My army makes sure of it.

Dress shoes clicking against stone pull my attention.

"Ah! *There you are*," Prince Hathin slurs. "Been looking for you *everywhere*, Queen Veya." The foreign prince hangs in the stone doorway, holding himself upright in his embroidered cream suit, somehow without stains today.

This one is always drunk.

I smile sweetly, plastering on a well-practiced mask. "You found me. Well done," I praise in a honeyed voice.

"Indeed—"

Hathin begins an obnoxious tirade, droning on about how bored he is. I try not to sigh at him. He's been visiting for weeks, dragging on about his lack of amusement with all the hard work he's undergoing to expand his kingdom in the isles of the Sereia Sea. And I can't help when my focus returns to much more pressing matters.

I rest an elbow on the window ledge, letting my frustration exhale into the cold breeze, gaze sweeping over my kingdom—my entire heart.

This note from my scouts is infuriating. I'm so tired of waiting to take Goreon Kingdom. I've spent the last century eliminating evil on my borders, but this target remains out of reach.

"Are you *listening* to me, my queen?" Hathin demands.

I turn back to the prince, yanking my gaze from the lightening night sky beyond. "Of course. You were saying you needed some entertainment before we rest today."

He winks and steps his muscled form through the archway. Hathin is handsome, and he uses it like a weapon.

The male drinks me in, sauntering away the distance between us, and helps himself into my space. "I believe we'll be great together, you and I," Prince Hathin drawls, dragging his gloved hand down my neck like he already owns me.

I have no interest in joining our territories; our beliefs could not be further apart. Hathin is only marginally better than Nerian. This prince has forced his humans to expedite the construction of his cities under his *motivation* law, as he refers to it. One member of every human family is taken for vampire consumption, and in the wake of their unimaginable loss, that family is then threatened. Because unless they want to lose more loved ones, the remaining members strong enough to work are thrown into continuous labor. And that labor eventually, typically, results in their death. Innocent humans are required to make an impossible choice. Die now, or die later.

So I've led Hathin to believe we have a future together, I needed his trust to get this close in private.

Bells toll through the large open window beside us, warning of the sunrise. The light I need is just moments away.

"You know, I'm glad you found me, Hathin."

His strong hand grips my waist, pulling me closer with a curling grin, and I let him.

"Is that so, my queen?" he purrs, the liquor on his breath violating.

I hum at him, staring into Hathin's lustful blue eyes as the soft pink of dawn peeks behind him, and my heart races with adrenaline.

Fangs snap from my gums, and I lunge for the vampire, ripping out his throat in a single bite. Those glacier blue eyes blow wide, and I shove the stunned male with all of my strength, pushing him through the open window to his death.

I retreat into shadow and watch his body burn under the first rays of daylight cresting the horizon, eliminating his threat to my kingdom, and his own. I ignore the biting doubt that my methods are ethical, because I just saved *countless* lives.

As I spin to the stairwell, my gown rustles, a thousand swatches of layered plum and black tulle commanding more territory than the doorway I'm dragging it through. I descend the turret, relief flooding me as I wipe the cold blood of another eligible prince from my lips and chin. Two weeks of courting and lying, of disingenuous glances and empty promises, and feigning interest in his assets across the Sereia Sea. But I played the exhausting game I've perfected over the last century because this prince deserved a swift and quiet death sentence.

Cursing, I lift my skirts higher as they threaten to trip me down the stairwell in my haste to leave my morning behind.

"My queen," Emmanuel says at the bottom of the stairs, offering an elbow.

"Good morning, Em," I say, taking his arm. We sashay into the dazzling throne room, welcomed by the candlelight of a thousand flickering wicks dancing against the shining cream marble.

I survey my court enjoying the last moments of their night before resting as we walk the center aisle, the mountain of tulle trailing us. Emmanuel's rich black hair matching his fine suiting, sculpted cheekbones, and strong jawline turns heads as we stroll. Em is one of my best-kept secrets. His naturally brooding self is often masked behind a pristine smile, and no one beyond my trusted circle knows Emmanuel is my best assassin.

So good, in fact, that he'd been sent to kill me when he was human.

"Did you handle it?" he asks.

"It's done."

"Hathin was so drunk. I didn't think he'd make it up the damn stairwell to you," he laughs, that perfect smile pointed ahead.

"I'm thrilled he did," I say, glad Prince Hathin is in our past.

He peers at me with a tilt of his chin. "So, who's next?"

I chuckle at his eagerness and let my gaze drift to the Gothic carved arches above us, reaching across the broad expanse, as I think through my decision. I stare longingly at the only opening to the outside world in this hall: a darkened skylight, centered a few yards in front of my throne. It's spelled to become transparent upon my signal, burning and destroying vampiric threats as needed. Thankfully, I haven't used it on others in decades.

We approach the raised dais, and I know my answer. "We focus on the isles. Sereia Sea could be neutralized within the next couple of years."

*Goreon can wait a bit longer.*

"I agree," Emmanuel says, departing from my side as I ascend the seven steps to my throne, conversations echoing softly up the high stone walls. The corpses of each corrupt fallen ruler who stood in my way to secure the Night Kingdom territory are entombed in the stone below my feet, their names engraved on each riser I climb. The architect of this beautiful room grumbled at the offense of burying bodies in the stone, but I never want to lose sight of the pain we went through, the lives we lost. Especially in the pretty throne room. We will *always* remember what's important.

The room silences and bows to me.

"Please rise," I command, heart full as I look upon the trustworthy souls before me. My ambition and relentless effort have protected them, and all of the citizens beyond these walls, creating a place of peace and safety for vampires and humans alike. It's my greatest accomplishment and my greatest treasure.

The antechamber doors whip open, and my focus jerks up.

Second strides through them like he owns the place.

My second never gave himself a vampire name when he asked me to turn him centuries ago; he insisted his station was his identity, and that was enough. So, he's Second, by station and by name.

A grin pulls joyfully at my lips as he barrels down the grand hall. I'm grateful for his presence after my morning. We share my vision for this kingdom, and we've worked tirelessly together to see that vision come to fruition.

"You won't believe it," Second warns as his massive form and long gait close our distance in moments. That's a benefit too: He's a naturally made bodyguard.

My eyes land on the letter he clutches. "What is it?" I ask, my insides jumping. Second is the closest thing I have to a brother in this life, and I know him *well*—he's rarely flustered by anything.

"A letter from Goreon."

My body stills, the predator within me stiffening, and hushed whispers race through the room.

"You're right," I say. "I *don't* believe it."

We *rarely* correspond between kingdoms. Vampires and their secrets rule this world.

And that silence is how I've quietly eliminated so many of my enemies. They handed me a wide-open door to lure princes under the pretense of courting for the position of king and assassinate my way to securing our borders, ensuring the Night Kingdom's stability and way of life. Because no one talks, no one communicates their losses.

Second climbs the tomb steps two at a time to hand me the letter.

"Charlotte and Emmanuel, stay. Everyone else, please leave us," I say, and the throne room empties outside of my three most trusted counselors.

I run my fingers along the fine parchment before ripping open the gold-and-black seal and threading the letter out of its envelope. My eyes scan the scrawled cursive, and the giddiness of surprise curls in my chest.

I can't believe it: It's an invitation to his court.

I read the letter again and pause at the king's requested arrival time, which is within the week.

*Not a lot of time to prepare.*

My gaze flicks to Second. "Nerian's inviting us to his court for discussions."

He rakes back his chestnut hair, anger palpable—or maybe it's fear. "Discussions for what?"

"Our peaceful surrender."

Second belts a laugh, thick lips stretching into a confident smile. "Not a chance."

"Agreed."

I stuff the letter back in the envelope. The terms of our surrender include a marriage proposal to Nerian. I'm fairly certain Second won't agree to this visit if he knows what's at stake in our negotiations. But I'm willing to risk just about anything to get close enough to kill this king—like disappointing Second by withholding some of this letter, or letting Nerian think he might have a chance with me.

"This is our way in," I say, hope and eagerness twisting inside me at the opportunity I've wanted for so long. My fangs pop—I'm unable to suppress my joy—and my focus lands on Emmanuel and Charlotte. "How would you like to join me in Goreon as the queen's attendants?"

They grin, and Charlotte offers a bow, long blonde curls dipping toward me. "I can't *wait* to sink my fangs into some filth," she says, eyes flashing red above her perfect pink cheeks sitting atop high cheekbones.

"I couldn't agree more," I assure her, lip lifting in anticipatory excitement.

Charlotte is everything you could want in a diabolically dedicated courtier who plays chess and wields knives with equal skill. And she has been many things to me over the years, but most of all, she is my friend. Decades ago, she waltzed into my castle and *demanded* an audience with me. The human girl got on her knees, swore her fealty, and begged me to change her. I don't wish this existence on anyone, but there was something about her power and poise in that commanding moment, standing in front of her queen and choosing the life she wanted for herself, that had me bending my own rules. I don't like to turn others—I don't want to live with the guilt of the decision they may someday regret. So, I rarely do it.

But I've never regretted turning Charlotte. And neither has she.

Second paces the dais.

"Something to add, Second?" I ask.

He stops mid-stride and turns to me, face stern. "I don't fucking like it." The vampire wears the agony of losing his humanity like a cloak, always shrouded in it, and his temper runs hot from the pain still itching at his skin. But it makes him focused, callous even, which produces an effective second to the crown. Although I still hate that he suffers as much as he does.

I'd take the burden of it from him if I could.

Second soothes the pain of his losses by protecting those who remain in his life. So a risky, borderline suicide mission to Goreon disguised as a cordial peace discussion has him seeing red.

"Of course you don't like it," I laugh, trying not to roll my eyes at the poor male.

"*Don't* make light of your safety," he snarls back.

My lips press into a thin line, and I let his words wash over me. He's one of only a few I would ever tolerate such a tone from.

"You're right," I say finally, nodding at him.

He scoffs. "Of course I'm right."

"But we have to go," I say, holding up the letter.

Second crosses his thick arms and tosses his head back to stare at the ceiling. "I know," he says after a long moment and dips his chin to look right at me. "Doesn't mean I have to like it."

"We've been trying to orchestrate a way in for decades. This is our best shot."

"I know that, too. And I wouldn't ask you to pass up the opportunity to walk through the front fucking door," he says and then points a finger at me. "But we need a plan. We need to be sure of your safety there."

"I agree."

"Good. I have a meeting with Officer Maya upstairs; there's rumors of a stirring in the Southern Continent. Join us when you're done so we can strategize our visit up north," he says, spinning on his heel and speeding down the hall. "And I'm going with you to Goreon!" he shouts, disappearing through the doors before I can tell him any different.

Charlotte clears her throat politely. "You won't talk him out of it."

I ease back into my throne, slipping the letter into my pocket. "I rarely do."

Emmanuel lifts a blood pitcher off its warming candle and pours himself a glass. We don't drink from the vein. A single bite will turn a human, and doing so against someone's will is punishable by death in the Night Kingdom. But those who live here have no complaints. We *chose* this way of life.

Bicep flexing as he casually swirls his goblet, Em looks up at me. "Did the letter say when they're expecting us?"

My eyes meet his. "Within the week."

Emmanuel curses and slams the contents of his glass. "I need liquor."

I'm about to walk into Goreon, and failure isn't an option—for my kingdom, for the human lives in Goreon, and for the long-held promises I made to nullify this threat. I need to take the edge off. "Pour me one, too," I tell Em.

It's a heady feeling, being so close to what I've wanted for so long, yet I know what this letter is.

A trap.

Emmanuel's dress shoes clack along the marble to the cabinet beside the dais. "Charlotte?" he asks, snatching the whiskey bottle.

"Gods, yes please," she sighs.

Vampires digest one thing well—human blood. Liquor hits us like the poison it is, and vampire tolerance is pitiful when stacked up against that of humans.

Emmanuel pours the auburn liquid, serving me, then Charlotte, then himself. "Well, I guess we're spending a full moon in enemy territory," he laughs. "It's going to be interesting."

I groan loudly, I haven't thought that far ahead yet.
*The full moon.*

For one night, every month, vampires are forced to relive our humanity. The torment of our memories comes to life, and we dreamwalk through them. We don't get to choose what we experience when trapped in our human reality for a night. We're thrown in, reminded of all we've lost, and then we wake up—wholly broken all over again.

Our memories *never* fade. We endure pain we can *never* push past. Because it's always there, haunting and relentless. But since we're all equally vulnerable on the full moon, including the king, it's nothing more than an inconvenience in enemy territory.

I look my people in the eyes and raise my glass. "To the king we're going to kill. No matter what they put in our path."

I will do this. I have to do this.

*With all that I am.*

Emmanuel nods at me, and Charlotte winks before we drink and numb ourselves for the day.

I enjoy my last sip, body finally calming against the onslaught of nerves. "Go rest," I say. "We'll leave at sunset and stop by the estate and wherever else you'd like to remind ourselves of what we're walking into enemy territory for."

Emmanuel's eyes shift to mine. "I don't think any of us need a reminder."

"Fair. But I need to say goodbye. Just in case."

Charlotte sighs and plops down on the steps, her chiffon pooling around her in a giant pink puddle. "It won't be goodbye."

Emmanuel looks down at her, swirling his drink. "Well, if Char *says* so."

She tilts her chin, pinning him in place with a glare. "Watch it, Em. Positivity is never a bad thing."

"It is when you ignore reality with it."

She scoffs around her smile. "Good thing you're coming along and will never let us lose."

He peels a finger from his glass and points at her. "Good thing."

*Gods, I adore these people.*

"I'll see you both in a few hours. Thank you in advance for what you're giving," I say.

They nod and exit through the large wooden doors as I fall back into my seat.

My gaze shifting to the skylight, I summon the transparency, and blinding morning light beams down in front of me. Sighing into the stillness, I descend toward the enticing sunshine.

Slowly, I extend my fingertips within reach of the warmth, and the burning rays of light drench me in memories of my humanity, of the life I loved with every fiber, every now-dead piece of me. A life I was forced to abandon as the fangs of death turned me.

My anger surges, and I plunge my hand into the sun streaks and watch myself sear, savoring the pain, as though it can burn away the anguish I still feel from losing everything.

With a press of my lips, I yank myself back into shadow before my skin melts, and I summon the window shut, blinking away tears but holding on to the pain that fuels me.

The throne room's doors fly open at the flick of my wrist, and I depart to the war room to meet Second.

I stuff my nerves down with a swallow. King Nerian is already setting me on edge. Because we need to leave by *tonight* to make it in time.

But our moment to force Goreon to its knees and honor its innocent citizens with the life they deserve is *finally* here.

# CHAPTER 2

## KADE

Two Hundred Years Ago – Goreon Kingdom

AN EMPTY BARSTOOL at Lou's is never a good sign. And the one beside me that's been vacant for a week has wrecked me.

Chin on my knuckles, I stare at the liquor bottles, glassware clanking around the tavern. Lou slaps a rag over his shoulder and pours out more drinks while my gaze drags to Mother Diane's barstool.

She warmed the seat since before I started coming here, and we're pretty damn sure she's been taken. Mother Diane isn't the first to disappear—she's one of thousands the Goreon king has taken over the years—but she was my friend and the mother of a fallen warrior.

The Hunter within stirs, needing revenge.

I grasp the whiskey glass staining a ring into the wood, my rage burning. This bar top should have grooves in the shape of my bone with how many hours I've spent on my stool over the years.

Lou pushes the bottle of bourbon my way, and I shake my head. "I'm good. Still saving up for that summer home."

The tavern owner chuckles as he pours himself a drink before placing it back on the shelf. "For the one month out of the year we see sunshine."

I snort. "We need a place away from it all, you know?"

He takes a swig of his drink before responding. "Yeah, Kade. I get it."

I blow out a breath. "Has anyone checked for Mother Diane today?"

Lou leans an elbow on the bar, bushy eyebrows scrunched. "I don't think so. I went yesterday. House was still empty."

"Aye. I'll stop by on the way home."

Lou pats the bar. "Thank you, Captain."

I nod. "Of course."

He leans in closer, voice dropping. "How are the men doing with Tuck?"

*Gods, it's been a shit day.*

I shake my head with a huff. "Never easy to lose a Hunter. Even if he wasn't truly one of us, you know?"

"Lesson learned, eh?" Lou says, sipping through a sigh.

"Yeah. Lesson fucking learned, Lou." I tip the rest of my whiskey into my mouth as he rests both elbows on the bar to look me square in the eye.

"You tried, boy," he says. "It was worth a shot. We need more Hunters out there."

*Don't I know it.*

I groan, sore body shifting in my chair, and my glass thuds onto the bar top. Thankfully, I know how to squelch the anger from my losses, to bury it so fucking deep and catalog the pain for later. "Yeah, we do need more men. And I'm about to send half of them to the Night Kingdom territories."

Lou clears my glass, swiping the rag from his shoulder along the bar in its wake. "Aye, I heard we're losing ground down there."

"Yeah, Southern Continent vamps are crossing the channel to take advantage of the upheaval. We can't give up all that progress."

"Damn straight, we can't." The deep wrinkles around Lou's eyes crease with his frustration. "We've been working on that territory for *too long*, and Mother Diane's son didn't die for no fucking reason."

"Agreed," I growl. "Forever may he rest."

"Forever may he rest," Lou replies.

We're taking it from all angles. In the south, the Night Kingdom territory is a mess with no ruler in place, but it's given us an opportunity to try to eradicate the unstable vampire population that can't put together coordinated efforts. Goreon is just the opposite: The Goreon king's speed and strength, his wealth and army, and his ravenous bloodlust have everyone timid; his court bows to his whims. We live in *his* world, but the time is coming—we can't continue with the way things are.

The era of the Hunter will dawn. Soon. And I've been training *our* army while we work tirelessly to protect our towns as far as we can stretch our warriors.

I throw a coin on the counter and snatch my cloak from the stool beside me. It floats over the knives sheathed at my hips, and I stride for the exit.

"See you tomorrow, Kade?"

I wave without looking back. "See you then, Lou."

The mangled wooden door slams, and my eyes adjust to the darkness within a second, my magic whirring, golden threads spinning and humming in my veins.

Mother Diane lives two streets over, and the doorknob of her cottage rattles in its hole when I let myself in. The house is dark, the air damp with the lack of fire and life.

I slip inside through a curtain of mildew and strike a candle. My eyes skirt to the unmade bed and piled dishes in the single-room home. Empty liquor bottles are littered about.

Remorse floods me. After all these years, I didn't realize she was struggling with the loss of her son to this extent; it's been over a decade. And she always wore a sly smile at Lou's tavern.

My magic is heavy, gold solidifying under the weight of a dead Hunter and the pain his mother endured.

Denying her own magic so her children would inherit it, and then losing her son when he was so young, is a cruelty I can't imagine.

Silence surrounds me as the curling wind blows snowdrift through the door.

*She's not here.*

And I wonder if Mother Diane chose her fate to escape this agony.

"Forever may you rest," I whisper, boots rooted in the entryway, staring at a Mother's sorrow too profound to hold. I wish I had known she needed us.

Perhaps that's peace: for this life to finally end. To discover what exists on the other side with the gods. The alternative, being turned into one of *them*, is far worse a fate. There is pride in death, at least where I come from. And we usually meet it defending human life, and that is an end I will always embrace.

I secure the door, breath billowing in the frigid air, and head toward home with a hand on a hilt, weaving the cobbled streets of Southend. After ten minutes of hugging shadows, with magic spinning and sensing for vampiric threats, the twirl of chimney smoke from our rundown, three-story manor beckons me toward warmth.

Climbing the front porch of the Hunter safehouse, I kick snow off my boots on the landing and curse when my sore palm encases the doorknob. I should've called it quits on training sooner and saved my grip if I can't even grab a damn handle.

Shoving open our weather-beaten door that's always stuck in the jamb, I enter and toss the front door closed, heat brushing my skin. I amble down the foyer of our welcoming home, glad to be here and ready to see my people. They always take the edge off.

I pause under the archway to the living room.

Only one of two things will kill me in this life: a den of vampires that's caught me unprepared for some unfathomable reason, or the sacrifice I'd make for the woman glaring at me beside our crackling fireplace.

*Grace.*

My wife, my love—my Gracie.

"I'm sorry I'm late."

"You promised," she growls at me, but I know what's coming next. The little tug at the corner of her mouth, the twitch she can never hide when she's not truly upset with me.

"What time is it?" I ask, eyes skirting to the kitchen. The dining table is still empty, and my entire body relaxes.

"Thirty minutes *past* when you were supposed to be here," she scolds. And there it is: the hint of the smirk that brings me to my knees every damn time.

*Gods, I love her.*

"Good thing dinner's not ready yet, then," I challenge.

Seated on the faded velvet sofa, she leans back on a hand and quirks a perfect eyebrow at me. "Good thing I started it late on purpose."

"How did you know?" I ask, my lips already starving for hers.

The playful twist of her mouth disintegrates my restraint. I drop my weapon satchel and rush her on creaking floorboards, capturing her mouth with mine.

"How did you *know*, Gracie?" I breathe into her lips, her smile spreading against me.

"Your limp was gone this morning. I knew you'd stay and train until something else hurt."

I grunt in agreement as her hands skirt along my biceps, her touch melting my pain and lighting a fire in my chest.

"I missed you today," I confess, balancing her beautiful face in my palms. "It was a rough one."

"Tell me." Her voice is feminine and fiery, this blend that feeds me and captivates me, and I can't help but trace my thumb along her jawline.

"We lost another trainee, and I don't think Mother Diane is coming back."

"Well, shit," a deep voice says from behind us.

We whip our heads to the top of the curved staircase as Riot straightens his shirt and shoves back his disheveled hair.

"Nice nap for you?" I jab at my closest friend and Central station leader for the Hunters.

His heavy bootfalls thud down the steps. "Don't start with me—you know it was my day off. And now I need a fucking drink." Riot disappears into the kitchen, calling back, "Where's dinner?"

Grace's green eyes spark like glinting emeralds. "We waited for Kade."

Riot leans against the doorframe, tipping the bourbon bottle into his mouth. "Which trainee?"

"Tuck," I answer, my hands sliding over Grace's shoulders.

"Damnit," Riot grumbles and lumbers to the sofa, plopping down next to Grace, the force of his weight bouncing her in my grip. "I just worked with him on his crossbow technique last week."

"It's my fault," I admit.

Grace's eyes snap to mine. "It's not."

I shake my head. "I shouldn't have bent the rules. Warriors with no magic don't belong in the Hunters. They won't make it, no matter how skilled. Tuck is case in fucking point."

Neither of them says anything.

My attempt to bolster our numbers failed with Tuck's last breath. It isn't a risk I'll take again—I don't care who begs for the chance to defend their loved ones alongside us.

My calloused hands glide down Grace's soft arms, her skin like silk as I exhale my guilt and stow it for later.

"Forever may he rest," Riot says solemnly.

"Forever may he rest," we answer.

Grace cups my jaw in her soft palm, and I melt under the feel of her fingers threading through my hairline. "Let's eat some dinner, okay?"

I nod, swallowing the lump in my throat, and follow her into the spacious but humble kitchen; its efficiency is my favorite thing about it. Sealed wooden counters line the walls, ready to bear whatever we need: parcels from the store, cutting boards brimming with our garden production, or the occasional suturing kit and bloody rags. The large range built to feed an army hums in the center like a heart. Grabbing mitts, I hoist the roast from the oven while Grace lays the table. Riot mutters curses as he snatches as many glasses as he can carry between his thick fingertips.

I park the roast on top of the range, and the smell hits me.

*Home*.

"I'm sorry about Tuck," Grace says, her graceful hands carving the meat onto our plates.

Riot drops his enormous ass at the long table that seats twelve, although we typically squeeze fifteen.

"Thank you, my darling," I tell her, landing a kiss in her hair and carrying our plates toward a salivating Riot.

"I'm starved," he growls.

Grace laughs. "We know." She leans out of the kitchen doorframe. "Boys! Come and get it!"

Riot stabs at the roast, shoveling a dripping piece into his mouth before Grace and I can sit down. Boots thunder overhead and then down the stairwell, rattling the candlelit chandelier above us.

"I deployed half of us to the Night Kingdom today. Eastern outfit is sending the most. They leave tonight," I tell Riot.

He stops mid-chew. "You think they'll make it in time?" he asks through his food.

I nod, but I have no fucking idea if I'm right.

"They won't know what hit 'em when our boys get there," he growls.

Grace stares at her food beside me, and I run a hand along her thigh. There's a certain pressure on the rest of us when we thin the Hunters like I've done today. Holding the line here gets riskier when our numbers dwindle.

"Damn right," I say, shoving meat in my mouth as the kitchen fills with Hunters.

Sam plops down next to his sister, and Grace sets a roll on his plate, his fork already stabbing into the platter of roast.

Rhett, Sam's stationmate and best friend, reaches over my shoulder to grab his own roll. "You didn't *wait* for us, Captain?"

"Sit your ass down and eat your food, Rhett," Riot scolds.

Rhett flops next to Riot, stuffing the roll into his grin, stubble stretching across his chiseled features, and blue eyes sparking.

"How does it feel to be three decades today?" Grace asks me, running a hand over my shoulder.

"A lot like two decades, but with more muscle," I laugh, and my wife grips me harder.

Grace hums. "I remember your two decades. You were piss drunk and wouldn't shut up about me."

My chin jerks to her. "How do you know that?"

She grins, shooting a look at Riot. "A birdie told me."

I drill my narrowing gaze across the table, and Riot's hands raise innocently. "I did you a favor. Look at you now."

"Bastard," I say as Grace trails her fingertips down my spine.

"I'm glad he did. Someone had to make the first move," Grace says.

I snort. "It's not like I could. I didn't need the wrath of your father aimed in my direction."

"*Or* her brother," Sam snarks next to his sister, eyes narrowed on Grace's hand over my shoulder.

"Give it up, Sam. It's been ten years," Grace drawls, her attention still aimed at me, and I lose myself in those green eyes that hold me in place no matter what else exists around us.

"I would have made a move eventually," I say, tracing her jaw, ready to show my wife all the ways I've loved the last decade with her. "There's no life for me without you. Whether it's five days or decades, we'll live them together the best we know how."

"And how's that?" she whispers.

"As Hunters. Swords at our backs, hearts at our fronts."

Her top lip curls. "Aye, Kade. What a privilege, isn't it?"

Riot shakes his head at us. Talking around his full mouth again, he says, "You two are cheesy as fuck. And we're trying to *eat*."

I point at him. "It's *my* birthday."

"And you'll be spending it alone with your wife if we have to listen to any more of this," Riot says, washing his food down with ale.

Rhett smirks at Riot, whispering, "Mommy and Daddy are fighting."

Riot fists Rhett's shirt and tosses Rhett off the bench before Grace's laugh hits my ears.

My heart is full, and I relax, gazing at the table filled with my Hunters from the Central outfit as Rhett clambers back into his seat. Then Grace douses us in an ice bath.

"It's a huge risk, splitting the legion," she says, bringing back our topic before the distraction of ravenous men interrupted us.

I turn to face her. "What would you have me do, Grace?"

"I don't know. But things are bad enough here as it is. I just—" She pauses, gaze locking onto mine. "I need you safe. I need you all safe," she confesses, eyes pleading. Her face softens, and she gives me a gentle smile that says she understands my position but doesn't want to live through it. Love and logic rarely collide in perfect harmony, like a woman who desires peace married to a warrior. And my graceful, loving wife not only was born to the only remaining Master of the Hunters but also is the Heir of the

Hunters, descendant from the most brutal and powerful line of magic that has ever run through our kinsmen.

But here we are, living the cards we were dealt. And I thank my lucky stars her birthright at least softened the blow of her falling in love with one of us.

I run a thumb along her jaw. "The Hunters are the strongest we've ever been. Our odds are fantastic," I assure her.

"And you have me, so—we'll win any fight we get into," Riot says, tone dripping with confidence around the teeth he's flashing us.

Grace lobs an eye roll in reply. "I want change in Goreon. I'm tired of walking past human pain on every fucking corner of Southend."

"Once we stabilize the Night Kingdom territories, then we make a plan to take back Goreon," I say, repeating the mantra that hasn't changed in the last year.

Hunter goals are slow-moving when we're up against a millennium of vampiric rule, solidified by a blood-obsessed king who foments fear and doubt from his perch in his iron-and-stone fortress.

"I'm sorry we don't have more warriors for you, Captain," she says, lowering her gaze away from mine.

And there it is: her guilt.

There's never been an Heir who didn't accept their Hunter magic.

I cup her face in my hand. "Look at me." Grace's eyes flick to mine. "I respect your choice, my love. I want what you want. And I plan to give you peace in Goreon, just like I promised I would."

She nods at me, eyes brightening at my comforting words. "Good—you'd better. Now eat your food. You're going to need energy for later tonight." Grace winks and shoves a roll in my face, and I chomp at it, wondering how I ever got so damn lucky in this life.

# CHAPTER 3

## VEYA

Present Day

W HAT DO YOU MEAN, you don't *know*?" Second glowers, the torches at the entryway of Prosperity Castle flickering over his face.

The royal guard backs up a step, and I press my lips together to leash my reaction.

*It's not funny, Veya.*

"I've never been across the border, sir. I don't know the way to Goreon Castle."

Second shakes his head. "You didn't think to mention this when you were assigned to leave ahead of us?"

It's a rhetorical question.

"*Useless!*" Second shouts, wresting his cloak from the line of hooks on the wall. "Looks like we're all traveling together then." He points his sword at the guard before sheathing it at his back. "Next time, I hear about a problem *when it surfaces.* Not *after* the fucking fact, not two minutes before we're supposed to depart, not when it's too late." Second crosses his other sword behind him, sheathes it, and palms his daggers. "Better yet, try some forethought on for size. See how that works out."

The guard backs up one more step. "Yes, sir. I'm sorry."

Second shoves the daggers in his hip sheaths. "I don't want to hear 'sorry' when I'm having to save this entire court from Goreon filth because we didn't follow the *proactive* plan."

"You're right, sir. Sor—" The guard clears his throat. "It won't happen again."

Second points a thick finger at him. "Good. Now bring the carriages around since we're all leaving *together*."

The guard sprints out of the front doors and down the wide stone steps of my castle before the words are even out of Second's mouth.

"This kid," Second mumbles to himself.

"We never planned for the guards to leave in advance," I say, confused.

Second sighs. "I know that, but he didn't. And it took him way too long to be honest with me. *And* he obviously didn't ask anyone how to get there. He needs to toughen the fuck up and stop being afraid of his shortcomings."

"You were testing him? Brutal." I laugh. "Theo's eighteen years old. He's learning, he's trying."

"I know," Second says, jaw ticking as he snatches his bag. "But our enemy doesn't give a shit about his age. His inexperience will get him killed. Better it be my temper than his life."

The pride Second has in the army he's built me has given him purpose over the last century.

I release a loving smile. "You've always been a big softy."

Second glares at me as the crunching of wheels filters through the open castle doors. "Do you have everything you need?" he finally asks, face softening as his eyes count the weapons on my person.

"Yes," I say, daggers strapped to my thighs, sword at my back, and seven wooden pins in my hair, gilded in innocent gold—along with a racing heart, sweating palms, and an eagerness ripping at my skin like it's already five miles down the road ahead of us.

It'll require three days to travel from Prosperity to Goreon Castle at the heart of their territory. We could fly, but that would completely drain our energy and leave us vulnerable for days while we recovered. Summoning our wings is a great feat.

*We're not doing that.*

Vampires rarely fly; it's not worth the vulnerability and mostly reserved for life-or-death moments. Snapping is preferred, but we can really just flit about a room with it, moving in a blink to a location we can see. We might be the apex predator, but the gods sure threw in some limitations.

Correction. We're *one* of the apex predators. Never lose sight of a Hunter.

"Why do you need *four* trunks?" Emmanuel admonishes behind us.

I turn to see him eyeing the stack of Charlotte's cases lining the wall as the staff prepares to load them. Emmanuel holds up his own modest bag.

Charlotte glares at him. "Because a queen's attendant needs to be well dressed. And two of them are for Veya, Em."

I sigh. We've prepared for the pomp and circumstance, even though I'd rather skip right to the bloodshed.

Five carriages line the front drive of the castle, accompanied by twenty guards, and I step out into the night and climb into the royal carriage, flopping onto the plush seat as Second barrels in behind me. Moments later, the carriage jolts forward, and we leave the castle grounds, passing the crop fields that feed our human populace in this region of the Night Kingdom. An early frost bites at the edges of the stables and garden sheds, and I shove my hands in my pockets, knowing we're in for a much deeper cold in Goreon.

We'll be at Castle Death by sunrise, with two brief stops along the way. The Night Kingdom barracks is our first destination. We need to appoint the temporary second to run things while we're in Goreon.

We ride past the artisan town of Meadowbrook and over the bridge that connects the two sides of the river, entering my army's territory. The vast estate sprawls along the river's edge and, with its surrounding village, houses seven hundred warriors, the rest of our legion stationed at the Northern Wall.

Our travel party comes to a stop in front of the stately three-story building, beautiful in its simplicity, with cream stone and tall windows.

"Let's make this quick," Second says, throwing open the carriage door. As the general of our army, he leads the way down the wide path into the estate, and we follow him into his domain.

We've stitched protection into the fabric of our culture; even those who don't serve in the army learn to fight. And any citizen of the Night Kingdom is welcome to train at the estate for as long as they desire.

We walk into chaos.

The officer lounge is busy, vampires rushing from table to table, inspecting maps and correspondence, voices raised and tempers raging. Second clears his throat, and the room turns and lowers to a knee when they notice their queen.

"Officer Cave, what's going on?" I ask the male we're here to see.

The room rises and returns to urgent duties while Second and Emmanuel join in at the map tables.

"My queen," Cave says, disheveled blond hair falling over his eyes as he bows. "Uprising in the Southern Continent. Nothing we can't handle, but they've lost an entire village to a coven attack."

Our control over the Southern Continent has been an uphill battle, but it's one we will never give up on.

"Were we able to save anyone?" I ask.

Cave's fangs pop with his rage. "We didn't make it in time."

I hiss. "Second," I call, and he joins us, hands on his hips and eyes red with his anger. "I'd like to move a hundred out of the estate to the continent. Sounds like we could use stability across the channel."

Cave nods in agreement, gaze shifting to Charlotte beside me.

"I'll assemble the team," Second agrees and disappears into the grand foyer.

"Thank you for your diligence, Cave," I tell him, and the vampire's eyes shift to the map tables, his shoulders tense with stress. This is why I chose him. He actually gives a shit and cares about his duty with the same ferocity that I do.

An upheaval in the Southern Continent makes our departure to Goreon even riskier. *Damn the gods.*

"Can we speak privately?" I ask, nodding to the private meeting room off the lounge.

Cave's eyes drag back to mine. "Of course, my queen."

Once we're in the room, Cave shuts the door for us, shoving his hands in his pockets. "What can I do for you, Veya?" The legion's head officer looks at me expectantly, and I realize there's no way to soften the blow, so I toss out what I have to say.

"I've been invited to Goreon."

The vampire blanches. "You're joking."

I shake my head, lip quirked with my excitement. "And I'm accepting the invitation."

Cave exhales, those tense shoulders drooping. "Fuck, Veya. Well, Second and I will handle things while you're away."

"That's why we're here," I begin, and his chin tilts in response. "Second is coming with me. Are you ready to sit on the throne in our absence?"

Cave's eyes bolt themselves to mine as he lowers to a knee. "I will protect the Night Kingdom with my life."

I huff a small laugh, motioning for him to rise. "I know. You've always done whatever is required. Please choose the command you'd like to leave in charge at the estate and position yourself in Prosperity until our return."

"It's done," Cave says as he rises.

"Good. Thank you."

"And Veya?"

I look up into his hopeful eyes.

"Give those vein-drinkers hell, my queen."

My fangs burst out of me, anticipation rooting, and a snarl rips through my throat. "I *promise* I will."

Charlotte pokes her head into the room. "Second is back, and we're ready when you are."

"We're done here," I say, and Cave follows me out into the lounge.

"I'll be at Prosperity before morning," he assures me before returning to the nearest map table next to Second, who is busy outlining the position of the hundred warriors we're sending.

"When do you think he'll finally ask me out?" Charlotte muses, staring unabashedly at Cave.

"My money is on fifty years," Emmanuel says from beside her, and she slaps his shoulder.

"He needs time," I tell her, leaving it at that.

I speed through the estate toward our travel party, my people following, and scurry into the carriage with Second. We need to keep moving to Castle Death before sunrise, but I promised Em we would stop in Lilygate before we left. We all need one last visit there—one last reminder of the humans we're fighting for.

After several miles, we clop into Lilygate. Celebration ensues around us on the last day of fall, before the nights get longer and snow covers the ground. Streets buzz with human teenagers and children running with their lanterns from porch to porch, collecting winter trinkets and homemade treats from doorsteps in their best dress.

"It's always the best fucking feeling here," Second says, his face glued to the festive view through the window.

We travel through the center of the human town, music floating out of taverns and lounges, conversation and laughter mixing into a charming blend that brings me so much joy.

"Yeah, it sure is," I say, catching my gratitude in my throat before my voice quivers.

We've worked hard for nights like this, and the generation skipping up to porches is the *first* to experience life this way in the Night Kingdom. Lilygate is evidence of how life can be for humans in a vampire world. It's our shining accomplishment and a special place. We knew if we ever saw this day, we had done *something* right. It was the dream of this town over the last century that kept me going when I didn't think I could anymore.

Before we're even fully paused in front of the tavern, Emmanuel opens the carriage door, lips about to stretch right off his face. "Thanks for this stop," he says to me and whisks himself through the creaking door of the bar. The cheers from within are deafening in response, even from outside.

"You'd think with all the money he wins off these people, they wouldn't like him so much," Second grumbles next to me. Second doesn't frequent taverns, and the vampire chooses not to drink, instead demanding focus on his duty.

"You know he just donates it right back to their community," I laugh.

"Yeah, well. Some of us have to buy love, I guess."

I roll my eyes at the male and cross the threshold of the bar. The dimly lit space is crowded and warm, humans huddled around tables with cards and pints.

Conversations halt, music dies, glassware thuds, and the room stands as I enter.

I raise a hand. "No need for all that tonight, friends. Please just let us join in the fun for a bit."

"My queen," the bartender says, tipping his glass in my direction and slamming a shot into his mouth.

"Thank you, Ben," I tell him with a laugh, and the tavern bursts back to life.

Ben's young daughter skids into Em's side, and he kneels down. "What are you doing up so late, Victoria?" he scolds with a smile.

She shrugs her tiny shoulders drowning in her red puffed-sleeve dress. "It's a holiday. I'm allowed." Victoria's eyes skirt to me, and she steps back from Em with a deep curtsy.

"You may rise, Victoria," I say, and her eyes twinkle as she wrings her hands in front of her, staring up at her queen. "And I brought you something."

A gasp escapes her small mouth. "What is it?"

"A snowflake."

Her eyes narrow. "Snowflakes melt."

"Not this one," I say, reaching into my pocket for the ornament and handing her the velvet pouch.

She gently pulls the crystal snowflake from it, holding it up by its string. It glimmers in the candlelight, and Victoria's responding smile fires into my heart. I never had the opportunity to have children before I was turned.

"I want to hang it by my bed. *All year*," she says, entranced by the reflecting light.

"You should."

"I'm going to do it right now," she says and begins to scurry off before bolting back and colliding with my leg, hugging tightly. "Thank you."

I chuckle and rub her back. "You're welcome, honey."

She races away, and I wink at Em. "Told you she'd like it."

"You were right," he laughs and parks himself and his sly grin at a table. Charlotte joins him as cards are dealt. Ben hands them pints, and they get to work while Second and I settle into a quiet corner together, surveying the bar in silence for a while.

"You're of few words," Second tells me.

Our eyes connect.

"Just taking it all in."

He nods, expression somber. "I'm glad we carved out time for this stop."

"Me too."

Groans and cheers spout from Emmanuel and Charlotte's table, and Second and I smile at one another.

I trace my finger along the edge of the table, staring over at my people again as they enjoy the moment. "You and I will either get our shot at the king or we're going to need to come back for the entire legion and start a war."

Second crosses his arms over his chest, his chair groaning as he leans back. "I really hope it's not the latter."

I huff. "The anticipation is eating me alive."

"You're not alone in that."

Ben saunters over to us, Victoria right behind her father, and she crawls into my lap. I wrap an arm around her, snuggling her close and shoving down the sorrow that I will never hold my own child.

"Word is Lilygate should be on our guard. Apparently, there's an uprising across the channel," Ben says.

Second stiffens. "Yeah. We've sent reinforcements. Nothing will touch our borders, though."

The bar owner shifts on his feet. "But just in case, is protocol still the same?"

I look up at Ben. "Yes. Do not alter course. Shelter in Ruthlessness."

He bows his head. "Thank you, my queen."

"We need to leave soon," Second says.

Victoria twists in my grasp. "You *just* got here."

"It's been twenty minutes," Second says.

Victoria whips her face to the general of my army. "Not long enough, sir."

I suppress a smirk.

"My apologies," Second replies. "But I must get your queen to safety before sunrise."

"Oh my gods, of course," Victoria says, leaping from my lap.

"*Language*," Ben scolds, and her cheeks flush. "Off to bed with you."

She gives me a final curtsy. "Goodnight, my queen."

"Goodnight, Victoria. Sweet dreams."

She dashes away as I stand, and Emmanuel's discerning gaze shifts from his deck—he always has one eye on his queen.

I jerk my chin, and he lays down his hand, the entire table groaning in response when he sweeps the pile of coins from the table into a pouch.

Emmanuel tosses Ben the coin purse. "Drinks and meals for the bar are on me tonight."

Ben beams at my assassin. "They'll be happy to hear it."

"See you soon," Em says, and we follow him out of the bar, every patron standing in honor as we leave.

Second lumbers into the carriage behind me. "Onward to Death, shall we?" he asks.

I grin. I always knew I'd love naming that stronghold for its intended purpose.

Castle Death holds the fence at our northern border, the one we share with Goreon.

"Onward to Death, my friend."

Second's palm bats the side of the carriage, and we jolt forward again.

There are three strongholds interspersed throughout my territory. Each castle represents the tenets of my command—Prosperity, Ruthlessness, and Death. Prosperity to those who obey the laws set to benefit all of us, ruthlessness to protect our kingdom, and death to those who challenge either of the first two. My main home is Prosperity because she's lovely, and I like nice things.

Lost in thought, we stare out of the window as the landscape passes by. And after several hours, mist begins to crawl along the edge of thick pine trees, the forest growing dense the further north we travel into higher elevation and harsher climates.

Before the sun crests the horizon, we pull up to Castle Death in the whistling wind.

I open the carriage door with fervor and beeline for my second favorite place, which sings to the predator caged within me. The Gothic fortress, with gnarled vines draping its iron and stone façade, is the epitome of darkness.

The sunrise warning chimes from the towers of the stronghold as guards haul open the iron doors, the Night Kingdom crest embedded in the metal. I step into a hall of deep purple and black walls, strolling into Death as daylight breaks through the darkness outside.

Second drops his satchel on the floor, and Emmanuel sweeps past him, spinning in the foyer.

"I forget how much I miss this place until I'm here," he says, staring at the ceiling, our wars illustrated in a moody, bloody mural down the long corridor leading to the throne room.

"I *know*," Charlotte says, breezing past him in her trousers and coat.

I grin at her backside as she struts down the entry hall of Death. It's rare to see Charlotte in anything other than her finest gowns.

I roll out my shoulders. "I need to rest," I say and hoist my own case toward the royal rooms. We don't keep steady staff at Castle Death, just guards. If we're here, it's for a reason, and we need warriors ready to fight, not staff to haul trunks full of gowns or dust the furniture.

After several stairwells, I step into my bedroom, pulling at the pins in my hair, and they quickly gather in my palm. I place them on the ebony dressing table and unsheathe the blade at my right thigh. I draw the other from my left and set my favorite daggers next to the hair pins.

Shrugging out of my coat to unclasp the first hook at the front of my bodice, my breasts puffing against my effort, I undo the next and the next until I can breathe and my ribs are free. *Thank the gods.* I unload my pockets, placing the contents next to the pins, and finally I slip out of my pants.

Naked, I stare at myself and the jarring reminder of my humanity in the mirror.

In the crook of my shoulder, the fang marks that turned me are a cruel deep purple on my fair skin, the last evidence I was ever human. A daily reminder of the choice I never had, a visual of the moment I lost everything.

*Damn the gods.*

Vampires don't scar, but the last brand to our skin *never* fades.

I slink into my soft bed, body begging for rest with daybreak. My being calms, and I close my eyes into the comfort of darkness and stillness, away from my fears surrounding this mission and pestering thoughts of failure.

Day passes, and I jolt awake, sensing my surroundings in the dim bedroom.

*I'm alone.*

Just nightmares waking me. Rattling fear filled my dreams instead of slipping away as I'd hoped.

Loneliness chirps incessantly, and I try to brush it aside while dressing. Looping my hair up into a tight bun, I wait for the door to swing open. And it does, right on cue.

"Ready?" Second asks from my doorway, twirling a stake in his hand while I strap on thigh sheaths.

There are no pauses in training, not even during travel, but I enjoy working on my fighting skillset. And Second insists on it. Because, in the end, a queen must defend her own throne.

"You're not even ready for me today," I warn. "I'm pent up."

Second narrows his eyes. "Anything I need to know?"

"Nerves. Fear of failure," I say.

"Let's work it out," he says, turning on his heel, and I chase after him, looking forward to this session.

We wind down the stairwells to the large, padded room we designed for this specific purpose. Second swings the door open, and the wall of weapons greets us—a collection so glorious my heart leaps in answer to it. The image captures my breath every time.

"What'll it be today?" I ask.

Second yanks two broadswords off the wall. "Your weakest weapon."

I sigh at the ceiling but know it's for the best. The broadsword is an important weapon for taking the head off a vampire. I prefer my daggers, though.

Second chucks the sword at me, and I catch it with ease. He lunges with no warning, his massive form challenging to avoid.

I skirt around him, dipping and thrusting my sword, evading and attacking with speed.

"Stronger forward stance, Veya," he corrects and jabs at me.

I push through my foot, bracing with my thigh, and thrust forward.

Vampires are strong; our transformation upon turning creates something unbreakable. But we aren't made equal, and the physicality of our humanity still plays a role. The older we are, the stronger and faster we become. So an ancient Goreon king, over a thousand years old, would be able to rip my head off, probably more quickly than I care to admit.

But that's why Emmanuel and Charlotte exist—and Second, of course.

"Good," Second praises, his bright eyes meeting mine. "*Again.*"

I swipe at him, my lungs burning alongside my determination.

Envisioning our success, I daydream what King Nerian's final moments will look like when my blades take off his head. The relief I will feel.

I huff a laugh through my next swing.

This evil tyrant, who's proposed marriage and joining our rules, can't possibly believe that I would agree to that. The irony is that Nerian's offer is an echo of my own strategy with the foreign princes over the last century. Maybe Nerian does believe I would bend to his wishes to save my kingdom from an invasion. But he doesn't know me well, and he's going to find out the hard way that I don't break for evil. I don't give up. And nothing will stop me from protecting the Night Kingdom from him.

With all that I am, I will thwart this king.

Second's blade slices across my wrist, and I hiss, gaze flicking to my wound as it begins to stitch itself back together.

"Damnit."

"Where's the focus, Veya?"

*Not on this training session.*

I lower my weapon. "I'm wasting our time today."

Second narrows his eyes at me. "You're never wasting my time."

"I'm eager to get on the road," I tell him, hoping to placate the curiosity spiking across his features.

"It's more than that."

I shrug. "Didn't sleep well, either."

Second cocks an eyebrow. "We should be practicing how to lie better, because you're failing *miserably* right now."

My lips pinch a smile into submission.

Second secures our weapons on the wall and loops an arm over my shoulder. "You're not going to tell me. That's fine. Let's get the fuck out of here, then."

I sigh under the weight of his arm before he pushes me through the door.

We're packed within the hour and on our way to the northern border.

*To Goreon.*

# CHAPTER 4

## KADE

Two Hundred Years Ago – Goreon Kingdom

GRACE THREADS HER FINGERS through mine as we stare at the stars while lying on the roof outside our bedroom window.

It's a rare, clear winter night, and we never miss an opportunity to spend time up here. Our version of peace. A little slice of privacy under the blanket of the gods.

My magic simmers beneath my skin as Grace trails her fingertips along my forearm. I twirl a lock of her hair between my fingers and drink in the curves of her in the wash of moonlight.

With no warning, the magic in my blood swarms, and my entire body tenses with awareness. All sense of calm vanishes, and I bolt upright and crawl to peer over the edge of the roof for whatever has my magic in a spiral.

Grace scoots to the roofline and lies next to me on her belly in silence, waiting while I assess this warning.

Vision sharpening, my eyes track movement in the shadows. Darting forms bounce between snow-covered pine trees, closing in around us.

"Vampires are approaching the house," I whisper hoarsely in the dark.

We scramble through the window, and I toss Grace my crossbow, her long, dark hair fluttering around her as she spins and catches it with ease. Yanking my blades from the wall, I palm the hilts as my veins rush with adrenaline.

The Hunter within prepares for war and death, my magic bursting to life and giving me the edge that every Hunter who accepts their magic carries—the physical capacity to take on a vampire. Everything inside me readies. Muscles become like stone, tendons like unbreakable cabled cords; my hands tighten as they prepare to wield indefinitely, my breathing steadies, my eyes become focused and responsive, and my heart sings. A call to protect transforms my body and mind.

And my magic dances.

"Not a single one left," I tell Grace.

"Not a single one left, Kade," she promises me, looping the stake belt across her torso.

I hear the chaos of blades erupt and open the bedroom door to hissing and Hunters yelling at the base of the stairs.

*Sounds like Riot and the boys have their hands full already.*

Grace positions herself at the top of the stairs, crossbow aimed below as I launch over the railing, my feet landing in a whisper onto the floorboards.

There are three ways to kill a vampire.

My blades swipe through the air, crossing in front of me to sever the neck of my enemy. Cold blood races down my wrists and sprays through the air, and the vampire's head rolls away and onto Grace's favorite rug.

*First way.*

Before I turn, a vamp snaps into existence in front of me, materializing out of nowhere with its telltale flitting movement, and I plunge my knife into its throat to pin the creature in place. Tossing my other blade in the air to free my hand, I snatch a stake from my belt, stab the wood into its heart, and splay my palm for my airborne blade, its hilt landing back in my grip. The vampire gurgles, and its eyes flash red, its anger and sorrow emanating. My magic simmers with approval as the ancient being shrivels and crunches, collapsing into a heap.

*Second way.*

I spin, Hunters fighting hard throughout the house, sensing all of my warriors through our magic.

Sam takes the head off a vampire with his broadsword as Riot throws the fire canister to me with one hand and stakes an intruder with the other. Grace's bolt takes down the vampire behind that one.

There's an entire fucking coven here tonight.

I snatch the canister from the air as Riot stomps on the vamp he's pinned to the ground, the force of his boot crushing its neck before he slices off its head with his sword.

"Behind you," Grace warns from atop the stairs, and I spin, flipping the switch on the canister and aiming the nozzle at my attacker.

Fire blazes and swallows the vampire, its screams shredding the silence of the night. Its body sizzles and sparks, burning and coiling until ash rains.

*Third way.*

Before I breathe, five more close in. And then another five, their striking faces taunting us with confident grins and elongated fangs.

This is an orchestrated attack. We haven't seen this before—usually it's just one, or a handful, hunting their next meal.

The first two attack in a blink, snapping into existence a breath from me. I slash through both necks before they've even fully materialized, my Hunter speed untraceable.

Spinning, I take the next two at my back, blades swiping, cutting through the foulness that captures and tortures our people.

My jaw absorbs a hit from the side, and my magic surges, sensing the speed of this vamp. We trade several blows before I gain an opening and shove its chest, my strength punching it back as my fingers jam into its eyes.

It stumbles, and I throw a stake into its heart before it has a chance to recover.

That one was trained—also not something we've had to deal with in Southend.

I'm a flurry of limbs as I kill the remaining three near the fireplace, Riot working his side of the room. Sam and Rhett fight hard in the kitchen now, plugging the funnel of vampires coming in through the back door. Two more Hunters defend the stairs, an impenetrable barrier between our enemy and their Heir on the balcony above. And the rest are spread about the first floor, moving with precision. The leader I've worked to become blooms with pride.

I sense every movement of my Hunters—the Captain's advantage. I know their actions like I'm reading a battle map and the status of their bodies. Our magic connects us on a visceral level.

The last vampire goes down under my knee, adhered to the floor with my strength, its beady eyes searching my face.

"Hunter, your time is almost up," it whispers.

My lips stretch over bloodied gums. "I can say the same for you. Last words, asshole?"

A tear slides down its cheek. "My name was Kyle."

My mouth parts at the confession, and I slowly push the stake into its heart. Sometimes it's difficult to consider every vampire my enemy; they were all human once. With names and lives, loved ones, and dreams. Just like us.

But once they cross the line, my empathy has to end. The Hunter has only survived this long because of that brutal line—there's no middle ground. Our magic ensures it.

"Fuck," Riot spits, heaving a headless body to the side.

My being transforms again, pulling back to its normal state, and my gaze climbs the staircase for Grace. She's already halfway down, crossbow dangling at her side, relief in her eyes.

"That was too many," she says.

I rise from the ground, blades dripping, adrenaline still coursing through me.

"That was a targeted attack," Riot adds. "They're growing bold."

Sam and Rhett skid out of the kitchen, cheeks pink with their effort and faces beaming.

"Good birthday, Captain," Sam says, and Rhett elbows him in the side.

I sigh, ignoring Sam, and turn to Riot. "I'd bet money the king was behind it."

Riot's eyes narrow. "Why?"

Unease slides along my skin. "When was the last time you fought that many *trained* vampires in Southend?"

Riot curses, and Grace answers for him: "Never."

The tea kettle screams.

Riot sweeps up the last of our enemy's ash as I head for the kitchen. Dawn sheds her first light through the frosty windows, and icy rain patters on the roof.

Grace pulls toast from the oven in the soft glow of morning, and the vision of her paints into my memory with sweet reverence.

I snatch the kettle off the fire.

"What's our plan today?" Grace asks, piling eggs on plates.

I slice a lemon beside her and the spritz of its juice zings in my nostrils as I squeeze a quarter into Grace's tea. "I want to get to Lou's. Riot and I need to discuss last night's orchestrated attack with the rest of Central."

"Aye," she says, dropping toast on each plate. "Horrible timing."

"What is?"

Her green eyes glisten with unfallen tears as she peers up at me. "We're at half strength, and we've got the king's dogs on our doorstep." Grace carries the responsibility of our fate in her heart like she's the only one allowed to bear it.

*But she's right. It is bad timing.*

I run a thumb over her lips. "We'll handle it. I swear it."

Riot lumbers through the kitchen, swinging open the back door and dumping ash into the slush. "Is breakfast ready yet?"

Grace piles another scoop of egg onto his plate. "Yes, you beast."

"You love me," he says, closing the door and grabbing the plate Grace holds out for him.

"I do," she says, and I hand Grace her teacup, china chattering against the saucer as we make our way to the table and clamber onto the benches.

Grace runs a hand over my shoulder, sipping her tea with the other.

Riot speaks around a bite of toast. "Have you sent the call to the outfit yet for Lou's?"

I huff a laugh. "I was trying to let Hunters sleep until a reasonable hour."

Riot stuffs the rest of the bread in his mouth. "Good point," he mumbles and gestures to the window as he swallows. "But sun's up, Captain."

I glare at Riot. "Aye."

Closing my eyes, I pull at the threads of my magic, feeling them dance along my skin. Like rivers of gleaming gold running through my veins, my power babbles and bobs in its dormancy. I summon it to attention, and the whoosh of rushing energy roars in my ears and rolls like thunder under my skin, power curling and preparing.

And then I fire my magic out across Goreon City to my fellow Hunters in the Central outfit. Their power senses mine, and our magic connects, allowing me to communicate my demands. Their responses trickle in, their magic thrumming and splashing as it washes against mine, each unique signature carrying its own feeling.

Finally, silence answers, and as though a door slams shut, my magic rocks to a faint tremble in my veins.

My chin jerks up, eyes fly open. "It's done. Lou's in eight hours."

Riot nods and stuffs a spoonful of eggs in his mouth as Grace leans her head against my shoulder.

My body sags in exhaustion.

"I'm curious what they'll make of it," Grace mutters, yawning and reaching for her teacup.

I drag a hand up her thigh. "Aye. Nothing good."

After a hearty breakfast, I slog toward the stairs for a nap.

Sam and Rhett are on the sofa, boots kicked off, a deck of cards between them—they're best friends first, stationmates second.

"Hell no, it's *not* your turn," Sam says, grabbing the deck.

I shake my head at them, climb the stairs, and then I sleep like the dead before Grace's arm curls around me. My lips sink into her soft hair, the sweet scent summoning my arousal.

"Time to go, my love," she whispers, and I tilt her chin up, taking her mouth in mine.

I groan, not wanting to leave this bed now as I grip her hip, and she smiles into my lips, her body pressed against my bare torso.

"Come on, Hunter," she drawls, trying to pull me with her off the bed, but I've got about a hundred more pounds of muscle than she does, and she fails instantly, flopping forward onto my chest. She groans. "Part of me is looking forward to your old age."

I scowl down at her. "Why?"

"I'll have a softer landing," she says, trying to hide her curling lip as she drinks in my abs, but the feral look in her gaze is unmistakable.

I laugh, stomach flexing, and her eyes spark.

She scoots from the bed before I can grab her, and I follow, not wanting to be late, either. I stuff my socked feet into my boots, my hungry gaze dragging down Grace.

She smirks at me. "Later," she promises, and I snarl, chasing her to the stairs. Her playful scream fires into my heart.

We gather in the foyer with the rest of our party and bundle into cloaks, my wife already rubbing her gloved hands together.

"Ready?" I ask, jerking the stuck door open and the nip of the air sails through the hallway.

Grace groans and then marches onto the snow-covered porch, a fresh layer of thick powder blanketing the land. Our breath billows into the late afternoon, and I wrap an arm over my woman, her cheeks already flushed against the burning cold.

Every winter is the same in Goreon. It always feels like it will *never* end.

A bright-red cardinal hops along a snowy branch of Grace's treasured tree, the mature pine planted by her grandfather long ago. She breathes deeply, her shoulders lifting under my arm as she takes in the smell of fresh pine— her favorite scent in the world.

"You'd think our blood would have adapted to the cold by now," she grits as we trudge down the stairs. I don't have the heart to tell her our magic aids us as gold spools under my skin, warmth curling.

"Stop complaining," Sam says, brushing past his sister, hand skimming the railing to collect snow in his palm.

My arm darts for Grace's hips, and I scoop her up, spinning us at the base of the stairs, just as Sam's snowball drills into my back.

"Shit," Sam whispers. "Sorry, Captain."

"You're only sorry because you missed your target," Riot laughs, his retaliating ice ball clocking Sam in the face.

"Ah, bastard!" Sam yells, batting at his neck.

"Whatever, Sam. You deserved it," Grace spits, prancing past his struggle under my arm.

I look back over Grace's shoulder, narrowed eyes pinned on my Hunter, and shake my head. Sam drops his newly loaded snowball with a scowl, and Riot smacks him over the head.

Rhett stomps ahead of us, hands shoved into his pockets, and leads the way as ten Hunters tail us out of the house. We snake the back trails of Southend, snow piled to the edges of cobblestone streets and muddied paths. Human citizens bustle about their afternoon, our party receiving curt nods and curious glances from storefronts, and children scurry home from school. The Hunter legion is revered, but we're nothing more than bedtime stories for most. Our existence is intentionally kept quiet, whispered—legend. Of course, vampires know we exist, but we keep our numbers and locations as discreet as possible. After last night, though, it seems our king might be very aware of our strong presence in Southend.

We reach Lou's bar, and I yank open the door.

"As I live and fight, *Captain Kade*," Lou says, his warm smile stretching to his ears. "Never seen you in the daylight hours."

My party files into the tavern as I prop the door.

"Sun's almost down, Lou."

He chuckles at me, embracing Rhett barreling into his side. "How's my son?"

"Good, Pops. Captain taught me a new move last week."

Lou eyes me over his son. "Is that right?"

"He's good with a blade," I admit.

Hunter Rhett will be a station leader someday, I have no doubt about it. He's a skilled fighter, but he's also intelligent and reads people well. Much like his father.

Sam and Grace greet Mother Hollie before Rhett wraps her in a hug, and then they all make themselves comfortable at the corner table while Lou steps behind the bar again.

Lou and Mother Hollie have run this tavern for as long as I can remember, and Rhett knows he's a lucky Hunter, with both loving parents still alive.

"What brings you in here so early?" Lou asks, pouring three fingers of my favorite as I sidle up to the counter.

I tip the liquor into my mouth. "Safehouse was hit last night. Pretty sure it was an orchestrated attack by the king. I called a meeting for the Central outfit."

Lou narrows his eyes at me. "No way." The old man was one of the best Hunters we've ever had before he retired, and he knows Goreon vampires and their habits better than anyone.

I shrug. "They were trained, Lou. Infiltrated the house with strategy, hit us on all sides."

Lou takes a swig right out of the bottle, wipes his mouth clean, and meets my eyes. "Fuck."

"Aye," I mutter, staring into my whiskey and wondering if confrontation with the Goreon King and his soldiers is in our near future now and no longer on our terms after the Night Kingdom territory stabilizes.

My gaze flits to Lou's stern face, but his eyes are twinkling. "Goreon is due for a flushing."

I snort. "Been due," I say, tilting my glass for another sip.

"Well, if anyone is going to do something about it, you're the one to do it," Lou growls.

My magic simmers at his words, in agreement and with excitement.

*Interesting.*

"Mother Diane wasn't home when I checked last night. Any news on your end?" I ask, changing the subject before we're overrun with Hunters from Central.

"Damnit," Lou grumbles. "No, haven't heard a whisper." He shakes his head. "She's gone."

I nod. "Yeah."

"Forever may she rest," Lou says, clanking the bottle against my glass.

"Forever may she rest," I say, and we drink.

Lou spins, surveying his shelves. "I better make sure all the glassware is washed if you've got all of Central headed my way."

"Thanks. My apologies for the last-minute intrusion," I laugh.

He turns and points a knobby finger at me. "Whatever you need. Name it, boy. *Always*."

"Don't embarrass me in front of the outfit, Lou," I tell him, suppressing a smirk and endlessly thankful for his presence after I lost my father over a decade ago.

He pats the bar. "I wouldn't dream of it," he says and then fingers dirty glassware, dunking them into the wash basin below the bar. "The era of the Hunter is close, Kade. I feel it in my fucking bones."

His words are music to my ears, and my magic twirls. "Forever may we reign."

Lou grips my shoulder with his wet hand, his kind eyes connecting with mine. "Forever may we reign, Kade."

"Aye," I say with a nod, clutch my glass, and cross the bar to Grace and Sam, Riot's arm slung over Mother Hollie.

Boisterous laughter rings out from our table, and my attention jerks to Sam. Rhett is now pinned under his arm in a headlock, blond hair flopping over his eyes, and Grace counts out the seconds.

"Time! You lose, Rhett. Drink!" Grace commands.

Sam releases his stationmate, and Rhett tips his shot into his mouth.

"Lawless. The lot of you," I scold, forcing a scowl to hide my amusement.

"You just don't want to risk losing, Captain," Sam jabs.

My eyes land on Sam with a dare gleaming from my irises, and my brother-in-law clears his throat and pours out two shots.

"Challenge accepted," I croon, stripping my knives and cloak.

"Heads or tail—"

A loud crash cuts Sam off as the bar door slams open. My magic races, sensing a threat, and before I can move, a bolt flies through the air from outside. My eyes widen as it sinks into Lou's neck, blood spilling down his front, and his shocked eyes stare at his open bar door.

Lou clutches his neck, then collapses forward onto the bar and falls to the floor.

*Dead.*

My magic screams, curdling with the death of a Hunter, gold flooding with black. I can barely focus under the weight of it, and my anguish consumes me staring at Lou's vacant eyes.

The Hunter within releases, and I leap from my chair, blades in my palms and dive for the door, ready to block whatever or whomever dares to pass the threshold next.

I take the first three vampires before they make it through the doorframe, swiping my blades in a cross at the front of their throats, then sidestepping to the left as Riot hurls stake after stake into each.

The next five snap into existence throughout the room. I spin and lunge for the closest one.

"Behind you," Grace warns, suddenly in front of me and jabbing her stake through a heart. I turn, keeping her at my back, and stab a vampire snapping into existence in front of us, fangs yellowed and aged.

"Get your back against the wall in the corner," I yell through my panic. Grace doesn't have her knives, and this bar has no strategic position for her to perch in or protect herself.

My wife ignores me, face alight with anger, and challenges the next vampire, ducking and twirling as it chases her. She takes her opening and stabs its heart.

The bar swarms, filling with our enemy, and my mind and heart are torn between duty and protecting Grace. But a Hunter is supposed to protect without discrimination.

*Fuck that.*

I race for Grace, scooping her around the waist as I slice the head off a vampire simultaneously.

"Against the wall, Grace, before I lose my damn mind," I yell and move to shield her.

No one is getting past me.

She can fight. She's brilliant at it. But one bite and I lose her.

And I won't fucking have it. Not my Gracie.

Sam and Rhett defend Mother Hollie, who won't leave Lou's body. All around me, my Hunters are staking, slashing, and lunging with their swords, decapitating vampires who don't stop coming.

Our magic pushes us to unnatural limits. We don't tire. We don't stop.

This bar has never been attacked, and my rage boils as I take on two at once.

A sea of cloaks and blood spray fills the room, and my boots slosh through pooled blood while the tang in the air fuels my magic.

Riot takes on three snarling vampires, but another five slip past him, heading for Mother Hollie. They swarm her, but I know my Hunters can handle it—I've trained Sam and Rhett well.

A slice across my arm stings, and my focus shifts to the two assholes in front of my own face.

Finally, the consistent funnel through the door stops, and I smash the last vampire up against the wall, pinning it there with a knife in its shoulder, and a stake aimed at its heart.

"This bar is off limits. It pays its dues to the king. Why in the gods did you dare enter here tonight?"

The vampire stares at me.

I twist my blade in its shoulder, and it winces.

"A big mistake for such an insignificant little thing," I growl, holding the struggling vampire in place. "*Why* did you come here tonight?"

"Orders," it whispers, eyes bouncing around the room to furious Hunters.

Mother Hollie wails over Lou's body.

"Orders …" I repeat, letting the word drip out of my mouth, coated in disdain. "Your orders were to kill us?"

Its breathing skitters into thready nervousness.

The vampire nods slowly.

"Why would you want to pointlessly slaughter helpless humans who work hard to make the king rich?"

The vampire's rapid breath stops, a sneer overtaking its bloody gums. "This is no human bar."

My eyes narrow on it, magic racing around my veins and coiling like a poised serpent. This is another orchestrated attack on the Hunters.

"Who gave the order?" I demand.

"Not my secret to tell."

I scoff. "Surely you're not that noble."

"I have loved ones to be noble for," it spits.

"Aye. So do we. *Whose orders?*"

The vampire, to my absolute shock, places its hand over mine and pushes the stake into its own heart. It crumples to my feet, and I turn to Riot, my eyes raking over the destruction of the bar—blood spatter, broken glass, and headless vampires everywhere.

"*Fuck!*" Riot screams and throws his sword on the ground and then a table at the wall. The wood splinters in a hundred directions, his Hunter strength still warping and whipping at his edges.

Shocked Hunters and smashed furniture I've sat in for a decade rip a stark pang through my chest.

Our normalcy is shattered.

Sobs snag my focus. *Lou.*

My heart wrings. This man meant the world to me.

Grace rushes past, spinning in the center of the bar, her expression wild.

My brow scrunches. "Grace?"

Her panicked eyes meet mine. "Where's Sam?

# CHAPTER 5

## VEYA

Present Day

W E PAUSE THE CARRIAGES at the massive gates of the Northern Wall, and while the guards unlock the series of barriers, I climb the stone steps of my ramparts to greet my people. A queen does not just pass by those who serve and protect—she gets out of the fucking carriage and *honors* them.

I step onto the landing of the wide wall, a frigid breeze sweeping past and into my bones. Males and females stand at attention under flaring torches as far as the eye sees. Cloaks billow and eyes flash red as I stride down the line of devoted soldiers who fight for the Night Kingdom with their entire heart.

They offer a bow as I pass.

I walk the entire wall, acknowledging every warrior, and it takes over four hours before I snap back toward the gate.

Time well spent and time we planned for in our tactical session yesterday. Ideally, we should have been resting, and I have no doubt Nerian is enjoying the thought of our discomfort from the moment his letter reached me and what it would take to get to him in a timely fashion.

And if this visit to Goreon results in war, I need to see my warriors one last time before hell rains down on us.

"Queen Veya, it's an honor to see you this evening. I just got your note an hour ago," Officer Holton says at the top of the steps, voice unusually tight with his concern.

My admiration for this male ignites my smile as I gaze up at the officer in charge of the Northern Wall. "How has the last week been?"

He shoves his hands in his pockets. "Nothing abnormal, no change." His deep laugh floats between us. "Outside of winter setting in. Always makes life at the wall a bit unpleasant."

Second steps beside me. "I don't miss living up here," he adds jovially.

I jut my chin.

*Not helpful.*

Second clears his throat. "As our correspondence stated, we hope our time in Goreon is no more than two weeks. But we'll send word if it's going to be longer than that."

"Understood. And we'll attack as planned if we don't hear from you."

"Good," I say, a shiver clanging through me as the wind whips around us. "Thank you."

Officer Holton looks down at me, eyes flashing red. "You've built a kingdom worth protecting. We will always bleed for it, Queen Veya. And no one will get past this wall."

Warmth weaves through me against the nipping chill. "We'll see you in less than two weeks," I say firmly.

Holton steps aside so we can pass. "See you then, my queen."

Second and I descend the wall and settle into the royal carriage, the bite of winter following us into the velvet-covered interior. We jolt forward through the gates and into Goreon territory.

The land on the other side is desolate, scarred with abandoned villages, crumbling buildings, and bare farmlands. Only the dead husk of vibrant communities remains.

Humans left this region centuries ago, before I was alive. They either escaped to the old Night Kingdom territories before it was a kingdom with a ruler, or they were captured by Nerian in the early days of his bloodlust when he bled his southern lands dry with his hunger.

Gnarled tree roots thread the unkept road, rocking the carriage and spinning my nerves along with it. I can hope our journey to the enemy stronghold is unobstructed, but this is Goreon. And under my nerves, in the pit of my stomach, is the dread of no return. Because I love the life I've built and the people in it. But the fate raging in the distance might steal everything from me.

I breathe deeply and pray to the gods that this assassination goes as planned.

"We're five hours from the sleeping house," Second says, and I nod, flopping back into the seat to get comfortable.

The journey from the Northern Wall to Goreon Castle takes two days, which means we need to make a stop for daybreak. Dotted throughout any vampire territory are refuges from the sun. They're shelter, they're survival, and they're known to be safe places, no matter who you are.

"Whoa!" the coachman hollers, and my body flies forward into Second.

He catches me and tosses me to the side as he darts from the carriage. "What's going on?" he demands, slamming the door in my face as I try to join him.

I glare at the velvet and whip the curtain away from the window to peer out.

"Movement across the road up ahead," a soldier says.

Something shifts beside me, and I turn with a snarl, my heart in my throat.

Emmanuel offers me a cheeky smile, daggers in his palms.

I didn't even hear the carriage door.

"Gods, you scared the shit out of me, Em," I growl.

Emmanuel's ability to sneak into rooms without anyone ever knowing he's there is annoying when you live with him, but lifesaving in every other instance.

"Sorry," he says with a shrug.

"You're not sorry."

He winks at me, and I refocus on the window I'm forced to look out of.

"There!" a guard calls.

Second curses and throws open the carriage door I'm plastered against. I start to tumble out but Emmanuel's hand is on my belt, suspending me in the air before I even have the chance to catch myself.

"We've got company, Em," Second warns, pointing at him.

I roll my eyes, not surprised in the least.

"We'll be here," Emmanuel says, pulling me back. I recover into my seat, pulling my own daggers into my palms now.

Outside the carriage, the clash and clank of blades mixes with the snarls and hissing of vampires. And I can't see shit out of the window into the night. The soft glow emanating from the carriage torches is infuriatingly limited.

"We should assist," I say.

Emmanuel sighs. "We should not."

He's right, because I promised Second I would hang back when possible, one of the agreements I made to ensure my safety in enemy territory. But it doesn't soften my urge to leap from this carriage and slash some Goreon throats.

It only takes a few minutes before we hear a guard yell from further down the road. "Clear!"

"Same over here!" Second says, opening the door again and barreling inside, spattered with blood.

"Fuckers were completely feral with bloodlust. Probably smelled our stores."

"Must have been cut off from the royal stash," Emmanuel muses, exiting our carriage to ride beside it on his horse. He latches the door, and we're moving a moment later, not wasting any more unnecessary exposure on this road.

"Did we know vampires were being pushed out of Goreon City or cut off?" I ask Second.

He shakes his head.

There's no food source down here; it doesn't make sense for them to be here. Unless—

"I wonder if they tried to leave but got stuck between a king who won't feed them and our wall."

"Fuck," Second spits.

I sigh and try not to blame myself, if that's even the true story.

Our carriages finally pause at the sleeping house, and Second and the twenty soldiers with us enter the house first while Em stands guard outside my carriage.

I wait, trying not to fidget.

Pulling a pin from my bun, I lock it between my fingers and stare at the front door of the inn, counting the minutes. Finally, Second's form fills the doorway, and he jerks his chin.

I climb out and join him inside, Charlotte and Emmanuel behind me.

Second sheathes his sword, and I shove the pin back in my hair.

"It's empty. I've secured a room for you at the end of this hall. And I'll be sleeping on your floor."

I smirk at the blood smeared across his face. *Seems reasonable.*

I see myself to our room, and Second joins moments later, squeezing through the doorframe and flinging a featherbed he filched from another room onto the floorboards.

It takes us over ten minutes to fully disarm ourselves, and just before daylight, the front door of the house slams.

My eyes dart to Second. "A visitor."

"Indeed," he growls and grabs his sword, edging to the door and listening.

My muscles twitch, nervous energy ricocheting as I race to my daggers.

Footsteps tread confidently down our hallway, and the door across from us opens and shuts.

Second bolts our door, slides his featherbed in front of it and plops his heavy ass against it.

"They're going through me if they want in here," he says, leaning back, sword across his lap.

I smirk. "You'd be more intimidating on the other side."

"I like the element of surprise better," he lobs back.

"Of course you do." I glance at the door. "I don't hear anything else, you?"

He shakes his head, ear against the door.

"I should've locked this place down," he growls.

I frown. "We're not sentencing someone to death because we happen to travel through. And you know sleeping house rules. Safe space."

Second cocks his chin like I've spoken another language. "And you know how loose the rules can get here."

*True*. But I'd still make the same choice.

I ease into the bed, exhaustion setting in. It requires great effort to remain awake during the day.

Second thuds his head against the door and shuts his eyes. "I can't believe we're doing this."

I snort. "Me neither."

"But I'm also so fucking ready," he says as I stare at my closest friend.

"Me too."

Second's torso bounces as the door knocks him forward, and he's on his feet before I can track him, shoving the door outward and breaking it from its hinges. He pushes the slab of wood into the hall with whoever is on the other side of it.

"I didn't mean any offense, sir!" a female yells, voice muffled.

I leap, daggers in hand, to the center of the room to get a look into the hallway, now crowded with our entire party.

Second has the vampire pressed against the wall, body squished between plaster and wood. "You shoved your way into our room. Pretty offensive in a sleeping house," Second growls.

"I'm starving. I'm sorry," she pleads, her fire-red hair falling into her eyes. "I tried to control myself, I swear it."

I let my daggers dangle at my sides.

"Are you in control now?" I ask, and her panicked, green-eyed gaze flicks to mine.

She nods, peering over the door in her chest.

"Release her," I command, and Second steps back, dragging the door in one hand with him.

The wood scrapes against the floor as the female fidgets with her ratty clothing, skinny fingers shaking.

"I saw the carriages and knew there would be blood somewhere in this inn." She shakes her head at herself, eyes locked on mine now. "I'm not usually this person."

"Why are you starving?" I ask.

She sighs, slumping against the wall. "I refused to participate in the taxes in Goreon City. And so I was banished, but there's no easy way out of Goreon anymore."

My eyes narrow. "What are the taxes?"

"We have to turn in one human per month to the king."

*Oh my gods.*

Emmanuel spits on the ground, and Second tosses the door into our room.

Charlotte approaches the female. "Come on, I'll get you something to eat. And you need a new dress," she offers kindly. "I'm Charlotte."

"I'm Penny."

They disappear down the hall to Charlotte's room.

"What the fuck," Second hisses. "When did that start?"

I scrub at my face. "I'm guessing Penny can tell us."

Emmanuel sheathes his dagger. "What are we doing with this woman?"

"We could send her to the wall with one of the guards," I suggest.

"I'm not keen on lessening our numbers given the wild state of things we've seen so far," Second challenges.

"Are you keen on sentencing her to desiccation or suicide? Because those seem like her only options here."

Second rolls his eyes at me. "Obviously not, Veya."

I raise my eyebrows at him. "So …"

We step back into our bedroom, and Second rearranges his featherbed. "Let's ask her what she wants. Night Kingdom, or with us to Goreon."

"She was banished. Can't imagine bringing her with us is going to win favors," I say.

"Let's sleep. We need to be at our strongest tomorrow. We can figure out Penny then," Emmanuel says and disappears before we can respond.

*He's not wrong.*

We rest fitfully in our doorless room; no other threats will be arriving during daylight, so we don't bother with the effort of switching. As the sun sets, we find Penny and Charlotte waiting amongst our travel cases in the entryway.

"Penny," I say, and she turns to me, cheeks flushed with a meal in her belly. "You have two options. You can go to the Night Kingdom with one of our guards, or you can come with us to Goreon Castle."

Penny pales, shaking her head vigorously. "No. Please. The king's men took my daughter and turned me when I refused to hand her over—" Her voice breaks, and she inhales deeply, gathering herself. "I have nothing left in Goreon City and no desire to go back."

"I understand," I say, her sorrow edging its way into my heart.

I eye the young guard Second lectured before our departure, his kind eyes softening at Penny's words.

"Theo." The guard's gaze darts to mine. "Please escort Penny back to the wall and see that she is settled in Prosperity until our return."

"Yes, my queen," he says with a swift bow and hightails it out of the front door to ready his horse for them.

Second eyes me, tamping a smirk as I choose to send Theo back to safety.

Within the hour, our party is packed into the carriages, Penny and Theo headed in the opposite direction.

In my travel dress, with a dozen stakes stitched into the bodice of my corset, I'm stuck upright with wood encasing my ribcage. As the carriage rattles along, I savor every stiff jab against my bones from the stakes that will stab the hearts of my enemy.

I peer out of the window during the last stretch of our journey. The night doesn't hide the ramshackle human towns covered in snow or the posturing wealth of vampire estates lit with torches and boasting cleared, private drives. We edge into Goreon City toward the stronghold, hooves clopping on frozen cobblestone shining under fire lamps, and my nerves whip and snap.

Second looks at me as we come to a stop in front of Goreon Castle.

"Be bold and be brave, my queen."

I swallow, heart racing. "With all that I am," I promise him.

Second flashes a rare smile and opens the carriage door into the swirling snow.

It swings wide, and I glimpse the shadowed stone steps ascending to the giant iron doors of the Goreon stronghold.

*I'm finally here.*

# CHAPTER 6

## KADE

Two Hundred Years Ago – Goreon Kingdom

RHETT CARRIES HIS WEEPING mother into our house while Riot holds the door.

The entire Central outfit files in through the foyer, forty Hunters filling our space beyond capacity.

"If anyone needs suturing, I'll be in the kitchen," Grace says, striding for the doorway to hide the tears pooling on her lashes.

Riot follows her.

"Mother Hollie," I say, kneeling next to the couch as she sobs into her hands. "I am sorry. Lou meant something to all of us, and we mourn with you. Know that you're not alone."

She looks up from her hands, her strawberry hair matching the blotching in her face. "Thank you. And you have nothing to be sorry for, Kade."

I swallow. "Forever may he rest."

She nods, tears running before her voice quivers out, "Forever may he rest."

"We'll travel to Mortifer tomorrow to bury Lou."

She shakes her head. "He wouldn't want you to waste the time with what's in front of you."

I huff a laugh. "Gods, isn't that the truth—"

A forced smile cracks her dried lips.

"Rest, Mother Hollie. We're going to Mortifer," I assure her as she leans into Rhett's side, and he holds her as soft cries tumble out of her again.

Rhett's sad eyes meet mine, and I tap a fist against his knee.

After two orchestrated attacks, a captured Hunter, and the death of one of our own to be entombed in Mortifer Fortress, we need to convene *everyone.*

All of the Hunters left in Goreon will travel to Mortifer.

Because this is war now.

I push up from my knees and head for the kitchen, leaning into the doorframe.

"My office," I tell Riot and Grace, and they follow me in silence down the dim hallway and into my den.

I cross the midnight blue area rug to the fireplace, wood-paneled walls encasing the room in a hickory warmth. Once the door thuds shut, Riot's mouth spills a slew of burning curses that might set fire to the logs I'm stacking.

"We share the same sentiment," I confess, snatching the canister from the mantle and blasting fire into the hearth.

"I can't *fucking* believe this. Let's just take the castle in the morning."

"We're not doing that," I tell Riot as Grace flops into my armchair, tears streaming down her cheeks.

Riot snorts. "This is why you're the Captain."

I tuck the note that was nailed to Lou's tavern door into my journal, signed by the king of Goreon. There's no doubt who has Sam, but we won't be following the instruction written on that parchment: "Consider him lost."

*Yeah fucking right.*

Riot slumps into the armchair next to Grace and scrubs at his face.

I glance down at myself, blood crusting on my exposed forearms, my clothing soaked. This is why we have leather chairs. Much easier to clean.

I inspect the deep, seeping slice across my wrist. They sent talent into that bar tonight.

"They knew how to fight again," I say, glancing over at Riot.

He leans forward. "Yeah. They did. How many was that?"

"Forty-six," I say, my magic sparks in response, droplets pattering against my veins.

"How many more do you think they have?"

"An army," I say.

"Yeah, well, so do we," Riot growls.

I grab the suturing kit from my desk to work on my arm.

Riot's rounded shoulders droop forward as he sinks further into the armchair. "Anything from Sam?"

I shake my head, taking the third seat, and thread the needle. "I can't feel his magic."

Grace curls around herself, my enormous chair swallowing her.

Riot exhales, his bloodied boots gleaming as he stretches his legs out. "Shit."

"Why did they take him?" Grace whispers, staring into the flames.

"I can think of two reasons. And you're not going to like either of them, Grace," I say, stabbing at myself with the needle.

Her shining green eyes meet mine, begging for an answer.

My lips press into a thin line. "I think they intend to study their enemy and force our hand to attack."

If the Goreon king is aware we're at half strength, that makes his play even more strategic.

Grace's face darkens. "We're getting him back. I'm not letting my brother rot in that castle."

Riot stands, striding for the bar behind my desk. "I need a drink. All that fighting ruined my buzz."

He pours out three shots and brings them over, along with the bottle.

"To Lou," he says, handing me one, and I pause on the suturing.

"To Lou, forever may he rest," I say, clinking my glass with theirs.

Grace scowls at my half-sutured, filthy arm. "Hunter," she scolds, batting my hand away from the needle and lowering to her knees between my legs to work on my wound.

"Thank you, my love."

She peers up at me. "We need a plan. I want into that castle as soon as possible."

I sweep the bangs out of her eyes. "Aye."

Looking above her to Riot, I address my Central station leader. "I'll send the Hunter call to travel to Mortifer. We'll convene every Hunter left in Goreon and prepare for war."

My magic spins with approval.

Riot's eyes blaze. "At half strength, in the dead of winter, with rage boiling over a captured Hunter—" He slams another shot. "Perfect timing, Kade."

A laugh huffs from my chest as Grace ties off the suture in my arm. "We don't have a fucking choice."

Riot grins. "You mistake me. I *love* the plan; it's perfectly insane."

*Yes, it is.*

The Hunter within simmers with the call of duty. "We leave in the morning. Make sure Central is ready to move out."

"Aye, Captain," Riot says, standing and yanking open the door.

He pauses in the doorway, eyes landing on Grace. "Swords at our backs."

Grace spins on her knees to Riot. "Hearts at our fronts," she responds, voice shaking.

He smiles sweetly at her. "We'll get Sam out of there, Grace."

She nods, and Riot disappears behind the closing door.

I exhale a heavy breath, and Grace turns back to me, climbing into my lap.

I wrap my arms around my wife as her head finds home on my shoulder. "I can't believe it's time," she whispers.

I squeeze her tighter. "It's our moment in history, and I can't wait to share it with you. But I'm sorry this is how it's happening."

She nods against my neck, and my palm encases her thigh as she lifts her head.

"Forever may we reign," Grace whispers, a tear sliding down her cheek.

I swipe it away. "Forever may we reign."

She peers at my face. "You need rest."

My body droops at her words. Our magic takes a toll on our physical selves. Our power hands us the ability to wield and perform beyond what our physical body is capable of, leaving an aftermath that feels like I ran up a mountain and back down it in a single day. But sleep heals and resets us.

I scoop Grace into my arms, standing with ease. "Do I?"

"Yes," she says, kissing me as I stride for the door.

I carry Grace upstairs, and we wash and settle in bed, falling asleep entangled together but not before I send my magic's call across Goreon, summoning everyone to Mortifer.

If war is what the king wants, war is what we'll give him.

And then I offer a prayer to the gods to guide us to the other side of it and give us our Hunter back.

Blowing out a breath, I stare at my breakfast and know I should eat, but the weight of our future spasms inside me, and my appetite is somewhere beneath the mayhem.

I've been reaching out my magic to Sam all night, but there's no response. They must be keeping him unconscious.

*At least he's not dead.*

I just need Sam to hold on for a couple days. And I know he can; he's stubborn and strong.

"Papa is going to lose his shit," Grace whispers beside me, her meal also untouched.

*Gods.*

Master Hull is a fierce man and the eldest Hunter. He resides in Mortifer Fortress, overseeing our libraries, our training facilities, our weapons, and our dead.

And the king has his son.

I'm going to get my ass handed to me today.

"We need to move out," I say, standing and leaving my breakfast behind.

"Aye," Riot says, lumbering into the living room. "Hunters! Round up!" he yells.

We bundle into coats and emerge into the dreary winter morning, all of Central gathering in the small courtyard of our manor.

Rhett and five Hunters march down the steps; Lou's body is wrapped and suspended on a cot between them. Mother Hollie is the last out of the house in mourning black, and we wait for her to descend the creaking stairs.

Lou leads the way, our procession following his body to Mortifer.

Hunters from all over Goreon—Northern, Eastern, and Western outfits—are all traveling today to join us. We've spread out over Goreon Kingdom the last several decades, protecting towns as far as we dare to reach from our fortress.

Eagerness pulls me toward this war like a beast to blood. Instinct I can't ignore yanks a cord taut within me, tethering me like a vessel to an anchor at the bottom of a vicious ocean. There is no other path but one.

One destination. One mission. One result.

And I will plunge into whatever depths are required to take out my enemy and save my Hunter.

We march away from Southend toward the eastern mountain range, snaking back trails and plunging our way through thick forests and deep snow. Grace's breath heaves beside me as we trudge through winter's misery.

After hours of hiking and frozen feet in our boots, majestic mountains rise before us when we emerge from the dense forest. Slabs of rough rock and glistening stone reach into the clouds, disappearing from view, like the gods dripped the mountains from their fingertips.

The height of this range makes crossing over it next to impossible. We've never attempted it.

We trail across the plain to the edge of the closest mountain, and I watch Lou and his bearers disappear into it. The rest of Central follows, and then Grace scurries through the crevice in the thick stone wall, Riot bringing up the rear behind me, and we vanish into the mountain range at the edge of Goreon territory.

Our boots crunch against gravel, descending and spiraling into the dark caverns of Mortifer Fortress. I remove a torch from the wall and strike it to life, the sizzle and pop of flame echoes into the silence, and warm light dances along the slick, cold soapstone.

Mortifer Fortress is my home, my training ground, my identity, and the sanctuary where our heritage pulses and lives like a breathing ancestor.

Twenty minutes of winding tunnels and correct turns through the labyrinth spit us into the hidden entry chamber. I cross the great carved chamber, centuries of stories honed into stone, memories and lives hallmarked for eternity. My fingers thread the chain around my neck, pulling it from beneath my shirt, and I insert the rock pendant of the Hunter crest into its home.

The familiar whoosh of air whips through the chamber as the massive stone door sinks into the floor before me, grinding and rumbling its way to reveal the fortress beyond. I take Grace's hand and step over the threshold while we lead the Central outfit into Mortifer.

We emerge into the grand hall. Carpeted lounges dot the room, and dining for a hundred splits the center.

"Took you long enough."

The scratchy, deep voice floats out from the barracks hallway, one of several doorways leading away from the main hall like spokes on a wheel.

"Master," I say as he hobbles our way.

"It's good to see you, boy," the old man croons, his crooked smile barely visible under his thick gray mustache and beard.

With a quick flick of his wrist, his blade flies through the air, and I catch it between my fingertips. "You too, sir."

"What about me?" Riot admonishes, unloading the packs from his back onto a sofa.

"You too, Riot," Master Hull says, opening an arm.

Grace rushes into his side, tucking in and squeezing. "Papa."

He kisses the top of her head just like he always does. "My baby." Master's gaze finds mine. "So, it's time, then?" he asks. Grace's smile falters under her father's arm.

I nod. "Yes. For good reason."

He snorts. "There's a thousand reasons to finally take this king out."

I unsheathe my weapons and pile them on the long dining table. "Hunters will trickle in by tomorrow," I inform.

"We're ready for them. Beds, food stores, ale, weapons."

I try to steel my confidence for the conversation we need to have. "Good, I had no doubts."

Master laughs. "My blood is buzzing. Haven't been able to sit still since I felt your call. Eastern outfit is already here."

I nod.

Riot crosses the room and pours himself an ale. "Where are they?"

"They're in the pens," Master informs, and then his gaze catches on Lou's body being carried across the massive room toward one of the hallways, a spoke I rarely traverse. I have yet to visit my father's stone.

"*No*," he whispers, staring at the stretcher. "Who?" he demands, tone fierce.

"I'm sorry," I say, knowing Master Hull and Lou were stationmates back in their heyday. "It's Lou."

Master's face drains, and his arm drops from Grace's shoulders. "Aye," he says, voice shaking. "Forever may he rest."

"We'll perform the burial once everyone has arrived," I say.

There hasn't been a funeral in over a decade; no Hunter has died under my command. Until Tuck. And now Lou. Even if Tuck were allowed to be buried here, we don't have his body.

Master Hull shakes his head, shoulders drooping as he walks to the ale barrel. "We hadn't seen each other in five years—" He swigs his beer and then looks me dead in the eye. "How did it happen?"

I take a few steps toward my father-in-law. "His tavern was attacked. They hit us fast and hard. It was chaos."

He nods. "Well, Lou would be thrilled to know he's the reason we're finally going to end this fucking king."

I swallow. "He's not the only reason, Master."

Hull's eyes narrow on me.

Grace moves to her father's side before I speak.

"They took Sam."

Silence rips between us, slashing open the vat holding my guilt as I watch Master's eyes widen in surprise and fear.

"*How could you let that happen, Kade?*" Master snarls, arms blowing wide as he barrels toward me.

Riot steps between us. "It was chaos, Master Hull. We didn't even see them take Sam."

"I'm not talking to you, Riot. Step back," Master growls.

Hunters filter away from the main chamber, giving us space.

"They must've knocked him unconscious in the bar. I didn't feel his magic struggle or call to me," I say, not looking to assuage my guilt with excuses but trying to give a father a reasonable explanation. "I'm sorry I lost sight of him."

*I was worried about protecting Grace.*

Master Hull shakes his head, turning away from me. "There's no apology that will *ever* suffice for this."

"I don't expect your forgiveness," I say, fists clenching at my sides. "And I'll get him back. I swear it."

Master ignores me and hobbles to the couch by the roaring fire. I don't blame him. I would need time to process this, too. But, selfishly, I can't stand his disappointment in me.

"Come, Mother Hollie. Let's sit by the fire in the library," Master Hull says, offering his arm to the sniffling woman on the couch.

Grace approaches me with kind eyes and squeezes my hand before she walks off to join them.

Riot blows out a breath and refills his ale. "Want to check on the Eastern outfit?" he asks, side-eyeing me over the pint.

"Yeah," I answer, gathering my discarded weapons and making for the tunnel to the training pens. I need a distraction, and I need to climb out of this sea of guilt before it fucks with my ability to strategize and get Sam out alive.

We enter the weapon hallway. Every inch of wall houses varying styles of stakes, swords, knives, guillotines, crossbows, fire canisters, and every other Hunter invention from the past few centuries.

"I always feel more at peace here," Riot says as we walk the hall designed to support a single purpose—death.

I can't help but smile.

*I agree.*

Sweat and steel hit my nostrils, mixing with the earth and salt of the stone hallway like a spice blend crushed and ground from our bloodline. Shouts and clanking vibrate through me, beckoning me toward my men as Riot and I jog to the arena. We exit the tunnel to stand on the edge of the underground cliff and gaze down into the cavern filled with fighting pits and training pens. The aged, fraying rope outlines the stone fighting ring in the pit, black lines tracing a merciless border. The gray rock is stained and chipped from centuries of blood and weapons trapped in this pit, their beholders taught to never surrender, forged with fealty to one higher power—the call of the Hunter. The training pens are built into the rockface surrounding the pit, cages serving the purpose of learning to fight in confined spaces.

Below us, warriors attack and defend in captivating choreography, every movement intentional and exact.

Riot crosses his thick arms over his chest. "They look good."

I nod. "Can't disagree. Let's get down there."

I grab the rope tethered beside us and swing down, landing silently, Riot right behind me.

"*Hunters*!" I bellow, my boots scraping over the stone quarry as I dip into the center ring.

My men still and lower to bended knee.

It's an intimidating job to be in charge of every Hunter, every life. And in a moment like this, when I've already failed three of them, the pressure on my chest is suffocating.

"Are you ready to kill a king, brothers?"

I doubt we're getting Sam out of Goreon Castle with anything less. They've never had their hands on one of us before, and I can't imagine the king will let Sam out of his sight. But that's still a blind guess. I don't know where they're detaining him.

The cavern reverberates with hollers and cheers, warriors brimming with pride and purpose.

Everyone knows about the recent attacks—it's why we're here—but I kept the news of Lou and Sam close to the chest until we had the chance to inform Master Hull in person. And I won't inform the legion until everyone has arrived.

"Rise and let's eat together while we wait for our kinsmen."

Men I've respected my entire existence surround me. Muscled, sweaty flesh with the warmth of human blood quivers and flexes as warriors stand.

I nod as they pass; one by one, they acknowledge me before climbing the cliffside.

"*Captain*!"

My head jerks toward *that* voice. "Uncle Brachett."

"Get in here, boy," Brachett says.

The fiercest man I've ever known wraps me in a hug, clapping my back before his large, gnarled hands grip my shoulders.

"Can't believe it's been ten years," I say, looking into his kind eyes, identical to my father's.

"It's been hell in the East," he grumbles. "I'm glad you're finally putting an end to all this."

"Good to see you in one piece, Uncle."

He steps back with a laugh, shoving his hair from his eyes. "Barely, although I hate to admit it."

My eyes narrow, magic stirring. "What do I need to know?"

He yanks down the edge of his collar to reveal the ragged fang marks on his fair skin. "Fucker got me. An entire hoard attacked us on the road."

When we accept our magic and make the choice to devote our life to the Hunters, we can't be turned against our will. When we're bitten, it heals just like any other wound.

Well, unless a Hunter *chooses* to turn. But no one ever would. And no one ever has.

"Shit," I mutter. "Go clean that wound. Looks festering."

Brachett huffs. "Bite before this one took a month to heal. I'm gettin' too old for this shit." He winks at me before moving on to greet Riot.

Uncle Brachett has held the East his entire career, and I've enjoyed adopting his tactics.

Which is really just one—*no mercy*.

Riot turns to me as Brachett climbs up the wall. "Ready?"

I grunt. "Let's go drink like war is upon us."

"Poetry to my ears," he replies and leads the way, scaling the rockface.

My fingers grip the rough surface I've touched thousands of times, and I pull and push up the cliff, hoisting myself over the ledge with ease.

"Do we talk strategy tonight?" Riot asks as we amble back through the tunnel, orbs above lighting our way.

I unclasp the bracers from my forearms. It's time to get comfortable.

"No. We'll wait for the others. Tonight, we ensure the men remember what they're fighting for."

Riot peers over at me.

"Tonight, we *live*."

At that, Riot picks up the pace into the grand living room to male Hunters milling about, tossing shirts over heads, treating themselves to overflowing pints, and taking their seats at the dining table.

It's been decades since a female Hunter honored us with her service. Grace is the only one, sort of. Vampire bloodlust hit a peak fifty years ago, killing humans at an alarming rate, and our parents' generation answered with a rebellion that failed, losing half of our Hunters and severely weakening us. Our women chose their service as Mothers exclusively after that, passing on their Hunter magic to their children to rebuild our warriors rather than accepting the magic for themselves.

When we kill this king, we can go back to how things used to be. When the female choice to accept her magic as a warrior, or to become a Mother, was based on more than survival of the line. And I'll be so grateful for that, because I've learned so many things from the way Grace fights.

The contributions from our women are greatly missed.

But the gods demand balance with our magic, and our women pay the price for it.

Life is so fucking unfair sometimes. And I despise the fact that Grace has had to choose. I can't even fathom the force she would become if she accepted her magic.

The room stills at the sound of grinding stone from the carved chamber. A minute later, the Northern outfit marches into the grand room, and cheers roar.

"Thank you for coming," I say in greeting, their faces wearing exhaustion.

Northern station leader, Longton, clasps my hand with his. "You shittin' me? Never been more excited for anything in my whole damn life."

I clap him on the back, and he disappears into the throng. Riot and I welcome the Hunters filtering in behind their station leader.

Once everyone is settled, we grab our own pints from the ale station and saunter toward the head of the massive table.

And then, like a punch to the gut, Sam's magic splashes against mine.

# CHAPTER 7

## VEYA

### Present Day

OUR CARRIAGES ARE BARELY paused outside the black stone castle when the steps fill with Goreon courtiers and guards snapping into existence.

"Here we fucking go," Second growls and exits the carriage.

I try to keep my nerves in check. The opportunity I've been working toward is here, and I can't mess it up. Every innocent life is at stake, in this kingdom and ours.

I plaster on a confident expression and emerge.

My heeled boot lands on royal Goreon grounds, and then the other, and I bask briefly in the moment of this milestone while staring upward at countless spires needling into the snowy night sky.

"Queen Veya of the Night Kingdom, we welcome you," a male says in a tone I'm *certain* is not genuine.

I shift my gaze from the imposing fortress, blinking snowflakes from my lashes, and I'm met with his red eyes piercing me with disdain above his armor and forced smile.

"I'm General Balor. You can follow me."

I know who he is. He's been Nerian's henchman as long as I've been alive.

Second positions himself inches from my side, Charlotte and Emmanuel behind us, and our guards beyond them.

The frosty chill clings to my skin, a numbness I'm unsure will fade as we climb the stone steps of Goreon Castle, wind blowing my cloak and biting at my eyes. I haven't felt bitter cold like this in a long time. The bleak weather magnifies the sneers and smirks around us, my gaze snagging on frigid, unwelcoming faces. Like they all have a secret of their own, too.

General Balor saunters down an ornate grand foyer, and the walls are a twisting blend of carved ebony stone and thick veins of gold, a swirling fire in the night.

It's admittedly striking. And almost as beautiful as my own castles.

But unlike the Night Kingdom, Goreon didn't build their wealth on the backs of those who could bear the weight; they built it on the spines and from the pockets of their humans.

"The east wing is our guest quarters. I'll escort you there first, and then you have a session with the king and dinner afterward."

General Balor's orders grate along my skin.

*No one tells me what to do.*

Second tilts his chin to look over at me as his hand skirts to his hilt. He knows that, too. But we're guests here, and I plan to play nice until I can't.

"That sounds just fine," I say, agreeing with the agenda.

General Balor glances back at me, eyes narrowed. "It wasn't a suggestion," he informs sternly.

*Well, I'll play nice with boundaries.*

I smile pleasantly at the male. "General Balor, everything out of your mouth is a suggestion when you address a queen."

His lips part, and he jerks his chin forward, lifting it higher than it was five seconds ago.

Balor has something to prove, and I'm looking forward to putting him in his place during my visit.

We trail Goreon guards to the east wing, my heart stuttering all over the fucking place as my eyes leap to every corner and open doorway for threats, for horrors known to exist here. But there are no drained bodies or snarling, feral vampires, just a very long walk amongst lavish wealth.

Finally, we're ushered into a series of royal rooms with a central parlor.

"We'll be back to collect you in an hour," Balor states and doesn't wait for a response before snapping his way down the unending hallway.

It's an affront to my station, a clear one. This invitation has nothing to do with respect or a desire to see me as their queen, exactly as I expected.

*He'll learn to watch his mouth before this is all over.*

Emmanuel lets out a sigh like he flew over an entire kingdom and collapses on the sofa. "That was stressful, and we just got here."

Charlotte sheds her coat and tosses herself next to him, and he loops an arm around her shoulders, hand squeezing her bare arm.

"You need a bath," she says, wrinkling her nose.

Emmanuel sniffs himself. "Told you I was stressed out."

"You're an assassin. How do you get stressed out?" she laughs.

"Swords and words are very, *very* different weapons, Char."

She snorts, leaning her head against his shoulder.

It's such a rarity to see vampires touch—a single touch to the skin can trigger an eternal bond between us. But Charlotte and Emmanuel tested that boundary decades ago, fairly sure they wouldn't bond.

And they didn't.

Just like Second and I tested it a century ago. We didn't need any surprises, and we prayed to *every* god that fate didn't want us aligned in that way.

They listened. For once.

Second opens the tall double doors to an adjoining suite and then through to another.

"Veya is in the middle. We'll take the rooms on either side," he says, slinging my five-foot dressing chest toward my room like he's carrying around a pillow.

"Come, my queen," Charlotte coos, skirting past me. "Let's get you dressed to dine with the King of Goreon."

I'll be lucky if I keep anything down in his presence, my desire to slice off his head included.

General Balor yanks the gilded throne doors apart, and my eyes catch on the ancient king draped over his seat in an obscene amount of furs and black velvet.

I want to rip his throat out.

But the love I have for the Night Kingdom and all of the souls within it, the duty I swore to uphold, keeps my instant rage in check. The moment needs to be right. We *need* to be strategic.

You don't crush a millennium-long rule with rash action, and I cannot afford to fail, especially to emotional whims. Nerian's faster than me, aged well beyond my years. It must be a team effort. So I'll play along, show restraint, and we'll take King Nerian once an opening presents itself and we understand just how disadvantaged we are against his ancient strength.

Second keeps pace with me down the long, decadent hall, with the king's court loitering and staring with rapt attention. My gaze flits about the massive, high-ceilinged throne room, arches pulling my eyes to the chandeliers lining the length of the hall, their crystal filtered light in a dazzling display around us. None of it feels like it belongs together; the evil that is known to breed here and the stunning, vast castle shouldn't be such intimate companions.

Chin held high, I let my top lip curl somewhere between a snarl and an alluring smile.

I met Nerian briefly, long ago. I doubt he even remembers.

The king doesn't bother to sit upright, his slicked blond hair glowing in the candlelight. I'm sure many find him handsome, but all I see is death and corruption.

"Queen Veya, your reputation precedes you," he says, petting the fur across his lap, staring at the ceiling.

*How does he know anything about my reputation?*

I hum at him as we come to a stop at the base of the dais. "I can say the same, King Nerian."

He sits up finally, his hand littered with extravagant bejeweled rings, gripping the arm of his throne to pull himself upright, and then his arms spread wide in greeting.

"Ah! *Yes*. I can't wait to show you what I've accomplished as we join our kingdoms into one glorious rule."

"That's presumptuous of you," I retort, offering a slight bow.

He returns it with a tilt of his pointed chin and a garish grin. "I enjoy a challenge. I'll win you over in the end."

I nod demurely through my disgust and hatred. "I'm honored by your upcoming efforts."

The Goreon king jerks his head to the side. "This is my second, Deleos."

My gaze flits to the most gods-blessed vampire I've ever laid eyes on as a male steps out of the shadows. Raven black hair, a jawline that could cut stone, muscles sculpted and stretching his fine suiting are captivating, but it's his bright plum eyes that have me mesmerized.

And they're looking *right* at me.

"It's Del, actually," he drawls, and his soothing voice reaches in and grabs my attention.

King Nerian glowers at his second, the corner of Del's mouth pinching into an intoxicating smirk.

Nerian's second pushing back at him makes me deliriously satisfied.

*What an unexpected moment.*

I drag my eyes back to the king before I have to pick my jaw up off the dais.

With a polite clear of my throat, I turn to my second, waving a hand toward him. "This is Second."

The king's eyebrows perch at his hairline, and then his upper lip curls before his words slur out. "*Ruthless* queen. Won't even let your court have names."

I don't correct him. I am ruthless when I need to be.

He licks his lips, eyes running up my bodice. "An enticing choice for a wife."

Second steps forward with a hiss, a pace before me. "*Not* on the table."

The king glares at Second. "You're an assertive one, aren't you?"

I raise my hand. "I look forward to our discussions," I say vaguely, keeping tempers at bay for now.

Second's head jerks to me, and with great effort, I ignore him. Nothing was going to stop me from this visit, even if it meant keeping the contents of the letter private.

*Bold and brave.*

*With all that I am.*

The king clicks his tongue. "Let's dine, shall we?"

"I fucking hate this guy already," Charlotte whispers into my ear before stepping toward the king and cooing, "I'm starved."

I turn to look at her, pinching my lips to suppress my grin.

She tosses King Nerian a sweet smile.

Charlotte's conniving and manipulation will have the best at any court wondering what happened when she's done with them. She's been integral in wooing and distracting my foreign princes' companions while I worked on the larger target.

Nerian's gaze rakes her up and down next. "You're a lovely thing. Do *you* have a name?"

She bows deeply to her knee, gown pooling around her and breasts spilling over green silk.

"Charlotte, my king," she purrs, her bright blue eyes drinking him in.

"It's a pleasure, Charlotte," Nerian drawls as he stands from his throne, his slim build drowning in fur. "And who is your other companion, Queen Veya?"

Emmanuel steps to my side.

"I always travel with my most entertaining attendants. This is Emmanuel."

Nerian eyes Emmanuel, and my assassin offers him a curt nod.

The king snorts and descends the dais. "I'm no fool, Queen Veya. And I didn't expect you to travel to Goreon with anyone less than your best."

I try not to sigh. Nerian is right—a vampire who's survived this long as a ruler is no fool.

The royal Goreon guards shift to attention, lining the entirety of the hall, their red eyes soulless but alert, like once-vibrant cranberries now crushed beneath an unforgiving boot.

Second and I step to one side as the king passes, Del descending after him, and I hold the breath and nerves in my chest, still in disbelief that I'm a few feet from Nerian.

Del's eyes skirt to mine, piercing and captivating.

"I can't believe you came," he whispers, and my gaze narrows on him as Nerian marches ahead, Charlotte accompanying the king and feigning interest over his impressive throne room while fielding his complaints about how long human labor takes to build such things.

"Who was I to ignore an invitation from the King of Goreon?" I say to Del, trying to keep the salt out of my tone.

With the manners of a perfect gentleman, he gestures for me to walk beside him, and I do.

"Of course, no one denies King Nerian," he says. I glance up at Del, his thick lips turned upward in a playful smile.

"Ah! And that's my favorite painting!" Nerian calls, pointing high above at the mural staining the ceiling near the entrance.

Unsurprisingly, it's a depiction of war.

"It's lovely," Charlotte replies, following Nerian into the antechamber.

I refocus on Del, working to keep my stride long enough under the weight of my layered, black silk gown. "I won't be quick to accept anything beyond his invitation, I assure you."

His beautiful eyes flare. "Careful, Queen Veya. People around here might think you have a sharp mind and your successes haven't been all luck."

Is that the rumor? That I've been *lucky?*

I hum at him and face forward, picking up the front of my dress to relieve some of the friction slowing me down.

Del shortens his stride in response, and I try to ignore the warmth in my chest from the small gesture.

We accompany the king to the dining room, *surrounded* by guards, and they spill through open gilded doors. But I can't imagine Nerian is really that threatened by us. Which means it's intimidation he's after.

General Balor cuts me off, stalking into the dining room first.

I glare at his back, and Del's fists clench beside me as we filter in behind Balor.

*Interesting.* Del and I already have something in common.

Two marble fireplaces twice my height roar on opposing sides of the flickering dining room, and candelabras line the walls, the bleed of light dancing about. It's romantic, designed and set for an intimate gathering. A draft brushes against my skin, and I wonder where the hidden doorways in this room might be. There's never just one exit in a space frequented by royals.

Gold and onyx servingware dot the cream-covered table, and a line of fire burning in oil threads the center. Several place settings decorate the two sides of the table, but there's only *one* setting at the head. The other end is empty.

I pause as I watch King Nerian settle into his head seat.

A queen does *not* sit at the side of the table.

My gown gleams in the firelight, and I let my expression darken and my eyes flare red.

Del walks past me and pulls out the chair opposite the king.

My gaze runs up Del's finely tailored suit, hugging his muscular form in all the right places. Yet the intensity of his appearance is nothing compared to the penetrating look locked on my face, and his lips purse as he waits for me to take the seat he's boldly offering.

I step confidently toward him, and King Nerian glances up as I lower myself into the plush chair, his red eyes narrowing and jaw ticking from the other end of the table. I meet his gaze as we stare each other down across the licking flame between us, our companions hesitant at the fringes of the dining room.

Del leans over me, his cologne whispering like a hushed secret in the air, stealing my attention. He transfers the three empty tasting goblets from the place setting on my left, his strong hands arranging them before me.

"An oversight," Del says, blazing plum eyes finding mine again as my chin tips up to look at him.

"*Was it?*" the king barks, and I wonder why Nerian even has a second—he seems to barely tolerate Del.

I swivel my attention to the king. "Surely one of the demands I'll be making," I say with a pleasant smile uncomfortably adhered to my face.

Del clears his throat and sits to my right as the king tries to grin at me, but it comes out as nothing kinder than a sneer. And I almost laugh at how horribly he's failing.

Second stomps around the table, fingers three glasses from another place setting, and sets them up on my left, replacing the ones Del moved. He plants himself on my other side, crosses his arms over his broad chest, and leans back with a huff.

Charlotte sighs dramatically, sitting herself next to Del, and Emmanuel pulls the chair next to Second across from her.

Silence breaks with the pop of Charlotte's fangs. "Perhaps some champagne to toast to our queen. And yourself, of course, King Nerian," she says, playful grin and pink cheeks aimed shamelessly at our host.

"I can see through you, girl," King Nerian accuses, taking off his crown and tossing it on the chair beside him like he can't be bothered with the weight of it.

She doesn't even flinch. "And I hoped you would. It's no fun when the game isn't fairly stacked."

He assesses Charlotte for a brief moment before grinning at her, eyes gleaming. "I do *love* a good game of court."

"I'm the best," she promises with a wink. "Now about that champagne."

*Charlotte will always get what she wants.*

King Nerian raises a finger, and the butler procures a bottle.

Charlotte scoots her champagne glass to the side as the king snatches the bottle, pops the cork with a flick of his thumb, and stands to pour her drink *himself.*

*Charlotte won this round.*

Nerian clears his throat, cheeks pinking slightly and perhaps very aware of what Charlotte just accomplished.

The butler swipes the champagne from the king, pouring out the other glasses for the table while Nerian takes his seat.

The Goreon king extends his glass in the air, his eyes shifting to mine.

"To *negotiations*," he says, the words dripping from his mouth like a poison, mysterious and deadly.

No one expects a happily ever after between the King of Goreon and the Queen of the Night Kingdom. A truce, a peaceful surrender to save the lives in my territory, a marriage for appearances to save my reputation in the wake of submitting to a threat—perhaps. But I would never consider these as options.

Yet I'll do my best to convince Nerian I would, to buy us time, even if he is just playing with me. Because we need to be here long enough to remove the head from the male across from me and claim his throne.

We hold our glasses, waiting for Nerian to take the first sip.

My people are trained well. In all things. Court, weaponry, words, and not drinking the fucking wine in enemy territory before the host. Poison won't kill us, but being weakened by toxin would be a death sentence here.

Everyone is still as stone as we wait, glasses held in suspense, bubbles racing to the top in silence.

"Oh, for *fuck's* sake," Del says and tips the champagne into his mouth in a single gulp.

I pretend to sip to hide my amusement, staring at Del's thick throat and full lips. And if I'm being honest with myself, I'm looking forward to a tipsy Del to soften the sharp edge off the evening.

Del's eyes flick to mine, catching my stare.

*Shit.*

I dart my gaze to the king as he drinks half his glass.

Second, as usual, ignores his liquor.

We need a topic of conversation before the awkwardness of this evening becomes blistering.

"Your letter mentioned the desire to explore the isles of the Sereia Sea as our first joint endeavor," I begin.

*Probably because the Night Kingdom has ships.*

Nerian raises his hand, and the butler comes to his side, receiving a whispered order.

"The first course will be ready shortly," Nerian informs. "And there's no talk of business tonight. I'd like to get to know you, Veya."

He leaves off my title like it never belonged, and my gaze narrows at the blatant disrespect.

Setting my glass down with intention, I look Nerian in the eye. "If 'Queen' is too cumbersome, I also accept 'Your Majesty' or 'Your Highness' as alternatives."

He sighs, tracing a finger along the tablecloth in a swirling pattern I can't decipher. "Since we're to spend time together and surely address sensitive subjects, I propose informal names to be appropriate."

"If the standards are equal, I have no objection, *Nerian*."

He slaps the table, his mood shifting to jovial in an instant and giving me whiplash. "*Excellent!*"

I already have concerns about this male's sanity.

Second shifts in his seat. Apparently, I'm not alone in that.

"Do you enjoy male or female blood more, Veya?" Nerian asks bluntly.

A personal question, but I don't miss a moment before responding. "I've indulged in an array of men, but I can honestly say, I haven't sampled anything worth savoring."

Del clears his throat and suppresses a smirk through a sip of his refilled champagne.

The king snorts. "So, female then."

"I enjoy both equally," Emmanuel offers.

"In every sense," Charlotte laughs.

"Look who's talking," Emmanuel fires back.

Charlotte shrugs her petite shoulders and bats her lashes before placing her lips around her glass again.

"Straight from the vein?" Nerian asks me, sucking the life from the room.

"Everyone must eat, but there's still a choice in how we consume, Nerian," I say sharply.

He laughs. "Thankfully, we've solved that problem. There's no shortage here. Drink up—I've procured some of our best for the evening from the cellar."

*Gods, stake me now.*

"We don't drink from the vein, Nerian," I say to clarify any possible miscommunication.

The candlelight dances and shadows taunt the secrets of Goreon in the extended silence that follows.

Nerian's features darken, and I'm nervous my welcome in his court will be over before it's begun, and then his words drool out of his mouth: "Just a taste, my queen. I promise I only offer the best."

The butler door opens behind the king, and he turns his head, listening.

"Ah, our first course. It is my honor to serve you, Veya."

The king stands, Del rising in custom, and Nerian disappears through the door beside the fireplace.

Del lets out a low whistle, taking his seat again. "Such a tense evening for the supposed betrothed," he says, silken tone confident and commanding as he traces his finger around the rim of his glass, his thick lip curling to reveal perfectly white teeth.

"They are no such thing," Second growls across from him.

The males stare each other down.

"Gentlemen, let's not get ahead of ourselves," I whisper, nerves spiking as I wonder what Nerian has planned.

I thought I could get away with sipping from goblets during our stay here, not an outright moment like this testing me and my boundaries.

Our attention is drawn to the Goreon king dragging a human girl through the butler door, her eyes frightened and naked body too lean, ribs bared like teeth against her skin, angry and jagged.

My insides kick, and I *force* my expression to stay neutral, hiding behind my champagne.

Before I can decide how to handle the situation, Nerian sinks his teeth into her perfect skin, drinking deeply.

From the vein.

My glass shatters in my hand at the sound of her scream, anger flooding.

He's killed her, whether it's death or vampire. I watch her human life float away like a soundless cloud no one will ever notice.

Nerian uproots his fangs, blood dripping down his chin through a feral smile, and drags the girl toward us by her neck.

"*Appetizer, anyone*?" he snarls and tosses the naked, whimpering girl on my lap.

# CHAPTER 8

## KADE

Two Hundred Years Ago – Goreon Kingdom

I DOUBLE OVER, beer sloshing onto stone as agony rips through me from Sam's magic.

He's in pain. Lots of it.

And as quickly as his magic called to mine, it disappears, the connection slamming shut between us.

Riot's wide eyes scan me as I straighten, Hunters around us silent and staring.

"What the fuck was that?" Riot whispers.

I catch my breath, my adrenaline subsiding in the wake of unexpected pain. "Sam."

"He's alive?" Riot asks, and I nod.

We were pretty sure of that already. I would've felt the loss of his life the way I did Lou.

But now we know.

And now I know a few other things, too.

Sam *is* in Goreon Castle.

"I think he's being tortured," I say. Hunters from East and North glance around the room in confusion.

The cavern rattles, and moments later, Ned, station leader of West, barrels into the fortress with his men.

"Just in time, Leader Ned," I call. "Sorry for the abrupt announcement, but we need to get moving on a plan."

Ned eyes me, frost clinging to his beard. "Captain Kade, what's going on?"

Hunters drop heavy satchels of gear around the massive room, filling us to capacity as they flop onto sofas and pull out dining chairs to stuff their mouths from the laden table.

Everyone is here now, and the last time all Hunters assembled, the Great Divide War was won, and Goreon lost the south, forging the Night Kingdom territories from the blood of my ancestors. I feel privileged to be the one to lead us once again.

I post at the head of the table, the fire in the massive stone alcove roaring behind me, spitting and crackling like the blood in my veins. An energy courses through me, and my magic plumes to a bright glow. Power I've never felt floods me like the gods are preparing me for war and the responsibility of shepherding my men to the other side of it.

Sensing this within themselves, Hunters still, their focus shifting to me, and all is quiet.

"Hunter Lou has been killed in an attack by the king's soldiers," I announce. Murmurs race around the stone room as mugs crash onto the tabletop. "And one of our own has been captured."

The murmurs turn into roars of outrage, and I give them a moment with their anger before lifting a hand to silence them. "Hunter Sam, the son of our Master, is being held in Goreon Castle."

"Fuck," Riot spits, and my gaze catches on Grace, leaning in the doorway of the library tunnel.

I refocus on the long table filled with Hunters and then around the room at the full loungers.

"We have a Hunter to rescue and a king to kill who should have been dead a long time ago."

Deafening shouts and the rhythmic thumping of boots and pounding fists echo in support.

"You were *born* for this. You've *trained* for this. Are you ready to answer the call of the Hunter?"

The thunder of warriors rattles glassware and threatens to shake the tears from Grace's eyes, her soft smile aimed right at me. Her pride reaches in and grabs me in a way no one's opinion of me *ever* could.

"Enjoy your meal, and drink all the ale. Station leaders, please join me in the library to discuss our battle plan."

The entire room stands in salute as I exit.

"Gods, I'm lucky," Grace whispers, her hand running up my shoulder blade when I reach her side.

I look down at her. "Because you landed the most handsome of the Hunters?"

She rolls her eyes. "Because I get to stand with you and change our world. Even though I hate that Sam is part of the reason for it."

I drape an arm over her while we walk. "I'm sorry."

"You don't have anything to apologize for. We were all there; no one saw it happen. All we can do is *fix* this." She leans into me. "And, Kade—"

I gaze lovingly at my wife, endlessly thankful for her understanding and support.

"You *are* the most handsome of the Hunters."

I scoop her into my arms with a kiss threatening to unleash us into a frenzy of heady need.

There's always been something about Grace. I've never been able to resist her.

The call of the Hunter is one thing, but the summoning to protect this woman, to make her mine, to give her my life and my love with everything I do has made me whole. Our world demands balance. Grace is *my* balance. Just like the oceans don't break without a shore to wash upon, and the skies don't end without the land they touch—I don't exist without Gracie to ground me.

She wraps her slender arms around my neck and kisses me fiercely. Fingertips bite into my skin, letting me know she wants me just as badly as I need to throw her against this wall and lose myself in her. I rip my mouth from hers, searching those green eyes I never tire of drowning in.

"I'm the lucky one, my love," I tell her, and she kisses me again, pressing her full lips into mine before we're interrupted by station leaders entering the library.

Grace slides down my body to her feet as Master Hull emerges from the back alcoves of the library and plants himself in his usual leather chair nearest the fire, encased in his favorite fur. The chill in this underground fortress is unforgiving.

This massive library was designed to educate and preserve Hunter heritage. The treasured volumes range from fighting skill and our history to vampire knowledge since the dawn of their existence. My own journals from the past decade line one of these shelves, alongside those of the captains before me.

Hull's sad eyes meet mine, but he offers me a nod, his anger dissipated, and a Master looks back at me, ready to hear the plan.

Station leaders settle into armchairs, and I stand with my back to the fire to address them.

"So, Captain Kade—what are your orders?" Longton of North asks, wasting no time. He's always been business before pleasure.

I've thought about an attack plan since I began training in these caverns, working toward a moment like this my entire service.

"We infiltrate the castle during the full moon. Half will be knocked out on sedative serum, and the others will be dreamwalking their humanity and losing their minds."

And not a single human will be on guard the following day, staying well the fuck away from the chaos of the monthly dreamwalking.

Riot grins at me, and Ned of West leans back in his seat, eyes skirting to Grace briefly before speaking.

Ned grunts, his auburn hair gleaming in the firelight, and drapes his burly arms over the sides of his chair. "It'll be dangerous with their feral state and unpredictability, but I agree. Best shot we've got of gaining access. No one will be standing guard, day or night."

*Exactly.*

I nod. "We get in during the chaos of the night and attack. They'll be exhausted by sunrise, and if we aren't done with them yet, they'll have to fight through the day without slumber."

Uncle Brachett twirls a blade between his fingertips, his tongue tracing the hole no longer housing a canine. "The full moon is two days away. That's not much time to prepare."

I chuck a few logs on the fire. "I don't think Sam has much more time than that."

I ease into the chair beside Master Hull, and Grace perches on the arm of my lounger. "We let the men rest for the night and then filter into the safehouses in Southend and the city tomorrow. I'll take my outfit to estimate current numbers inside the stronghold and determine our best entry point."

Riot chimes in, peering apprehensively at me. "Your father always said the best entry is the waste dump access through the dungeon."

"I won't trust old information," I grit out.
*Although he's probably still correct.*

Riot throws his hands up in silent defense.

I address Ned, Longton, and Brachett. "Take whatever you require from the fortress to aid you. I'll send one of my men with each group to our ten houses. Please split your men as you wish."

Ned shakes his head. "This is insane, Kade. We're at half strength, we're tired—"

"What if it was your boy?" Master Hull snarls at Ned.

Ned's jaw ticks as they stare at one another. "I'd make the same foolish choice."

"Aye," Master spits, sinking back into his chair.

"And what about you?" Ned asks, turning to Grace.

She starts at his forceful tone, and I glance up to her narrowed eyes and pinched mouth. "What about me, Ned?"

"We're all about to risk our necks to take out this king and save your brother, and you're going to deny us the strongest magic in the legion."

I leap from the chair, my growl burning out of my throat. "*How dare you,*" I snarl, fisting Ned's collar and dragging him to standing. "You have *no* rights to her choice."

Grace decided long ago that her magic would belong to our children.

Ned glowers at me. "It's been a long time since a woman has accepted. Would be nice right about now."

"Give it up, Ned," Master Hull growls. "Unless you want me to throw you in a pen with Riot."

My Central station leader stands, towering over both of us.

Grace places her hand on mine, and I release Ned as she steps between us.

The eldest offspring of the last Master outranks me, the authority of the Heir is honored by all, but there's never been an Heir who didn't accept their magic. Until her.

"Make no mistake, Ned. I'll be fighting right beside you," she promises. "But if you speak of my magic again—" She takes a step closer, getting in his space. "I'll send you to the Southern Continent, and you can start working on that territory *alone*."

He blanches at his Heir's words—a certain death sentence.

Ned huffs, dropping into his chair, and Grace steps back. "Are we clear?"

His eyes flick to the fire and then up to Grace. "My apologies for the overstep," he says in a defeated tone, although I'm uncertain of his sincerity.

Riot smacks Ned across the back of the head, and Grace's lip quirks. "You're forgiven. Now grow some balls so we can win this thing."

Longton chuckles beside Ned, eyes creasing under his thick black eyebrows.

Ned clears his throat. "The Western outfit will need more clothing until our blood and belongings have adjusted from the temperate climate of the coast." He rubs his rough hands together. "I'm already missing Broadbank, to be honest."

I let my anger simmer, trying to cool it down from the boil that's still raging.

I jerk my chin toward my father-in-law. "Master Hull has quite the collection of furs. He'll see to it your men are dressed."

Master snorts. "After all these years of shit talking, my clothes finally save the day."

"Your service is noted, Master," I say in jest, although every word rings as true as the Hunter sword swings.

Master Hull pushes himself to a teetering stance before steadying and striding to the door. "Come on, Ned, let's raid my closet."

Ned rises, gaze lingering on my wife. "I'm sorry," he says and spins on his heel, Longton filtering out behind them.

Riot takes his chair again, stretching his massive legs toward the fire. "Well, that was awkward," he drawls, and Grace bursts into laughter.

Uncle Brachett cracks his knuckles. "That Hunter has always had something to say. Pissed me off more than once."

Riot looks at me as I finally sit back down. "I'm so ready to get into Goreon Castle and kill some assholes. I still think our access is going to be through the dungeon, like your father said."

Riot has been a strategist since the day I met him; he can't help himself.

"I need to vet it."

He nods. "I'm not arguing with that."

"Have you forgiven him yet?" Uncle Brachett asks suddenly.

My eyes flick to him and his pointless question. "You know that day will never come. Unless you can bring my mother back from the dead."

Brachett sighs. "I miss that beast of a Mother. Gods bless, was she a force." He leans forward on his elbows, his bushy eyebrows furrowed and features shadowed in the firelight. "Your father didn't have a choice, Kade."

"He had a fucking choice. He just made the wrong one," I growl. "They're both dead—why bother with forgiveness, Uncle?"

"It was all of us. It was his Hunters or your mother."

I look him dead in the eyes. "It was the *wrong* choice. He acted too early. He doesn't deserve forgiveness for the price he chose to pay."

Brachett shakes his head at me and stands. "Death is a faraway thing until it touches us. Don't let it poison you, Kade."

I stare into the fire, watching flames lick the wood, momentarily wishing I could hurl myself into it to escape this conversation.

"I'll see you back out there," I tell Brachett and wait for him to leave.

His boots finally scrape into the distance.

Grace slides into my lap and curls herself around me, my being softening from stone underneath her. My head finds home against her collarbone.

"Let's go have some fun with the boys. We need to take a break tonight before all of this is upon us," she says.

Grace knows how I wear my stress, like a thick, heavy chain around my neck, and it tightens and coils until I can't breathe.

And right now, I can't stop thinking about Sam. And Lou.

"Sam is stubborn, and that makes him hard to kill," Grace says, a small smile playing on her lips. "Believe me, I've tried."

I shake my head at her with a creeping grin. Grace walks through life with confidence and mental strength like no one I've ever met.

I stand us up, Riot leading the way back toward the hoard of Hunters dining and drinking in the main chamber.

Stuffed bellies, half-empty kegs, and outlandish fighting bets land us in the pens an hour later.

"Now *this* is living." Riot beams as he drops the gate to a pen, locking himself in with Rhett.

Nothing like training in a cage to fish out the feral. Because when a Hunter feels trapped, look the fuck out. I'm just glad our magic heals cuts and bruises with a little rest; otherwise, this wouldn't be our wisest pastime before battle.

"You're not winning," Riot informs Rhett.

Rhett scoffs, muscles quivering as he strips his shirt. "I've got a hundred coins on my own neck. You're going down, you beast."

Grace crosses her arms over her chest, assessing the fighters. "Just get after it already. I want my money."

Riot points at her. "You're next, pretty girl."

"Big talk from the boy who could never outrun me."

Riot rakes his hands over his enormous, chiseled physique. "Don't need stamina."

Grace shakes her head at him, and I bask in the absurdity of my gods-blessed life.

"Riot," Grace whispers. "Seriously, don't lose. The savings for the summer home is on the line."

Riot blanches, and my focus swivels down to my wife.

"You didn't—" I say.

She shrugs. "Brink of war and all that. Does it even matter?"

*Kind of.* We've been saving up for years.

And no. I'd give every coin I have to the men in this cavern.

I grin at her and dart a serious expression back at a pale Riot. "Don't lose."

Riot shakes out his tree-trunk arms and sets up at the far end of the metal cage, staring down Rhett fifteen feet away on the other side.

"Ready yourselves," I cue and grip a cage bar, my magic fizzing along my skin and into the metal. It vibrates and pulses beneath my touch, glowing and burning to a bright molten orange, and the cage door disappears as the metal molds together into a seamless prison. This is the only external use we have of our magic, sealing and manipulating cages—which is highly valuable, considering a vampire is powerless against a cage locked with our magic. Vampires can still reach through it, summon things between the bars, but they can't open it. Serving a single purpose for us: *to trap them.*

The Hunters' forms hone, eyes piercing with intensity, and muscles contract, hands flexing and skin rippling, magic sensing their surroundings.

The pens aren't intended for weapons training— brute strength and fighting talent only, to test survival, to test what you have when no weapons remain, no help is coming, and all that is left is you.

"Begin," I command.

The Hunters collide in a demonstration of precision and strength that makes my blood sing, and the captain within sparks with pride. I don't give a shit who wins—the show is worth the price I'll pay if Riot loses.

"*Come on, Riot!*" Grace screams.

Riot lands a punch to Rhett's jaw, and a tooth flies into the metal bars, disintegrating on impact.

Riot is going to win this one. He's five moves out.

"Come on, Riot. Please gods," Grace whispers next to me.

I glance down at my wife. "If you lose us the summer house, you owe me a new blade for not asking me first."

She glares up at me. "It's *our* money."

I raise an eyebrow at her. "Right. So it should have been *our* decision to bet it on Riot's big ass."

She huffs and bolts her hands to her hips, attention pinned on the match again.

"Take him, Riot!" she commands.

I clear my throat to hide the smirk burning at the edges of my mouth.

Riot lands a blow to Rhett's gut and then a victory punch into his chin as the Hunter goes flying, landing just short of the scalding cage.

Grace spins, eyes and smile plastered wide. "We won!"

"Congratulations, my love."

She presses herself into my side. "And Captain—" Grace whispers. "I commissioned you a new blade last week for your birthday."

I pull away to look at her. "You're too good to me."

"You need a token of my love at your hip. Don't feel too special, though. I got myself one, too."

My grin widens. "Good." I kiss her temple. "And Gracie—"

She runs her fingertips down my forearm. "Hmmm?" she hums at me.

"You can bet our entire fortune I'll start over anywhere with you."

Her lips part, and she unleashes a sparkling smile that has me starving for her mouth. "Your words have always been your best weapon, Kade."

Rhett stomps over to the bars separating us, face bloody, and shoves his blond hair back. "Stop eye-fucking each other and let us out of this damn pen."

# CHAPTER 9

## VEYA

### Present Day

I SWALLOW AS THE HUMAN girl curls in my lap, trying to hide herself.

I keep *every* instinct in check. Fangs. Hunger. Desire. *Rage*.

My insides burn, fighting my control. The smell of her pumping blood calls to the monster within.

I only have one thing left I can offer her.

*A choice.*

"Look at me," I tell her kindly, keeping my hands fisted in my skirts, not touching her.

And I don't rush her.

Nerian prances in place, feet tapping with his excitement beside us.

I ignore him and pray the gods tip fate in my favor and sway Nerian toward leniency if this doesn't go how he wants it to. It isn't my intention to start a war or overstay our welcome on the first night of our visit.

Second and Emmanuel already have palms on their weapons, though. I can't blame them.

The girl sinks, her knees resting on the floor, and peers up at me, sheltering her breasts in my skirts.

*She looks younger than twenty years.*

"I'm sorry this happened to you. I need you to tell me what you want. Do you understand what I'm asking?" I say.

She nods, her greasy blonde hair glistening in the firelight, tears streaming from her sapphire eyes.

"I want to join my family," she cries.

I give her a kind smile. "And where are they?"

She looks me in the eyes. "With the gods."

"Are you certain?" I ask, my heart breaking for her.

"I'm certain," she says, her voice dropping to a low growl.

"Whatever you wish, brave girl. Would you like me to do it?" I ask, my eyes skirting to Del as he shifts in his chair, his knuckles white as his fingertips grip the edge of the table, Charlotte pale beside him.

I'd be convinced Del was trying to restrain himself from drinking, but my own rage is written in his eyes— another thing we have in common besides our dislike for Balor.

*Surprising, for Nerian's second.*

His expression disappears in a blink when Nerian moves behind Second and into his view.

"Yes, I would like you to do it," the girl whispers, and my gaze finds hers again.

"What is your name?"

"Christine."

"It's my honor to send you to your family, Christine. Know that I will remember you for the rest of my existence."

She smiles at me through her tears.

*Gods.*

I slide a hand up my skirt, reaching for my dagger.

"*Drink from her, Veya,*" Nerian demands excitedly through a crazed sneer.

My gut plummets, fear sliding along my skin. I don't want to be anywhere near the temptation of bloodlust or breaking the rules I steadfastly live by.

"Do it," Christine commands bravely, her gaze narrowing at the king before she climbs into my lap, my eyes connecting with hers. "Don't anger him over me—just drink."

Her hopeful expression begs me to listen, and I consider the risk I would put my people at if I upset Nerian. Their lives are my responsibility.

And we only *just* got here. I can't waste this opportunity.

My heart tears open as I choose to protect our mission and my people over my morals and the risk of bloodlust.

My fangs release underneath the smile I offer Christine, the last one she'll ever see, and I dip my mouth to her neck, jamming myself beneath her tender skin.

And then I *drink* from her.

Something I haven't done in a very, *very* long time.

Her warm blood coats my throat and seeps into me with a power so delicious I can barely breathe. Her aura, her essence, her humanity calls to the monster within, and I take everything. Euphoria, tantalizing and teasing, skims along my skin. Her life force clings to me, pooling pleasure in the starved alcoves of the vampire nature I ignore.

The donated blood I usually consume pales against the vibrant energy of life flooding me.

My hands leave my skirts, and I grip her, my body alight with pure intoxication.

And then, with tears running down my cheeks and desire coursing through my veins, I do something I've *never* done.

I drink the life from her.

Christine sighs, her breath whispering along my collarbone, and she loses consciousness in my arms, the throb of her pulse slowing.

Just a few more pulls.

With my eyes scrunched in grief, I pray to the gods to take her.

And then I *feel* the moment she leaves us.

I wish I could go with her.

King Nerian claps. "Ah, see! It all worked out. Everyone got what they wanted. And didn't she taste fucking fabulous?"

My eyes snap open. "If you'll excuse me, Nerian," I say, voice wavering. I'm balancing on an edge and just might ruin our welcome in this court with the rage and sorrow running through me with no mercy and no end in sight.

*I need to get out of this room.*

Nerian grins at me. "Of course, my dear. Go *enjoy* yourself."

I rise from my chair with Christine draped in my arms and walk out of the dining room without another word, her body and my soul dead.

"I'm so sorry," I whisper to her over and over, heels clacking amid grave silence while Goreon guards lined along the hallway assess me suspiciously. I see myself through the grand foyer, and males pull open the iron doors of the entrance as Balor comes up behind me, barreling past and cutting me off.

"Where do you think you're going, Queen?" he demands.

"Where are the wood stores?" I ask.

The guard beside us eyes Christine and steps forward, face softening so slightly I almost miss it. He nods his chin to the right.

I brush past General Balor as he turns his scowl on his guard. "Who the *fuck* gave you permission to step out of your line?" he growls and launches his soldier into the wall, along with a fuming lecture as I walk away.

*Asshole.*

Second and Del chase after me as I snap to the edges of the enormous stronghold and find the firewood storage.

"Veya," Second says.

I spin, clutching Christine.

"Let us help you," he offers gently, eyes reflecting the burden neither of us thought I would ever bear.

I nod, standing aside, and hold Christine while the males build a pyre.

I might be in Goreon territory, a place I doubt a pyre has ever been built for a human, but I'm the Queen of the Night Kingdom, and this is how *we* do things.

Enemy soil or not.

The freezing wind whips at my skirts, and I pull Christine closer to keep her warm. My pointless act shreds my heart, and it bleeds out as I squeeze a dead girl tighter.

Del and Second lift the final log and secure it before turning to me, their breath heavy with their quick effort. I place Christine atop the structure, her frail frame freezing in my memory as her blood courses through me.

"May the gods keep you and hold you," I tell her, brushing hair from her face and closing her sapphire eyes.

Second steps up next to me, threading his fingers through mine. "May the gods keep you and hold you."

Del moves next to the pyre with a torch and looks at me, the firelight dancing in his violet eyes. He gives me a sad smile, waiting for my command.

I'll never forget the kindness Del showed me tonight. No matter how all this ends.

I nod at Del.

"May the gods keep you and hold you, Christine," he says like he knows her and sets fire to the kindling.

We remain in silence until ash settles into the snow slush. Dawn is just a whisper away, and if I didn't have a kingdom to watch out for and promises to keep, I would let the sun take me.

The three of us snap back to the iron entrance and stride through the gold and ebony foyer.

"I'll leave you both to your rest," Del says, offering me a bow before turning down the hall to the west wing.

I watch his broad back, his suit soiled and dress shoes muddied, as he walks away, shoving his fists into his pockets.

"What do you make of him?" I whisper to Second.

"He doesn't belong here. I'm not sure what keeps him at Nerian's side."

"Agreed."

Second and I snap to our suite of rooms, Night Kingdom guards stationed in the hall. I nod as I pass them, and they bow to me, faces mournful.

My people know what tonight meant to me. My trusted guards are privy to most everything about me.

Charlotte and Emmanuel jump when we walk through the doors.

"Did you burn her?" Charlotte asks, eyes like glaciers, brilliant blue shining through tears.

"We did," Second answers, striding to the wash basin and wetting a cloth before bringing it to me.

I stare at the rag in his calloused hands, knowing exactly what it's for.

Lifting my chin, I let Second wipe Christine's blood from my mouth. He works the cloth down my throat, where I felt her life force flow, a serpent teasing my sanity as I let it snake along my skin in that dining room. Each dab and sweep of the rag threatens to crack the thin control I cling to.

Emmanuel stands in the corner, throwing his blade at the wall and summoning it back to himself over and over.

The consistent thud is comforting while I watch the knife carve his intended design.

The Night Kingdom crest etches into Goreon plaster.

"We will take this kingdom before it's over," I promise them.

"Yes, my queen," they respond.

Second towers over me, his eyes finding mine. "You and I need to talk."

And I know what it's about.

I nod at him to follow me to my room, and we close ourselves in.

"What was your plan? To tell me there was a marriage proposal when we fucking got here?" he asks, tone harsh but lacking bite.

I groan, slinking onto the edge of the bed, my gown pooling around me. "I'll do whatever is necessary to get us close enough to win."

Second paces the room. "Bedding that foulness will never be a necessity. We'll find another way."

"I'll do whatever it takes," I snarl dishonestly, the rawness of my evening screaming at my edges. I would never sleep with Nerian.

Second stops pacing, and his kind eyes make sure to secure mine before he speaks. "You've built a kingdom that will fight for you. *We* will fight for you," he says, gesturing to the closed door with Charlotte and Emmanuel behind it, my trusted guard beyond them. "For what is right. Don't *ever* forget that."

I fall back on the bed. "I'd prefer to only risk myself until we've exhausted every option." I wave a hand in the air. "You can always take over if I miss the mark."

Second yanks me by the ankle, and I bolt upright to face down his finger in my face. "Remember who you are, Veya," he commands. "We go before you do. In every life, godsdamnit."

I close my eyes to shut out my reality for a moment. But the stillness only heightens the sensation of Christine's blood coursing through me. I despise myself.

My gasping cry escapes before I can stop it.

I open my eyes, fangs out. "I still *feel* her. I can't do this," I say, my voice cracking.

A girl is dead, and the only consequence is ecstasy rocketing through me.

This is why vampires lose themselves to bloodlust. *I can see why now.*

Second assesses me for a brief moment, then abruptly tosses me over his shoulder, strides into the bathing room, and flips on the wall fountain. He walks us under a freezing sheet of ice water and stands there with me drooping over him. Each chilled drop feels like a ping of reality against my skin, pelting away at the pleasure consuming me.

"It won't last forever," Second whispers as I sag against him, the heat blazing down my core finally cools.

After several minutes, I pat his shoulder, and he sets me down.

I peer up at Second, recovered and drenched, water cascading down soaked black silk. "We were supposed to scout the west wing while everyone was resting today."

Second smirks at me. "I'm still up for it."

*And I'm desperate for a worthwhile distraction.*

"Let's get some dry clothes on, then."

Second looks warily at me. "You good?"

I nod, trying to ignore how shaken I feel, and he spins on his heel to get changed.

Killing the fountain, I step off the tile onto the fine carpet of my bedchamber, stripping my dress as I go. I opt for a thick sweater and leather trousers and stuff my feet into tall boots.

"Ready?" Second asks, peeking in as I thread another gilded wooden pin into my bun.

"Ready."

We snap down the east wing hallways and stairwells to the center corridor, skirting by human daylight guards with ease, and land at the edge of the west wing.

"Emmanuel said there are two main corridors that intersect at their end; he believes Nerian's rooms are beyond that. These halls are galleries, drawing rooms, and offices. But that's as far as he got," Second whispers.

I snort. "Of course Em's already been down here."

Second looks at me. "He made use of his time after dinner."

As any good assassin for the crown would.

"All right, let's each take a hall to confirm and meet at the end. Then we try to find Nerian's chambers from there."

Second posts his hands on his hips. "In what gods-blessed world are we splitting up?"

I roll my eyes. "Em scouted these halls, but I need to ensure there's nothing of interest here. I want to check the offices, learn what we can."

"Which we can do *together*."

I shake my head at Second in frustration. "We've already lost time today, and I don't know how long we're going to be here, given how difficult the first few hours have been. This could be our only shot."

Second groans at my reasoning. "I already know I'm going to regret this."

I start moving down my hallway before Second can change his mind. "See you on the other side in twenty."

Snapping to the first door, I let myself in.

A drawing room—with surprisingly stunning artwork. I wonder who painted these as I run a finger along a frame's edge, the manicured garden blooming with spring and dappled in moonlight, the depiction of Goreon Castle in its background not nearly as ominous-looking as it is now.

I abandon the painting and slip back into the hall and through the next door.

First office.

Beelining for the desk, I yank open the top drawers and riffle through papers, scanning scrawled cursive and crests.

Correspondence with the Old Tritan territory, dated only a decade ago.

Interesting. And *noted*.

The Night Kingdom will be paying a visit to our eastern mountains.

My spine tingles as I leaf through more communication from across the Sereia Sea and territories north of Goreon. Perhaps correspondence between regions is more common than I thought. Perhaps it's just the Night Kingdom that has been cut off.

*Shit.*

I slam the drawers shut and move to the cabinet on the wall.

Ledgers and banking. Many of Nerian's nobles are in debt to the king. Also noted.

My twenty minutes are disappearing quickly.

I sprint back into the hall and snap to the next door, hand on the knob—

The slap of bare footsteps on stone freezes me in place, and I pause in a shadow as Nerian patters down a hall to my left.

*Oh my gods.*

I ready to follow him, pulling a pin from my bun.

I won't try to kill him, but I want to see where he's going in his bare feet in the middle of the fucking day. I truly thought everyone would be in rest right now, and I'll take this unexpected opportunity without hesitation.

Nerian disappears around the corner, and I step forward quietly to tail him.

Panic spins down my spine as I'm grabbed from behind and pushed up against the wall.

"*Are you fucking kidding me?*" Del snarls in a whisper, his lips a breath from mine, bright eyes searching for an answer from me.

He's stronger, and his hips have me pinned to the marble at my back.

The scent of him hits me—first, the sensual traces of jasmine and cinnamon, then a warm, woodsy pine curls around me.

And the grip of his fingertips at my waist plumes desire I'm not prepared for, and my insides twist against my will. Heart racing, I stare into his eager plum eyes that hold fear, not malice.

Del's hand braces on the wall beside me, caging me in like he's trying to hide me from sight. "Nerian will kill you without blinking, Queen Veya."

*I already know that.*

I swallow, lips parting as my gaze flicks to Del's mouth, and I press a hand to his firm chest, pushing him away to catch my breath.

I'm here to kill a king, not be distracted by stunning gentlemen.

Del steps back, and I don't miss the graze of his fingertips along my hip before his hand drops to his side.

The sensation of his touch lingers.

Del's eyes flash. "Why are you in the west wing? *Please* speak."

"*What's all this?*"

I suppress a groan at the sound of Balor's demanding voice, and my pleading eyes connect with Del's.

His mouth quirks into a playful grin before disappearing into a neutral expression. Del spins to face Balor, his disheveled black hair falling into his eyes.

Goreon's second puts himself between the general and me.

But it's my fault we're in this, and I need to rescue us both.

I edge around Del. "I couldn't sleep. I took myself for a walk."

Balor rolls his eyes at me. "You're pretty, but, unfortunately, not dumb. Why are you in the west wing, Queen?"

This man has a serious problem with women.

"Come off it, Balor. We had a drink in my chambers," Del says. "She was a mess after dinner."

*That's a decent lie.*

I force a sway, sidestepping into Del, and he catches my sweatered elbow with perfect timing.

"Easy, Queen. Liquor and blood hit hard," Balor laughs. "I can't wait to tell the king about this secret dalliance tonight."

"There's nothing secret about it," Del says. "We're in the damn hallway, *General*."

Balor ignores Del. "Where's your second?" General Balor looks down the hall behind me. "I'm surprised the brute let you out of his sight."

Few things make me boil with anger after the life I've lived, but insulting Second is one of them. Thankfully, Balor thinks I'm drunk. I can act out with some leniency.

"Don't be a dick, Balor. I'll put you in your *place*," I slur. Del's chin turns sharply to me, eyes on fire with maybe a little malice this time.

Balor's pallid face flushes as he takes a step toward me, and Del's fingertips wrap around my arm, pulling me into him.

I try not to be distracted by the strong hips pressing into my leathered backside, or the fact that I want to melt into the stone chest behind me.

I kind of *feel* a little drunk, actually.

"Watch your mouth," Balor growls.

"You can't speak to a queen that way," I insist.

"Says who?" he asks with a sneer, spinning around in the empty hallway.

"Says *me*, asshole," Second bellows from behind us. "Get your hand off her, Del. Right the fuck now."

Del drops me instantly, and my step lurches.

I feel woozy. Like a hangover, but different.

Second snaps next to me, and I prop myself into his side.

"I was just about to deliver her back to your rooms," Del drawls at Second. "She had a bit too much, I'm afraid."

"I see. How disappointing," Second says, shaking his head at me.

An honest reaction for the situation I've put us in.

"The first intelligent thing you've said," Balor chirps, and Second's face whips to him.

Second doesn't say anything else. Which, if Balor knew him better, doesn't bode well for their future interactions.

"Come, my queen," Second says and pulls me away as I look over my shoulder at them.

"Get some *rest*, Queen Veya," Del calls after us, his smirk lighting a fire inside me that's going to require another icy shower.

My eyes blink open as the sun sets.

I'm still foggy. But I didn't drink the champagne.

*Christine.*

Reality crashes down on me, the weight of a bloodlust hangover encases me in something akin to shame.

Because I promised myself and everyone in my trusted circle that I would never take a life in that way. We all know I did what was needed, but it was never supposed to happen.

And Christine is dead for no reason other than for her to be Nerian's *appetizer*.

My rage burns like a brilliant star blinking at me in a sea of darkness. And I'm ready to wrangle it from the sky and douse Goreon in its fire.

I suppress a sob threatening to choke its way out of me, and my gaze lands on Second sprawled on a featherbed on my floor. Rising, I quietly pad around him so he can rest a bit longer. I don my dressing gown, strap my daggers to my thighs, and emerge into the sitting room of our suites.

Emmanuel glances up from the blade he's sharpening, lips stretched into a thin line.

When we met, the words it took to convince Emmanuel to join me were few. *"I've never drained a human, and I've only ever turned one other, and he's my second."*

Of course, since then, I've turned several more, like Charlotte. But only because they begged, and who was I to deny their decision for their own life?

This day is testing all of us. A broken promise lingers between Em and I, no matter how justified or humane the choice was.

"I'm sorry," I tell him, my chest unbearably tight. I can't stand the thought of disappointing Em.

He sets his blade on the marble table, the faint clack of steel on stone the only sound in the room. Emmanuel stands and crosses to me. "You've proven yourself more times than I can count. You don't owe me an apology for an impossible choice, Veya."

I nod as his words lay down a bridge between us and release a shuddering breath, trying to banish my sorrow and disappointment.

Charlotte yawns her way through the doorframe from her room and starts when she notices us, arms paused overhead. "How are you feeling?" she asks softly, arms dropping and mouth quirking into a hopeful smile.

I choose to tap into my rage instead of my depression. "Like a queen who needs to get to *work*."

Charlotte grins. "I packed you the perfect dress for that."

I follow Charlotte into her room and suppress a laugh as I glance around at what she's accomplished in a day—a makeup station laid out, jewelry and crowns arranged on a table, and gowns strung up with boot and heel options beneath. She struts over to my outfits lined against the wall, choosing a rich burgundy ballgown, the wide halter neckline designed to cover the turn marks at my neck.

"A commanding color," she says, fingers trailing along the velvet bodice studded with rubies and pink pearls before she plucks it from the hanger.

"I agree."

"What's your goal today?" she asks as I step into the pooled gown.

"To get a tour. I want to know this place like it's our own." Between the surprising correspondence in the office and getting nowhere in the west wing, we need more intel.

Charlotte drags the heavy train to the side and positions herself behind me to secure the buttons down my spine. "How in the gods are we going to convince them of that?"

My petite shoulders bounce under hushed laughter. "I'm still working on a plan."

Charlotte hums at me while she buttons. "This dress is lovely. You look stunning."

"Let's hope Nerian feels the same. I have no idea what he's thinking after last night. I hope I didn't ruin our welcome here."

I turn around as she pats my waist with the last secured loop.

"Why is Nerian bothering with all this? Why doesn't he just attack the Night Kingdom?" she asks, dipping her finger in the perfume on the nearby dressing table and then sweeping it over my collarbone.

I huff. "I've been wondering the same. I think he's bored and playing with his prey first."

But he's invited a warrior into his den. And I will dismantle it piece by piece.

Charlotte dresses herself in peacock blue, her eyes setting off against the color.

"Well, let's keep him distracted and his appetite whet, then," she purrs, drawing red onto her lips.

I smile at her optimism. "We're going to need a lot more than a commanding-colored gown."

# CHAPTER 10

## KADE

Two Hundred Years Ago – Goreon Kingdom

MASTER HULL AND GRACE lead the procession down the hallway to the Mortifer catacombs, with Lou carried behind us by Rhett and station leaders.

I master a neutral gaze to fight the sorrow in my chest while my memories of Lou spin inside me. I don't know if I'll be able to sit on my barstool at his tavern anymore, and my gut twists when I think about sipping from a glass he'll never pour for me again. Such a simple, stupid thing. And I'm going to miss it more than I ever thought I would.

But I have to go back to Lou's, every night I can, because he wouldn't want me to stop coming to his place, or Mother Hollie to lose business, or squander the comforting impact of the Captain's presence amongst the community.

We pass carved stones inscribed with names, ranks, and years along the cavern wall. I don't know which one is my father's; I've only visited my mother. Grace and I travel every summer to the Sereia Sea, where our Mothers' ashes were released, the gods sweeping their souls into the wind and carrying them home.

The procession pauses in the wide, spacious cavern beside the opening in the wall, and Rhett slides his father's body into its resting place with the help of Riot and Brachett.

Hundreds of candles flicker around us as Hunters hold their lit offering, and one by one, we pass the casket, dripping our wax, and saying our final words to Lou.

I'm pissed. I shouldn't be saying any final words to Lou. If I had just been a few tables over, I could have stopped that bolt with my bare fucking hands and this good man would still be behind his bar, smiling and laughing and bringing us all the joy we so greatly need.

*Fuck this king.*

I drip my wax and promise Lou, and all the gods, the revenge he deserves.

We bow our heads in silence and then depart from the sacred space to prepare for our attack on Goreon Castle. Usually, we're tipping back ale all night when a Hunter dies, but it's all business this morning with steaming coffee and station leaders gathered around the roaring fire in the main chamber.

Riot pulls out a map of Goreon City, splaying it on the table.

"We'll meet here on the second day. There's an abandoned underground tunnel system we'll hide in until nightfall." Riot indicates the location and then circles the structure next to it. "This tavern is our closest friendly outpost. Owned and operated by Mother Hollie and … Lou. There's tunnel access through their cellar."

"We're going to need to take out every vampire in that castle," Ned says, eyes pinned to the roaring fire, his jaw tight.

"No one left alive in the stronghold. It's the only way to change Goreon and get Sam back."

Riot grins. "I can't wait to sleep in a royal bedroom in two days."

Brachett tosses Riot his empty cup. "Fetch me another before your royal ass is too good for it."

The chair creaks as Riot stands to refill his coffee.

He eyes me and my full mug. "Anyone else?"

My nerves are getting the better of me. All these men. All these lives. Birthright, training, magic, the call—it's all supposed to numb the stress tied to sending every Hunter into battle on your command. But it doesn't. My worry is eating me alive like a poison. Ready to consume me with every life lost, every chest that will never expand again, every jaw that won't tick, eyes that won't blaze with love, voices that won't laugh, throats that won't swallow down the ale in our glasses.

Whether Hunters want to end the rule of this king, avenge Lou, or save Sam, we're all heading into this with our own reasons, but I'm still the one who has sworn to lead them to the other side.

"I'm good," I promise him, sending out another reach of magic to Sam.

No response.

Riot grips my shoulder before disappearing.

By late morning, all other outfits depart with their guides, and the thirty remaining Hunters from Central march in front of me through the carved chamber, Mortifer's massive stone door rumbling shut behind us. I watch the backs of my men as we venture out from the mountain into the slashing wind. Rhett and Riot hike ahead of me, their honed forms bundled in furs and bent forward against the gale, their boots crunching in the snow under the weight of countless weapons strapped to their backs and belts.

Our weapon stores haven't been this empty in a long time; every Hunter has taken all they can carry.

Master Hull and Grace trail me. The old man wouldn't stay, no matter what I said. Outside of chaining him to the fortress walls, I didn't have a choice. Or so he told me while threatening to douse me with his scalding coffee if I even dared to have an opinion about it.

With heaving breath, we trudge for hours through the icy wilderness back to Southend, and finally the familiar salted cobbled streets thud against my boots and the tension in my chest uncoils a bit.

"Home sweet home!" Riot announces, all but kicking the front door down and stripping armor and swords as he barrels into the kitchen.

Grace sheds her coat and assists her father with his belongings.

"Woman, I've got it," he snarks, and she backs off with a grin, going into the kitchen with Riot.

Men filter in, clogging the modest foyer, and with the last Hunter finally through the door, I slide the bolt and lock us in.

*Home.*

My favorite fucking place with my favorite fucking people.

"Food's in here if anyone wants some," Riot calls from the kitchen.

I escape into my study before I'm trampled by hungry Hunters.

The door snicks shut, and I find comfort in my large leather lounge chair after lighting a fire. I flop open the journal resting on the table next to me.

My pen scratches against parchment as I record the past few days—the decisions, the attitude of the Hunters, my magic that changes and grows with each passing hour since I sent the call across all of Goreon. Whatever unseen fate dangles in our future, my actions are reinforced by the approval of my magic.

The fire pops, and my eyes flick to the flames.

My study door creaks, and I don't bother to check who opened it. Only one person would ever dare such a thing. I set the journal on the table as Grace slides into my lap, her fingers tracing the Hunter crest chained around my neck.

"You need to eat," she tells me. "Should I bring it in here?"

My gaze finds her plump lips before skating up to kind eyes crinkling at their corners.

"I'm in the mood for something else," I admit, the feel of her body sending mine into a frenzy. Everything about our upbringing and magic calls us to protect and honor our women. With our words, time, and *attention*.

And I'd never trade it for any other skill in this life.

Grace runs her hands up my chest, humming as her green eyes sparkle at me. "Probably the same thing I'm in the mood for, Kade." I huff a laugh, and Grace sighs. "I could use a drink tonight, too, though."

My eyebrows pinch. Now, *that* is not a Gracie trait.

She thuds her forehead into my shoulder. "Do you think I should accept my magic before we walk into this thing—" Her voice catches, and I hate that she would even dare to second-guess her decision.

"You don't owe them anything, Grace," I growl as she hides in my neck.

She lifts her head. "I know. A part of me always wants to accept my magic, but I just—I want our children to have the choice."

I cup her face with my palm. "And I love you more because of it."

Magic or not, I'll bow before Grace until my last breath.

"I hate that I have to choose," she says, hands planted on my chest.

"I know, my darling. And I hate it for you, more than you can possibly imagine."

She nods, a small smile creeping out as she shifts to straddle me. "Stiff drink still sounds like the right remedy, though."

I huff. "Probably for everyone."

She hooks a tooth over her bottom lip, her eyes drinking in my hand encompassing her thigh. "I shouldn't get too drunk, though. I wouldn't want to pounce when you need to conserve your energy," she tells me with a straight face that I'm unsure how she's managing.

"Did you just insult my ability to perform my duties as Hunter *and* husband?"

She shrugs, but her eyes darken. "My needs are endless. And this war is important."

I scoff, getting hard beneath her as the heat between her legs threatens my sanity. "Grace Hull, I'm about to bend you over right here and put that baby in you."

She winks, rocking herself against my cock, and my hands tighten on her.

"Eat first, and let's have a drink with our men, *then* you can do that," she says with a velvet tone.

I growl and stand from the chair, tossing Grace over my shoulder. Her yelp pulls a huge grin across my face, and I snatch open the study door, marching us into the kitchen.

Riot looks up from his stew, spoon stuck in his enormous mouth.

"I knew she'd get you out of that office," he mutters around the utensil.

I give Grace's ass a hearty slap. "Conniving wife," I say with pride bursting from my chest.

I love my people. And I was stewing.

But I like to stew. There's nothing wrong with ruminating and internalizing. I can't be certain of my decisions until I roll them over so many times I've got emotional rugburn.

I slide Grace down my front, groping every inch of her as she goes, and my eyes devour her lips, and her piercing green gaze locks onto mine. My upper lip curls, my tongue remembering the way she tastes spread out before me like my own personal feast.

"I don't care how much liquor you have tonight, Grace. Your head will be spinning in bed regardless."

Her lips part as I stuff a ham sandwich into my grin.

"Drinks and swordplay in the basement!" I announce to the house packed with Hunters through a full mouth. "Follow if you want to lose more of your money to me," I shout from the foyer, throwing open the door to the basement.

Dishes and chairs rattle in response.

Grace is right—we need the men out of their heads and not stewing in the madness of storming the castle tomorrow night. And if they don't need it, I sure as fuck do.

I spiral down the stairs.

Striking a torch to life, I secure it in the wall holster and approach the long, leather-stuffed bag hanging from the ceiling and unclasp it to make room for a fighting ring in the center of our training facility. It's not as spacious or epic as Mortifer, but it does the job in a pinch.

Boot stomps rumble down the stairs as the room fills with Hunters.

"I'm going first," Grace announces, dragging a sword from the bin against the wall as Hunters position themselves around the room, leaning against the walls and getting comfortable to watch their Captain and their Heir go at each other.

I fell in love with Grace because of her undeniable beauty, her soft, fierce heart, and her *untamed*, extraordinary fighting talent. She's fast and intelligent. Her skill and training always match mine.

Working hard to ignore my need to ravish the woman sauntering toward me, I warm up my shoulders.

I met Grace when we were fifteen and Master Hull finally let her into the training pens. I couldn't take my eyes off of her. We grew up in the caverns of Mortifer, learning and fighting together from that day onward. And over a pint on my seventeenth birthday, I promised Grace that I would save Goreon and make it a place we would flourish in.

She rolled her eyes at me.

Grace tried to convince me our generation wouldn't bring forth the revolution in any way other than bloodshed and more despair. And I bet her that we'd be the ones to do it. Then she laid into me about the peaceful future she envisioned, but that Hunters are incapable of putting vicious pride and bred brutality aside to accomplish it.

Three years later, I fell to my knees and proposed to the loveliest person I'd ever known, and I promised her that our dreams were aligned. That we would bring peace because we weren't out for only revenge and short-sighted survival goals. Our vision spanned generations.

She didn't roll her eyes that time.

Grace spins her blade of choice, her body lunging and dancing through movements as she warms herself in the brisk room, her breath billowing and her eyes alight with an energy that only emerges when she's fighting. Those green eyes burn as they flick to me.

Gods, she's breathtaking.

"Hunter Kade," she coos, her smirk tipping toward her long lashes as she hits me with the most seductive glance over the edge of her sword.

"Wife," I challenge. "How hard do you want to go?"

She laughs, and her eyes spark. "Might be our last time for a while."

"So all in, then," I tell her with a broad smile and then let my face fall into seriousness.

"Yes," she growls.

I strip my shirt, shaking out the muscles in my arms as Gracie consumes me with her eyes, not giving a shit that we're surrounded by others.

She quirks an eyebrow at me, and I shrug innocently, flexing my abs.

Grace laughs. "Gods bless, Kade. The distraction tactic is *unfair*."

I blow her a kiss and release my most charming smile, only to be greeted by an eye roll and a groan as I yank a sword from the wall and set up across from her.

Grace lunges without warning, her sword nicking my belt, and Hunters cheer in response.

My eyes flick to hers.

Hunger looks back at me.

I scoff. "Are you trying to undress me in front of everyone?"

"You started it," she deadpans and attacks as Hunters holler.

I push her back, but she doesn't stumble; just like always, her nimble limbs carry her like a dancer across the floor.

"Come and get it, baby," Grace purrs, skirting around me, and I spin to track her.

"Aye," I promise with my sword thrusting, forcing her to dart left.

She swings her sword with no mercy, and I meet her, steel against steel, until we're both heaving for air. Tossing her blade, her strength waning without magic, Grace snatches the whip from her belt and cracks it through the air at me.

My eyes narrow, and my arousal spikes. "Not in front of the boys, my love." I duck away from the slashing leather, looking for an opening and catching her contagious, taunting grin.

Her whip snaps across my boots, and I dart for her, sweeping her legs before she lands another strike.

She hits the ground on her back but is already rolling away from my attack and springing from the floor. Grace collides with my body, the force of her lands me on my ass, and she straddles my lap, eyes fierce and wild.

My magic whirrs, and then pain rockets through me as Sam's magic trembles against mine.

"Fuck!" I yell and catch Grace's wrists, stilling her. Confusion crosses her face as my body contorts beneath her.

Rhett and Riot rush us.

"Is it Sam?" Rhett demands, worry etched in his eyes.

I nod, trying not to puke up my dinner.

My magic senses Sam's, deciphering and listening, and I send him the most important message I can, not knowing how long I have with him.

*We'll be there tomorrow night.*

And in response, his magic screams with warning before going dark again.

# CHAPTER 11

## VEYA

### Present Day

I CAN'T *BELIEVE* that was your first full drain last night," Nerian says, leaning forward in his throne, fingers threading a necklace of human teeth.

*Disgusting.*

It's the same dance as yesterday as I stand at the base of the dais, with Goreon guards lining the walls and a sneering court enjoying the show.

"Gods, what a privilege to witness a virgin drain. Honestly, I would've made more of a thing of it, had I known." He waves his hand at me. "I wondered, but—"

"That's enough," I say, eyeing the empty throne beside him, for the queen who no longer holds it.

Nerian raises his eyebrows at me.

I clear my throat, trying to recover my temper so I don't blow this, and smile brightly at Nerian. "Let's move on. If you'd be so kind."

"As you wish." He leans back in his seat, finally dropping his repulsive necklace against the rich fur collar he's wearing. "Where should we begin our discussions for the merger of our rule?"

My turn to raise my eyebrows. "I haven't agreed to anything of the sort."

Nerian cocks his head. "But you traveled all this way, my queen. Why risk such a journey and exposure in my territory without having made your decision?"

*To get close enough to kill you.*

"I'm a careful planner, Nerian. I don't do anything without all the facts."

"Ruthless and wise," he says, but his mocking tone is not missed as he drums his fingers on the arm of his throne.

*I prefer brave and bold.*

"Let's start with a tour. I want to know this place, how you run things, what you're *offering*."

He looks at me shrewdly for a moment, mouth pinching, and I can feel suspicion radiating from him.

I nudge Nerian in the right direction. "From what I've seen, my assets far outweigh yours."

He scoffs. "Definitely not."

I raise my hands, gesturing to the ornate hall. "I have *two* of these throne rooms. *Two* strongholds," I lie. Castle Ruthlessness is unknown, cloaked in endless fog and cloud, built into rock and lying in wait. And those who secretly reside within her are prepared to defend and protect the Night Kingdom whenever we may need them.

The king bolts out of his throne. "Goreon is unmatched, in *every* way," he snarls, fangs dropping.

I look at Del, standing at attention on the dais, and let a bored gaze rake him up and down. "Even your second is smaller than mine."

Del's thick lips part and his eyes gleam at my insult.

Nerian stomps down his steps, fur cloak dragging behind him.

"I'll give you a fucking tour," he says, sweeping past me.

I wink at Del, spinning on my heel, but not before I savor his narrowing eyes and growing smirk.

Second and I walk behind Nerian, Charlotte and Emmanuel behind us, and Del brings up the rear. Nerian's court is an array of judgment as we breeze out of the throne room, their faces screwed in assessment, like they can't decide if their king has any intention of joining forces or not. And it's red eyes all around, which means emotions are at an all-time high, good or bad.

Killing Nerian might be the easier task stacked up next to influencing his court into a new way of living. The Night Kingdom way is not for everyone. But we have had no problem ridding ourselves of problematic individuals over the years.

And I won't hesitate to do it again.

Nerian's long gait requires me to be on the verge of snapping to keep up with him in this heavy dress, but I don't regret my choice. The ballgown and train takes up space and forces vampires to step aside and make way for me.

Which is entirely the point.

Guards peel back, bodies flush against walls as I sweep past.

"Let's start with the army, shall we?" Nerian postures.

"Headcount?" Second asks beside me.

Nerian laughs haughtily, his voice echoing off marble as we wind toward the west wing. "I haven't bothered to keep it recently. We're in the thousands," he says, waving a hand in the air as he leads us along.

The Night Kingdom has one thousand.

But our army is loyal, well-bred, and well-trained. Based on how I've seen Balor treat his soldiers, I'd say Nerian might not have a single loyal warrior in his arsenal. And there's a lot that can go wrong when you can't keep the devotion of your people when the killing starts.

Nerian leads us to his army out of the back of the stronghold, and we snap through the snow for about a mile before the sprawling structure of the barracks looms before us.

It looks like a prison, not a place for a legion.

I wonder if they're chained to the walls in there, starved just enough to obey. I know I'd have to be.

Del steps in front of me, black cloak floating around him as he turns to face me. The set of his jaw and the intensity in his eyes have mine narrowing.

He's warning me—I just don't know what about.

But after his help with Christine and after he came to my rescue with Balor in the west wing, Del's cautioning is duly noted, and my nerves spike.

"Be on your guard, Veya," Nerian drawls. "I am king, but I can't control the whims of everyone."

*Great.*

Nerian steps through a stone archway, Del following, and I glance up at Second. The caw of crows echoes around us in the snowdrift, and flakes gather on my freezing cheeks. My best friend, the male who never shows fear, is laced with hesitation.

But I step a heeled boot over the threshold of the barracks anyway, following Nerian and Del into whatever this is.

To my surprise, the ground floor is empty, and our tour includes a series of vacant training facilities with blood stains no one bothered to clean penetrating stone and plaster. Outside of a few torches lighting the way, there is no warmth here. It's cold and damp and eats at my bones.

King Nerian flings open a door and descends with Del into the underground.

I hesitate at the top of the stairs. This route will offer limited options for escape if we need it. The only exit is likely the one we're winding down.

Images of half-starved vampires like Penny race through my mind, desperate soldiers willing to obey their king for their next meal. And it fires anger through me, heating my veins.

Charlotte threads her fingers through mine as Second positions himself at my back, and Emmanuel slips to my front.

Remaining calm is almost impossible as my fears prattle incessantly the further we follow Nerian into his army's heart.

They could slaughter us right now.

But I firmly believe Nerian's pride and desire to boast his wealth and power will get in the way of that for quite some time. His entertainment is the reason I'm here, and I don't think he's close to done playing with his new toy.

I steady my breath and straighten my shoulders against the onslaught of nerves.

The stairwell dumps onto a ledge, with an arena below us so massive I'm unsure how the ground above hasn't collapsed in on itself. And then the roar of warriors greets their king at such a volume, the pebbles rattle at our feet.

This is why our scouts never found his army. They're under the fucking ground.

"*Gentlemen*," the king calls out over thousands of males, and I try not to scoff. Some of my best fighters are females. And don't get me started on the assassins. Nerian has no idea what he's missing out on.

The feral response from his males fires a chill down my spine, piercing like a needle through each vertebra. Snapping and hissing becomes a frenzy below, like an untamed monster thrashing at the edges of the endless cavern, held back only by the walls that trap it.

Nerian turns to me. "We never let them out," he says like it's an explanation.

"Impressive," I tell him through a forced smile.

"When I do release them, they execute what I demand and are rewarded before returning to their shelter."

"What is their reward?" I ask loudly, voice screaming out of my chest over the roar of souls below.

I don't want the answer, but I need to know.

Nerian's eyes flash red, and his fangs elongate. "Anything they want, really. Most choose a visit to the farm."

My eyes flick to Del. His thick lips press together slightly before his features settle into a blank mask.

Clearly, he and I need a private conversation. It's obvious Del doesn't share the king's proclivities, but somehow he's the second of Goreon. And that just doesn't make any fucking sense. What is this game he's playing? Because it's a dangerous one.

"Is the farm our next stop?" I ask.

Nerian chuckles. "It can be. But given last night, you may want some champagne first."

I step closer to the king, gown snagging on the ground, but I rip myself from it without pause. "My beliefs don't make me weak, Nerian. Show me what you have to show me."

He bows. "As you wish, my queen."

Nerian makes for the stairwell, and Del nods for us to follow. I watch him grip the railing, his short, dark hair falling in front of his eyes, surveying the mob below.

"This is so fucked," Charlotte whispers in my ear, clutching two fistfuls of my gown to get close to me.

Her blue eyes find mine, and I drop my voice, tone determined: "Let's convince Nerian to show us everything. We *need* to know."

She nods and points her chin forward, holding it high, and struts her ass up the stairwell behind the king. "King Nerian, I did *love* the beautiful estates we saw on our journey through the city," she croons.

"Ah, thank you for noticing, my dear," Nerian drawls, voice echoing up the stairwell. "I built those for my nobles. They owe me their lives, really." He drones on about his wealth and the army as we climb and trail through the snow toward the castle.

Del whispers behind me, "You need to prepare yourself."

That's all he says, and my mind churns with how this could get worse.

Torches and tended fires guide our way as Nerian leads us east of the castle. The half-frozen bay glistens in moonlight beyond a series of immaculate gardens still clinging to the land despite the winter chill. The king stops at a set of tall iron gates flanked by twenty-foot hedges for as far as I can see on either side.

He bows his head before he flicks the gates open and ambles into the private garden, which I'm certain is stunning in the spring and summer. A grand fountain stands in the center of the meticulously curated horticulture.

"What a lovely garden," Charlotte says, walking beside Nerian.

My wine-red gown drags along freshly fallen snow as we follow the king to the fountain he's paused in front of.

"Not much farmland in a sitting garden, though," Charlotte says as I glance around, wondering what we're doing here and where the farm is.

"I don't keep precious things in plain sight," Nerian scolds her.

The king's fangs pop, and he pierces his own finger, blood pooling on his skin. Nerian traces his blood along the goddess statue carved into the marble fountain.

I jerk to attention, Second tensing beside me as Nerian draws a swirling pattern.

My lip curls. It's the same pattern Nerian absentmindedly drew on the tablecloth last night.

The spelled fountain unlocks under his blood.

The pattern is a key, and I play it over in my mind, memorizing it—just in case.

The marble splits down the center; a faint line I didn't notice before pulls apart to reveal a wide stairwell, stone shining in the moonlight.

Underground we go again.

It's intelligent, really. To hold so much where no one can see. Where no one knows to look. Much like the way I've done things.

King Nerian whisks himself down the steps, an eagerness moving his heels with purpose. His excitement spikes my unease.

The smell hits me first. The sharp tang of body odor and the metallic bite of blood.

Second stiffens beside me, Emmanuel curses, and Charlotte puffs her chest.

Del steps next to me, grabbing my arm with his gloved hand as Nerian hurries out of sight and earshot.

Emmanuel snaps, blade at Del's throat, but his grip doesn't loosen on my arm.

I wave my assassin off, and Em steps back as my gaze tracks from Del's grip up to his eyes, which are now full of sorrow.

"Know that I don't want this," Del whispers harshly, our breath unfurling between us in the dreadful cold.

He spins before I can reply, cloak floating behind him, and I watch his tall, muscular form descend into nothingness.

"We can leave *now*," Second growls, boots crunching in the snow as he steps to my side.

"I agree. We regroup and attack," Emmanuel says.

I turn to face my family and shake my head. "I'm not prepared to gamble the lives of our people yet. I need to know more. I need certainty we can't deal with this from the inside. There's still opportunity for us to take Nerian out during this visit."

Emmanuel and Second nod at me, but I can see the hesitation in their gazes.

I will always value their counsel. But I *will* listen to my gut first.

"Well, then, let's get down there," Charlotte says, voice sharp.

Second leads the way. My eyes adjust to the darkness as I clop down the steps.

At the bottom of the stairwell, Nerian and Del stand at another platform, their forms blocking whatever is below.

Del's head shifts to the side, sensing our approach.

"*Come, Veya!*" Nerian invites excitedly.

I move to the ledge. Holding myself together, with all that I am, I stare out at the *farm*.

My breath leaves me as tears prick my eyes.

From the platform above, my gaze sweeps over hundreds of humans chained and prostrate, with skin ports fixed into arms and ribcages, blood spilling down tubes. Iron stifles the air as humans slowly drip their life force into carafe after carafe.

Second hisses beside me.

"I control all food sources in my kingdom," Nerian begins. "Those who can afford to drink from the vein can purchase something fresh, but that gets expensive for the general population and the army." He leans over the railing, salivating. "This could all be yours, my queen," he brags.

"We're set for life here. Nothing can touch us. We *are* power."

I can't find my breath. I can't find my sanity.

Every dream will be haunted from this day forth. Every day I've stalled in taking this kingdom will *haunt* me, because with each sunset I saw, so many others were losing their lives, their freedoms, their mothers and fathers.

I had no idea it was this bad, that foulness to this extent existed here.

I sneak a glance at Del beside me. He's pale and still. A statue of honed, gorgeous marble. Outside of a ticking jaw.

*Prepare myself, indeed.*

My eyes drag back to the suffering below.

And then a door to the left beside a row of beds flies open, and guards stream through, humans shuffling and stumbling in their grasps. Balor enters last, holding a young woman by her neck. Her cries pelt at me.

"Please, I beg you, sir!" she pleads.

Balor throws her to the ground at his feet, then kneels and slaps a cuff around her wrist. "Don't fucking move, bitch."

"Ah! Taxes are here!" Nerian screams, bouncing next to me.

I grip the railing beside Nerian, needing to balance myself against the horror as Balor glances up at the balcony and *smiles* at us.

"My king, a very good haul this month," Balor says, and Nerian prances on his feet like a fucking child. "Besides *this* pain in my ass," he says, viciously kicking the cuffed woman.

I feel the assault in my own gut.

Balor snatches up the woman, dragging her to an empty cot. "Lie down."

She plants her feet and shakes her head.

*Oh my gods, lie down. Buy yourself time.*

Balor towers over her. *"Lie. Down."*

Second shifts on his feet beside me, probably about as ready to jump over this railing as I am.

Nerian clicks his tongue. "Settle her!" he yells at Balor.

The general tosses the woman on the cot, but she grips the edge of the bedding and pulls herself quickly to the other side, crawling off.

Balor sighs at the ceiling as the woman scrambles toward the doorway, and Nerian starts to laugh, a joyful, amused cackle.

I want to punch the sound back into his mouth.

The general snaps to the woman, hand around her throat before she's reached the door, and he glances up at Nerian. "Told you. Pain in my ass, this one."

"They can't all be winners," Nerian drawls, hanging over the railing like he can't get close enough to his new plunder. "Why don't you enjoy a well-earned lunch then, General?"

*No.*

Balor's eyes flash red, and his fangs drop. "That's generous of you, my king, truly."

Nerian waves him off and turns to me with a wide grin. "I've lost too many over the centuries by keeping them in the dungeons. This method has proven most successful. Wouldn't you say?"

I watch Balor sink his fangs into the screaming woman and drain her.

After her screams fade into silence, I peel my gaze away and look at the king. His eyes are wild with hunger, expression euphoric with his addiction.

A tear I can't control slips past my defenses.

My mission is set. We're not leaving here until I free these people and Nerian is nothing but a bitter memory. We *will* end this.

Nothing will stop me.

"Oh dear, I've upset you," he admonishes, swiping his own cheek to mimic my tears.

"No, it's the most striking thing I've ever seen," I say, forcing a steady and assured tone.

Nerian sighs, staring longingly below again before he looks me in the eye, gaze flashing red. "I know. And wouldn't you say our assets are more aligned *now*?"

I hum at him in agreement, bottling my rage. "Is this where Christine came from?"

Nerian's proud smile makes me nauseous as he tsks. "No, no. Special stock is kept elsewhere."

Dread pools in my gut. "Let's see that next," I demand, mustering excitement into my tone.

Nerian runs a finger along the railing, gazing at his farm. "I'd love to show you the cellar. We will visit it later this evening." His chin tilts toward me, and his red eyes spark. "First, I have an activity planned."

*Oh gods.*

"Oh?" I ask.

A thud below catches my attention, and I swivel my focus as Balor walks away from the finished "meal" he's tossed aside.

"I thought it best for you to get to know me, too, Veya," Nerian begins.

*You're a monster, that's who you fucking are.*

Del moves toward the stairwell, and I don't miss the disgust on his face behind his king. I force myself to pay attention, facing Nerian again and feigning interest. It feels like my body doesn't even belong to me anymore with the performance I'm compelling myself to give.

Nerian leans casually on the railing, flipping his cloak over his shoulder. His muscles flex under his suiting, and his mouth purses like I'm supposed to be drawn to his physique and his story. "When I was human, I loved hunting my food. Deer hunting was my favorite. Would you like to reminisce with me today?"

The king's eyes practically twinkle with his memories. I haven't hunted in a long time, but whatever gets me into that cellar tonight, I'll do.

"It's been a while since I aimed a bow at a deer," I confess, and Nerian chuckles softly.

"Oh, same for me. It'll be fun, regardless—I promise. It's a challenge in the night, finding them while they're sleeping."

I nod in acceptance.

He spins on his heel away from the farm, speeding up the stairwell. "Come, my dear! To the stables!"

With a final glance below, I stow my rage and horror, strapping it down tight, saving it for later. I straighten my shoulders with a deep breath and look up at Second. "We're *not* leaving."

Second's gaze flicks to the farm. "I support that decision," he snarls and whips around to lead the way to the surface.

Nerian and Del trot ahead on a cleared path, leading our party west of the castle toward a dense forest. Snow falls thickly, blurring my surroundings, and the only warmth is the animal underneath my sidesaddle as we trudge through the wintry storm.

Well, that *and* my enormous gown piled and draped around me, a sea of red in the moonlit white. And it's not so *commanding* when it feels like I'm drowning in vulnerability.

Nerian didn't even offer to let us change clothes before this hunting expedition.

I'm unsure how much more placating I can put up with, and we're only halfway through our second night in this hell. As we travel the frozen landscape, I let a tear fall while I battle the overwhelm surging through me. Nerian's bloodlust, his army, Christine, the farm, the correspondence in Nerian's office with the Old Tritan territory—that region was neutralized. Or so I thought. We haven't been over our eastern mountains in two decades, but Nerian's correspondence postdates that.

We missed something.

It all has me on edge, and I'm nervous what might tip me over it and break my restraint, putting all of our lives in peril.

Nerian didn't bring any guards with us, or even Balor, on this little excursion. Which tells me the king believes he could take us all if we attacked him. And that makes my heart sink. Our odds of success are stacked against us so blatantly, I can barely hold back my panic.

One night at a time. One step closer to finding a weakness, or an opportunity, that bolsters our chances.

My gloved hands squeeze the reins mercilessly as I grasp at control.

Emmanuel pulls up beside me. "Relax, Veya," he whispers, and I peer over at him from beneath my hood.

"Your fluency in body language is annoying, Em."

He shrugs. "Part of the job."

Charlotte comes up on my other side. "The cellar better be worth this pointless, freezing *activity*." Her teeth chatter as she rolls her eyes at Nerian's back.

I huff at her and look back at Emmanuel. "Remind me to tell you about a letter I found in Nerian's office," I say to him, and his eyes blow wide. "You're going to want to check the Southern Continent border on the other side of the eastern mountains when we get home. I think we've got unwanted company in our lands."

"*You went sneaking into offices*?" he hisses under his breath.

"Not the point."

"It *is* the point," he says, steering his horse closer to mine like the action might morph his opinion into fact.

I sigh at him. "You were out sneaking, too, when Second and I left."

His gaze narrows on me. "Part. Of. The. Job."

Nerian's horse halts ahead, and our focus whips front. He turns in his saddle, his red eyes burning through the snowfall. "Just around the bend now, weapons ready," he calls jovially. "Why don't you come by my side, Veya?"

Begrudgingly, I nudge my horse forward, joining the king with Second and Emmanuel on my flanks.

"Now, no cheating," Nerian drawls. "The rules are simple. You can't leave your horse, no snapping. Your limitations are human for this hunt. Let's see if we can still make a kill, huh?" He taps his bow and pulls an arrow from his quiver. "I'll get the competition going."

The king kicks his horse into a gallop toward the edge of the tree line. "Follow me!" he calls behind him before disappearing into the storm.

"What the fuck is this, Del?" I whisper, trying to rally any sort of strategy.

His amethyst eyes dart to me. "I honestly have no idea."

"Fuck," Second snarls, and we all trot forward to find Nerian.

We emerge into a meadow, and I know for certain there are no deer here.

The cottage in the center of the clearing is on fire, engulfed in flames, and the family that was sleeping within its walls is running for their lives into the trees as Nerian chases them around, taunting.

"On my mark!" he calls. "Pick your target. First one back with a kill wins!"

"Oh my gods," Charlotte says, the light from the blaze twinkling the tears in her eyes.

Del's horse prances nervously beside me. "*Fuck,*" he spews and races to the tree line after a woman in her nightdress.

"*That's it, Deleos!*" Nerian praises, and the king takes off after a man running in the opposite direction with a child in his arms.

We have seconds to make a decision. To do *something*.

My eyes find a young boy running after his mother.

"I'll get the boy out," I tell Second and Emmanuel.

They nod. "We'll see what we can manage with the others," Em says.

We all take off in opposite directions, and I pray to every god I know as I break back into the tree line behind the boy.

It takes me only a moment to reach him.

I leap from my horse, grabbing the boy, and slam my hand over his mouth. "Look at me and *listen*," I demand.

His wild eyes settle on my face.

"I'm going to lift you onto that horse, and you're going to get out of here, as fast as you can ride. Do you understand?"

He nods against my palm, but his eyes shift back toward his home.

"No. This is not the time for bravery or saving someone else. This is your *life*. Tell me you understand."

His gaze shifts back to me, and a tear slides down his pink cheek.

I uncurl my fingers from his mouth.

"I understand," he whispers.

I hoist the child into my arms, not wasting another second, and position him in the saddle.

"Grab the reins," I beg as he sits in his shock with winter raging around him.

His small hands grip the leather.

"Get into the city, get rid of the horse."

He nods, then I cluck at the horse with a firm coax on her hindquarter, and they race into the night. I spin back toward the clearing, eyes red and burning under my anger, and wade through the snow in my gown.

"You broke the *rules*, Veya!" Nerian laughs as I emerge into the meadow, struggling through the knee-deep snow.

"I fell off and couldn't get back up in this fucking dress," I say through a spine-shattering shiver. "I lost your horse in the process, too. I'm sorry."

He shakes his head with a snap of his tongue. "What a glorious failure, my queen," he laughs, and I don't even have to try to look defeated or disappointed.

"Indeed," I sigh, eyes catching on Second as he emerges from the tree line, empty-handed on his horse.

"I guess I won, then," Nerian says, the man he chased draped over his horse with two arrows in his back.

"I guess so," I say, wondering where the child the man was holding ended up. I'm not sure I can handle the answer.

"I would love to show you the cellar now. Back to the castle, shall we? You could use a drink, I think."

I nod, breath heaving, and beg the gods to get me through the rest of this night.

# CHAPTER 12

## KADE

Two Hundred Years Ago – Goreon Kingdom

"DO YOU FEAR FAILURE?" Master asks, warming himself by the roaring fire in the living room as my body finally calms down after Sam's magic ran through me like a blade.

My trance shifts from crackling logs to Master's weathered face. Rhett parks himself on the floor beside the fire.

"I feared loss of life, but not failure," I admit. "But now—"

Master nods stoically, and Grace shifts her head in my lap, her sculpted legs draped over the arm of the sofa.

"Sam was telling us not to come, but I don't know if it was heroic bravery, not wanting us to jeopardize ourselves for him, or something more than that," I say.

My magic is anxious, gold shaking in trembling pools as it awaits another message.

Rhett rakes his hands down his face. He lost his father and his best friend in a single moment, and I don't have anything to offer him other than my sword tomorrow night.

Master's expression is drawn. "We'll bleed more losses if we do nothing. Our veil has been broken; I won't gamble further discovery of our numbers or safehouses."

*I couldn't agree more.*

The front door crashes open, and Grace tenses against me. I grip her shoulder, running a thumb over it, and she relaxes again as Riot comes around the corner, dumping ten enormous logs next to the hearth.

Grace sighs, sitting up. "I agree. If the king found our home, and Lou's—" her voice catches, "they already seem to know everything about us in Southend. I still think we do this."

"Aye," Rhett growls, throwing one of the logs into the fireplace. "We're infiltrating that castle and getting Sam out. I don't give a shit what he's warning us about."

I don't bother to correct Rhett that he's not the one to make the decision because I was about to say the same damn thing.

Master pushes himself to standing, backlit by the fire. "Captain Kade—"

Grace lifts herself from me, and I stand at attention. "Master."

"We're moving forward with this war. And we're going to get my son out of that hell. I'm thankful you're the man leading us. Your father would be proud," he says, and my jaw clenches.

"Forever may he rest," Grace says softly, and I nod at them, falling back onto the sofa.

"You all need to head to bed. Big day tomorrow," Master says, shuffling toward his room, Rhett right behind him.

Big day, indeed. We're in the underground by late afternoon to meet up with the legion and infiltrating the castle by nightfall.

*Gods be with us.*

Grace steps between my knees and kisses me, and I let my hands linger on her hips before she pulls away. "I'll see you in bed, love."

"I'll be right up."

Riot rakes his hair back as she climbs the stairs, his face stern.

"We're leaving at dawn to scout the castle and make sure we've got that entry point," I tell him.

"Aye, I might decide to waltz right the fuck in there, though."

*He won't.*

"You know Grace won't stay behind tomorrow night," Riot whispers, and my heart thuds in my chest.

"I know."

"She can hold her own," he tries to encourage.

"I know that, too."

"Can't blame her. I wouldn't stay behind either. Nothing would stop me."

I shake my head, slapping my thighs as I stand. "When I married the woman, I made the decision to support whatever choices she makes. I won't stop her from performing the duties she sees fit for her life. Heir, mother, wife, Hunter. Magic, no magic. It's up to her."

"Aren't you just the perfect fucker?"

I huff at him, turning toward the stairs. "Doesn't mean I'm not tortured by it every day, Riot."

As dawn breaks, Riot, Grace, and I venture through Southend, strolling past Lou's, a single strip of black cloth hanging in the window, mourning the owner and warning everyone who passes. Black fabric is always hung during the day when warranted, discreetly communicating one message above all else: vampire attack.

Snow up to our calves, we slog through the forest bordering the bay that curves around the east side of the castle. Grace follows Riot, his form plowing a path ahead of her. Breath heaving from our effort, we finally break through the tree line and crouch to rest our legs and stay hidden at the edge of the forest.

Hail patters into the shimmering bay like diamonds scattering over glass, and rare sunshine streaks through spotty, heavy clouds. I shift beside Riot, my right thigh barking at me, and the stillness of the morning is eerie as fog curls across the water's surface, blurring the castle beyond. The clouds shift, finally blotting the sun.

"The men I sent to scout last night saw no movement in or out of the castle," I inform them.

"That's odd," Riot says, his boots scraping against snow as he lowers to balance on a knee and pulls the telescope from his chest pocket. "Are we still thinking dungeon access?"

"Yeah," I admit.

No matter what anger I have toward my father, he was the best captain the Hunters had seen in centuries, and I trust his assessment, but I need to vet its current status.

Riot peers through the telescope, and a damp wind gusts past and into my bones, fog rolling back like the gods are on our side.

Grace shivers beside me, hunkering down tighter in her squat.

"There's the usual thirty human guards on the rampart and another dozen in the turrets," Riot says.

"Let's go find our entrance," I say.

We jog the three miles around the bay to the waste gate at the base of the massive stronghold, the thick, iron dungeon door beside it that opens up onto the bridge crossing the bay.

"Wish me the luck of the gods," I whisper as Riot salutes me, and Grace giggles next to him.

I freeze the breath in my chest and step into deep sludge, the others remaining hidden against the edge of the castle wall. My magic simmers, reducing all bodily functions to a minimum to reduce the consumption of my breath and leave me with several minutes of no need for air.

And then I dive.

Under the foulness, I swim blindly for the rusted gate, and then my fingers find steel, and I yank at it.

No budge.

I feel along its edges to find the lock.

*There.*

My hand closes around the padlock, and I call my magic to attention. Muscles hardening, I pull at the steel, and the hinge of the lock bends and severs under my strength.

I drag the gate open in the soundless mud of waste and swim through.

Traveling to the right, I find stone and edge my fingertips upward toward a lip. Slowly, I float to the surface and peek above the flow to survey the tunnel I'm in.

The sewer is unguarded, as predicted.

I hoist myself onto the stone walkway and race toward the nearest door to test the handle.

Not locked.

*Fucking idiots.*

I'd worry about leaving a trail of sludge behind me as I explore, but it's obvious no one comes down here. The cobwebs, rats, dirty pathways, and mold growth are overwhelming.

Wiping my face to clear what I can from my airways and eyes, I finally take a gagging breath, vision blurring at the stench. I make a mental note to carry sacks of water to rinse with and sealed cloths to wipe if this is our only way in.

*I'm not taking down a kingdom covered in shit.*

After collecting myself, I assess the stone corridor before me. My goal is to find the exterior dungeon door access and confirm I can open it. I don't need all my men swimming through this if they can walk through the back door. And if I can get that door open, I can dunk my shit-covered ass in the bay, too.

The Hunter within prepares to track movement around me as I move forward, the shadowed corridor sharpening. Aged stone walls ooze with slime, like trails of blood crying with the despair of the kingdom. My magic surges to attention as I venture deeper into the dungeons of our enemy, my adrenaline spiking as my magic senses hundreds of vampires in the castle above.

I need to cut left and around to access the door beside the grate I swam through, so I follow the wall, waiting for my first opportunity to turn. My boots tap quietly against the stone floor, and I hit the first blockade.

The large wooden door is bolted shut, with a metal grate at its center. I peer through to a long hallway lined with holding cells and call upon my magic, strength bursting, and yank the pins out of the hinges before gripping the sides of the thick door. I push through my legs to release it from the wall. Spinning, I set the massive door to the side and race through the doorframe, clock ticking now with the evidence of my intrusion.

An unconscious body is slumped over in one of the cells, but based on the smell, the frail man is no longer with us.

*Monsters.*

I reach my magic out to Sam—*no response*. The Captain in me hates being this close to my Hunter and not being able to do anything to help him.

My first opportunity to turn left is just ahead, and my magic jumps as it senses movement around the corner. I halt in my tracks, but it's not a vampiric threat, so I plaster on a worried look before striding around the corner.

The human guard and I stare at one another.

His eyes widen as he scans my soiled clothing and the blades at my hips.

"Morning," I say brightly.

He fumbles for his sword before aiming it at me, and it shakes between us.

"There's no need for that," I tell the speechless guard, the dark circles under his eyes deepening with his stress.

"No one is allowed down here," he says, eyeing me as I step toward him.

"I'm just looking for my brother," I say, spreading my hands out wide. "Don't think he's down here, though."

The guard huffs at me. "Probably in the graves, I'm afraid."

"Aye," I say, wringing the shit water out of my tunic. It splashes between our boots.

The guard gags and recovers himself, shaking his head. "Sorry about your brother. There are no humans alive in the dungeons."

I grunt. "Why waste a good meal, right?"

The guard eyes me, clearly undecided about what to do with me.

"Care to show me the way out? I'd prefer not to go back the way I came."

The guard stiffens.

"So, is a failed rescue attempt going to cost me my life too, then?" I ask him.

"It's supposed to," he says, sword still pointed at my chest.

"I see," I say, praying to the gods I can convince the guard to let me out of here so I don't have to knock him out. "Any chance we can just forget we saw each other?"

He hesitates. Human guards are loyal to the king for only one reason.

I stuff my hands into my soaked pockets, watching the guard's nose wrinkle. "You know, if you ever want out of this life, there's a tavern in Southend that'll be looking for an extra set of hands in the coming weeks. Benefits aren't quite the same, but if you ever want out—"

"I won't trade my family's survival," he growls.

"Can't compete with that perk, huh?"

"No."

"Well, I have a family to feed *and* protect. And I don't have the privilege of working for the king," I say.

His face softens, a swallow tracking down his throat.

I let my eyes burn with the honesty in my statement. "Please. No one knows I'm down here."

His shoulders droop. "I hate this fucking job," he grumbles and aims his sword down the hall. "*Fine.* You're in front."

I grin and stride forward, passing the disgusted man.

My magic keeps tabs on the distance of his footfalls behind me and the threat of his sword while we walk.

"Thank you. *Truly.*"

He grunts, and I hear him sheathe his blade.

"Left turn," the guard instructs, and I head down the next hallway, passing through a round foyer of sorts, hallways jetting in every direction.

My eyes catch on the exterior dungeon door at the end of the tunnel, and I smile into the dimness.

"Stand aside. Hands on the wall."

I do as he says, peering over my shoulder to watch him insert a key into three separate locks and slide the thick bolts as wide as my forearm out of the stone wall.

A complication. But we can plan for it.

"If you want to leave, you need to help me pull it open," he says.

The iron door is so massive and heavy, it's impossible to move with one man. And there's no way a

Hunter could rip it from its locked bolts from the outside. An intentional design by the vampires. I could pull it open alone if unlocked, but he doesn't know that. So I help the guard heave the iron door, the scrape against stone echoing behind us through the dungeon.

The man's sad eyes meet mine as he steps back to let me through, and he gives me a half-smile before I step out into the chilled morning and push the door closed from the other side.

The guard locks me out, peering through the small grate.

"Until next time," I tell him with a wink, breaking into a jog across the bridge over the bay, knowing Riot is watching me through his telescope.

I throw two finger signals and make for home.

The dungeon is our way in.

# CHAPTER 13

### VEYA

Present Day

**M**Y EMOTIONS STILL in chaos from the farm and the hunt, I watch King Nerian prance into his cellar.

If hell designed a pleasure den, it might pale in comparison to the theater I'm standing in.

In the freezing underground of the castle, cages laced in fire surround us. Twenty golden prisons designed to keep hungry vampires at bay and barely dressed human girls warm within them dot the expansive cellar, all of them blazing, apart from one in the far corner.

The vibrant red hair and not-yet-starved curves of the girl nearest me catch my attention, and her bright green eyes lock on to mine. There's nothing but fight in them.

The siren within her calls to me.

I turn to Nerian and point. "I want that one."

Emmanuel's gaze flicks to me before he approaches another cage, following my lead. The soft, alert brown eyes of the girl behind the bars sear in my memory, a doe in a forest burning down around her. "I want this one," he says, and the doe flinches at his words.

Nerian's smile unleashes. "I knew my lifestyle would grow on you."

I hum at him, keeping my fizzing temper held deep within. I peer up at Second beside me. "Which one for you?"

His chin jerks to me, and understanding flashes.

Second pins his hands behind his back, forcibly restraining himself, and then walks the cages like he owns the place, and I fucking love him for it.

"I'll take both of these," Second growls, his eyes locked on two cages, dark braided hair in one and blonde curls in the other.

"You can pick *one*," Nerian scolds.

Second turns a raised eyebrow on the king. "You're courting my queen and my kingdom. I'll take both."

Nerian pauses at the gall. Finally, he acquiesces. "Anything for Queen Veya and her *second*."

"Excellent," Second says, and his hands move like lightning through the fire that could kill him, ripping the door of the dark-haired girl's cage off its hinges. Then he snaps, and the other barred cage door is slamming against the opposite wall faster than our eyes can track.

"Eager male," Nerian says, salivating and eyes flashing crimson.

"Always has been," I reply, my smile genuine as Second's girls peer at him warily, scooting away from the opening.

Charlotte strides to the unlit, dark cage in the corner. I can barely see the girl curled and shivering in the back of it.

"What happened here?" Charlotte asks, her hands gripping the bars.

"Ah, Violet is a naughty girl. Tried to escape."

*How?!*

Violet's eyes flash into the room, and bright plum sparks through the dark. Eyes like Del's.

"Show yourself, Violet," Nerian drawls, practically drooling on himself.

Frail, pale fingers grip the bars as Violet pulls herself into view, her raven-black hair and strong jawline make my breath catch as I stare at Del's spitting image.

*Holy gods.*

I leash any reaction. And I don't dare look over at Del and draw Nerian's attention.

"I'll take the naughty girl," Charlotte coos, drumming her fingertips along the bars in a taunt, and her fangs pop from her gums.

*Gods, she's brilliant.*

Desperate to get these girls out of here as soon as possible, I approach the siren. Her red-orange curls rival the flame licking around her.

"Will you join me in my rooms?" I beckon.

Her green eyes find mine again, emeralds gleaming in an abandoned mine.

"It would be my pleasure," she slurs, and my heart cracks for the drugged girl.

Nerian approaches the cage beside my siren and presses a mechanism that douses the fire and opens the door, the woman within cross-legged and ignoring him. He grabs her ankle and yanks her out of the cage, dragging her along behind him.

"If they're not turned or dead by sunset, it's your heads," he tells us as he hoists his girl up the stairwell and leaves us in his cellar, her soft pleas growing faint, and my soul mourning that I couldn't save her.

Or the others—fourteen cages are still filled.

I scan them, determination settling in my bones. We'll get them out, too.

*Soon.*

We all stand in stillness until we know Nerian has gone. Just the flicker of flame and the hiss of fuel until his footsteps disappear.

And in a blink, Del darts for the darkened cage, ripping the door off.

The whimper from Violet as she crashes into his arms threatens my sanity for the millionth time today.

I barge into our suite, the siren barely conscious in my arms.

Second ushers his two girls to the sofa near the fireplace and tosses logs into the hearth, quickly lighting them.

Cradling his doe, Emmanuel carries her toward the roaring warmth, her face hiding in his leathers. My assassin stands before the fire, and I've never seen him so still unless he's about to kill someone. He doesn't set her down, and it's a rare moment of tenderness from Em.

I place my siren on the sofa next to Second's girls, sweeping back the strawberry flame of hair from her emerald eyes.

"What's your name?"

"Sophie," she slurs, eyelids heavy.

"Why don't you rest for a bit, Sophie," I say and ease her back into the cushions.

She curls herself in the corner.

*Turned or dead by sunset.*

I storm to the window, throw open the steel shutters and then the windowpane, and breathe deeply. My eyes find the stars I memorized long ago, and I trace the pattern in my mind, trying to calm myself with familiarity and soothe insufferable frustration.

"He plays with us because he plans to kill us," Second says grimly. "There's no doubt there. We're not intended to walk away with this knowledge."

"Obviously," Charlotte replies, coming to stand beside me, her arm snaking my waist. I lean my head against her shoulder.

The suite door kicks open, and we whip around.

Del marches into our suite, Violet passed out in his arms. He lays her on the settee and beckons me with a jerk of his chin toward my room.

"We need to have a conversation," he says, face tight above his perfect suit.

I narrow my eyes at the male.

*Yes, we do.*

I sweep past him into my bedchamber, and his footsteps follow.

We face each other at opposite ends as the door thuds closed. The space between us feels like a battlefield to cross, but I'm unsure if this male is my enemy or my ally.

Curbing my temper, I start with a reasonable question. "Who is Violet to you?"

"Her name *isn't* Violet," Del growls. "The king names them after their eyes."

I swallow my disgust. "Understood. What is her name, and who is she to you, Del?"

His eyes meet mine, and after a breath, his shoulders droop. "Her name is Aurelia, and she's my great-granddaughter."

Which means he had a child when he was human, however long ago that was. *Gods.*

"Does the king know that?"

He shakes his head.

"Good." I sigh. "First things first: What are we doing with these women?" I ask, hoping I get the answer I want.

Del doesn't pause before responding. "We get them out. If they want to turn, we'll give it to them. But otherwise, we're getting them back to their families."

I offer him an approving nod. "We are in agreement."

He steps away from the door, closing a few feet of our distance. "Good."

*Time to be bold.*

"How do you stand by with all of that horror under your fucking feet, Del?"

I watch his throat track down a swallow, his gaze piercing. "I've been waiting for my chance. But I can't influence Nerian or the entire court alone," Del says calmly and takes another step toward me. "I've tried to find a way. I swear it. But vampire nobles love the way things are. How easy it is to maintain the control they've bred and orchestrated over the centuries. I am *one* man."

He rakes back the hair from his eyes and scrubs at his face, exhaustion radiating.

"I understand that challenge," I offer. "You're kind, Del. And nothing like the vampires here. Why are you second in Goreon? *How* are you second? Nerian dislikes you."

Del snorts. "I won the position."

*Oh, this is going to be good.*

"Please explain," I laugh, sagging under the weight of my snow-soaked gown and collapsing onto the edge of the bed.

"Nerian killed his last second. I don't know why. And then he hosted a series of trials for the replacement. Any nobleman could participate."

*So he is a nobleman.*

I loosen the laces of the corset that has me stuck upright and uncomfortable. "What were the trials?"

Del's gaze flicks to my bodice, the corner of his mouth lifting. "Nothing complicated. Just a fight to the death."

My lips part.

"I killed seven noblemen for my position as second."

*Impressive.*

"What is your goal? Tell me what you *want*," I demand, my eyes pinned to his.

He doesn't hesitate. "To kill Nerian and end the injustices in Goreon. With your help, of course."

I try not to let my eyebrows hit the ceiling as the treasonous words of the Goreon king's second whip through the room.

And my silence perches us on a knife's edge.

"You can trust me," he says, and I search his face for any hint of deception.

There is none. But it's never wise to trust a Goreon vampire.

I sigh. "We all know trust is earned. And even then, there's still a chance you're just playing the long game," I say, trying to think through this revelation and what to do about it. I tear at the bodice of my freezing dress I can't stand to be under anymore. "Entrapment isn't something I'm interested in, Del."

His eyes track my efforts, my undergarments peeking through the fabric, and I twirl a finger at him.

Del turns around so I can shed the heavy, suffocating, *commanding-colored* gown.

I struggle with the back button loops.

"Do you need help?" Del offers, and I can *hear* his smirk.

"*I've got it*," I bark and step out of the harmless-looking prison and slip on my dressing cloak, shoulders drooping in relief. "You can turn around."

Del moves to the sitting area near the cold fireplace and drops into a chair. "I just confessed to treason, and *you're* concerned about entrapment," he laughs. His strong hands drag down his thighs while I consider him. "Are you going to tell me what *you* want, Queen Veya? Because I know it isn't marriage to Nerian," he drawls, leaning forward, elbows to his knees, his gaze devouring me.

Disclosing my desire to conquer Goreon to its very own second is not in my best interest. I want to trust Del. Yet I still can't talk myself into it. I would consult with Second, although I'm fairly certain he'd prefer to die trying it ourselves than conspire with our sworn enemy.

Del's voice forces me out of my head. "It's taken me decades to plant the seed in the king's mind that inviting you here would be entertaining before we take your kingdom. I knew I had to get you here to stand a chance of changing Goreon. *Together*."

My mouth falls open; I don't bother to stop it. I did not see that twist coming.

"How clever of you."

"I'm excellent at *long-game* planning," he says, throwing my words back at me.

I glare at his smirk.

"Should I start guessing what you want? Should I surmise why you were in the west wing?" Del continues in my silence.

My eyes sweep to the door and the soft human weeping behind it, tearing at my heart.

"Because I think you want what I want, Queen Veya. I believe you need the horror to stop. And you want to reign over Goreon with the laws you live by in the Night Kingdom."

My face jerks back to Del. "What do you know of our ways?"

"I snuck into your kingdom after you built that wall a century ago. Credit goes to your sentries. They shot me down as I flew over but missed my heart by an inch."

I curse at their mistake.

"*Thankfully, they missed*," Del emphasizes, eyes burning. "For me. And for the sake of Goreon."

I plant myself in the chair opposite Del. "Your first opportunity to demonstrate trust, Del. Tell me what you saw and what you know of my kingdom, and I *may* spare your life for trespassing into my territory."

This isn't just some conversation about trusting someone with a family secret or money. This is treason, this is toppling kings and kingdoms, war, and everything and everyone at stake. And I will be nothing but careful and cautious with who I involve in that.

Del's mouth pinches before he speaks. "I'd like to point out that confessing to trespassing counts as my *first* demonstration that you can trust me implicitly."

*Says the trespasser.*

I ignore his comment, mouth pursed. "I'm waiting."

His face softens, and his plum eyes burst with a surprising brightness I haven't witnessed yet. "You should be very proud of yourself, my queen. You've built something truly remarkable."

I believe him because I know it to be true. I clear my throat. "Thank you. Tell me what you saw, what you know."

He rises and starts a fire while he speaks. "I know you have a kind heart by the way you treat your humans. With the laws you've enacted."

"You know *nothing* of my heart."

Del swivels his head to smirk at me like I can't talk him out of the obvious. "I know you've built an army so loyal and grateful they'll die in *this* life *and* the next for you."

*He's not wrong.*

He tosses a log into the fireplace. "You've made some bold choices in eradicating those who don't align with your beliefs."

*There isn't room for error with the fragility of life.*

"Where did you hear that?" I ask, leaning back in my chair and enjoying the heat from the blaze in the hearth. Del's gaze flicks to my exposed thigh as the dressing cloak slips, and I wish I didn't enjoy his eyes dragging up my leg as much as I do.

"Vampire taverns talk," he replies.

I lift my chin. "Nothing I've done to protect the Night Kingdom brings me shame."

Del settles back in his chair. "Really? Because I went to visit an old friend in the Southern Continent, and he wasn't there. Seems Prince Fash never came home from his travels over a century ago. And I wondered why that would be, because he was always intentional and cautious."

*Oh my gods.*

I swallow and leash my guilt into a neutral expression. I *am* ashamed of my actions with Fash.

A century ago, when I was desperate to understand the enemies on the borders of the Night Kingdom, I invited a neighboring ruler to visit. I had heard Prince Fash was a decent man, and he was—one of the only ruling vampires I've met who could possibly claim this. He would have been an ally for us. But to my shame, I panicked when he playfully grazed his hand along my bare shoulder and a bond began to form. The onslaught of attraction, the thread that seemed to be stitching us together, soul melding with soul, terrified me, both with sharing my rule and my life. I was not ready for a bond, nor did I want to open myself to brutal, heart-wrenching pain if it were ever lost.

So I slashed his throat with the daggers always strapped to my thighs and took off his head.

For years, I looked over my shoulder, waiting for the fallout of killing Prince Fash, but no one ever came with questions or accusations. And while my guilt still prods at me after all this time, Fash's death was worth something. Because my strategy was born that day. He showed me a way to eliminate powerful enemies discreetly. And a part of me hopes, if he knew what his life had bought, *maybe* he would forgive me.

But then the vampiric presence took advantage of Prince Fash's disappearance, and bloodlust became rampant in the Southern Continent. I've been trying to recover the territory ever since, and my mistakes haunt me. The continued loss of life is on my shoulders, and I doubt Fash would forgive me for that.

Del peers at me like he can see right through my façade, but I force myself to pin a prideful look on my face.

In the wake of my silence, Del clears his throat. "Given how the Night Kingdom seemed to quietly expand its territory since Fash's disappearance, I traveled east, into the deep mountains of the Old Tritan Territory, and the prince who ran them for the last five hundred years was missing there, too."

"Seems you gave yourself quite the tour," I bite out.

"I did," he says, crossing his arms, the lapels of his jacket pulling taut over his broad chest.

"I was lucky to spread the reach of my rule without bloodshed over the last century. Well, other than the first seven wars I won near the beginning," I add, closing the slit of my dressing gown.

Del's gaze tracks my hand and then finds my eyes, expression amused and challenging. "Of course. What well-timed, intelligent, ruthless *luck* you've had."

I don't dignify his words with a reaction. "Is there anything else you think you know about me?"

"Just one other thing," Del says, flashing a winning smile that turns his sharp features into refined handsomeness. My insides twirl, captivated by his face and the memory of his hips against me in the west wing.

*Godsdamnit.*

"And what is that?" I sigh, trying to release the coiling tension and not let attraction distract me.

"You have *three* strongholds. Not two."

My hissing snarl rages out of me before I can tamp it, and the gorgeous vampire in front of me morphs into my enemy in a moment.

Del tenses, raising a hand. "I swear I would die before revealing it to anyone. It's your best-held weapon."

"You just signed your own death sentence, Del. I can't let the knowledge you have continue to exist, especially in Goreon territory."

The male gets on his knees, and I watch his muscular thighs flex as he sinks back on his heels before me. "You must trust me," he says. "I live my life in service to saving Goreon, I swear it. We want the *same thing*." His voice reaches in and grabs me, the way it did the very first time he spoke, and I know he's being honest.

"Not good enough," I snarl.

His eyes are a plea before he speaks again. "My name was Patrick," he says softly.

My eyes go wide in shock. "*Why* would you tell me that?" I demand.

It's the most intimate thing he could have shared. We *never* reveal our human name. Our name is the *one* thing that still truly belongs to us from our humanity, and we don't share that, hardly ever, except with maybe a mate.

The firelight dances across his somber face. "Because, somehow, I need to convince you to trust me. And I'll lay my entire self bare before you, if that's what it takes. You're the opportunity I've been waiting for, and I won't let you slip through my fucking fingers, Veya."

He drops my royal title, desperation and honesty pushing out pretense, and I allow it for what he's given me to cling to, his name still ringing in my mind.

*Patrick.*

"Help me take down Nerian. Help me hand you another throne," Del says. "I *beg* you."

I exhale heavily, mind whirling with the consequences of agreeing to this if he's not who he says is. But my heart and my gut aren't balking; I believe he wants what I want, and that wins over any logic. My heart has *never* led me astray.

"I have an army and a kingdom to bring to the table. What do you have, Del?" I demand.

He smirks. "Goreon secrets."

# CHAPTER 14

## KADE

Two Hundred Years Ago – Goreon Kingdom

GRACE JAMS THE TIP of a blade into our dining table as the two of us sit down for a late lunch, my fork rattling on my plate from the force of it.

The knife gleams beautifully, its black hilt honed with the Hunter crest and gold inlaid throughout, mimicking Hunter magic. It's one of the most stunning weapons I've ever seen.

Then she stabs another into the wood beside it, its cream hilt carved with the same.

Twin blades.

"His and hers," she croons.

I twist to look at her. "Which one is mine?" It's a fair question, considering her favorite color is black.

"Your choice."

I pluck the cream-hilted blade from the table and twirl it in my palm. "It's lovely, Grace. Thank you."

"Want to test it out?" she asks, stepping back.

I adjust my grip and fling it across the room, the blade landing dead center at the top of the doorway to the living room.

Riot halts midstride through the frame, mouth popping open and eyes narrowing on me. "*Are you trying to kill me*?!" he yells, reaching up and yanking the blade from the molding.

"Not today," I deadpan.

Riot spins the blade on his palm, leaning against the wall. "She's a beaut."

"Give it back," I demand.

"Or what?" he challenges.

Grace's blade is airborne before his teasing smile fully forms, the edge of his tunic now pinned to the wall at his waist.

Riot scoffs. "Seriously, Grace?! This is my nicest shirt!"

She shrugs. "Give the blades back. I got you something, too."

Riot's face lights up like a child's on Winter Solstice. "Well, where is it?" he asks, spinning to glance around the kitchen, his shirt shearing. He groans, looking back at the torn fabric. After freeing Grace's blade and his shirt, he flings both blades at us, and we catch them with ease between our fingertips.

Grace jerks a chin toward the door. "Check the hall closet."

Riot's lumbering form is gone before I blink.

*"Oh. My. Gods!"* he yells from the entryway.

Boots rush back our way, and Riot reappears with a crossbow custom built for his size, which is *large*.

"You shouldn't have," he drawls, cheeks rosy as he eyes Grace over the weapon aimed at my face. The crossbow fires, and my body sings with magic as I snatch the bolt from the air an inch from my nose.

Riot pales and backs up a step, clearing his throat. "Guess the safety was off."

"Guess so," I growl.

Grace doubles over in laughter as Master Hull saunters into the kitchen, Riot stepping behind him and using the old man as protection.

"What's going on in here?" Master asks, eyeing our weapons.

"Just appreciating Grace's excellent taste," Riot says, face scrunched in apprehension.

I shake my head at him. "Just our Central station leader failing the basics today, Master."

Riot's eyes grow wide in embarrassment.

"It's nothing, Papa," Grace says. "Can I serve you lunch?"

"Don't fuss, I'll get it," he says, grabbing a bowl.

Admiring my new blade, I turn to Master at the stove. "Did you get what I asked for?"

"Aye," he says, setting down his bowl and unclipping a ring of keys from his belt. "Standard sizing and all twenty options we know to exist in the stronghold. Might take you a minute, but I'm confident they'll open that door."

"Thank you, Master."

He grips my shoulder. "You're welcome, son."

I swallow the scratch in my throat, thankful for the forgiveness he seems to have given me over Sam's capture.

"And I'm going with you tonight," he says, squeezing my shoulder harder.

My eyebrows pinch. "No, you aren't."

He pins me with a stern look. "I have a handful of years left at best, and my legacy is *not* dying in our fortress overseeing the dead, dusty books and sweaty trainees. I will fight to rescue my own son. And no one will take that from me."

*Fuck. Can't argue with that.*

I swing my attention to Grace. The death of her father puts her in charge.

A tear slides down her cheek. "Papa, I'm not ready to lose you."

"Lose me?" Master shakes his head. "That's uncertain. But participating in the opportunity of centuries *is* certain. I want my own chance at that king, too."

Grace shudders an exhale, like she's already trying to battle the grief. "Nothing will change your mind?"

"I'm as sure as your mother's ashes are in the Sereia Sea."

Grace's emerald eyes gleam. "I understand."

215

I wrap a hand around the back of Grace's neck, and her beautiful face turns to me. "We should get ready."

She nods. "Aye."

Taking Grace's hand, I lead us down to the basement, where our armor and weapons have been staged so we can dress in private.

"May I adorn you?" she asks softly, eyes skirting to the cabinet at the edge of the room.

I swallow. "I'd be honored."

Grace glides across the basement to the credenza and pulls open the drawer, fetches the satchel, and pulls the brushes first, then the tin.

"Stand near the light," she commands, face solemn.

Stripping my shirt, I pad over to the torch and turn to face my wife.

Grace runs the handle of the brush down my sternum before meeting my eyes.

"Are you ready, Captain?" she says, her smile reaching in and consoling my nerves around what's ahead of us tonight.

I nod, eyes gleaming, and my voice comes out low and certain: "Yes."

Grace dips the tip of the brush in the tin held in her palm and touches it to my skin, drawing the brush tip up my arm, the staining paint trailing in a thin blue line along my muscle.

"Listen to me, Captain Kade," she demands, and I lose myself in her eyes. "Your mind is as strong as the physical body you've honed." She drags the brush across my clavicle. "You've mastered both, and you will lead us into our future tonight. You will become the man this world needs."

The brush travels down my chest and over my heart.

"You are brave. You are worthy."

She dips the brush into the tin, scooping paint before dragging the tip up my neck, over my jaw, and up my cheek, her smile cracking through her fervor. "You will herald the era of the Hunter."

Every bristle of the brush is fire to my skin, and my magic twirls, listening to Grace and responding with the same fervor.

"Be sharp, be fearless, be the warrior you were *born* to be." Grace crosses the brush over my chest. "May your blades carry you to victory."

Her eyes pin to mine, and I capture her green gaze like I'm starving for the adoration in it.

"Forever may we reign, Captain Kade."

I swallow, my voice hoarse. "Forever may we reign," I promise.

Grace sets the brush in the tin while I draw my fingertips up her arm, bumps crawling in my wake.

"Your turn," I whisper.

Adorning a Hunter is one thing, but adorning an Heir—not many get that honor, and I'm the only one in this generation who will. I've looked forward to this day our entire relationship, and I've thought about every word I would say.

Grace turns away so I can work the laces loose on her bodice. I tug the fabric over her head and then her shirt, and my eyes consume her, bare before me. My fingers trail her spine, the curve of her plunging me into primal worship as I run my hand along her waist, gripping her hip to spin her gently.

"Are you ready, Grace Hull?"

Sparkling eyes meet mine. "Yes," she says, conviction reverberating in the silence of the basement.

I take the tin and brush from her and dip the bristles. My forefinger lifts her chin, and I grin as I press the brush against her temple and draw the first line across her brow.

"You are the Heir," I begin. "You carry the blood of our ancestors in your veins and ruthless warrior strength in your heart."

I draw the brush down Grace's throat. "You are the soul of the Hunters, the beat of our rhythm, the breath in our chest."

The paint leaves a line of blue down the center of her sternum, and I stroke across her ribs.

"You possess the strongest magic, the fiercest voice, and the will of us all. We will follow you into any battle and defend you on any cliff. Our swords will be the first to fall for your victory."

I paint around her joyful, tear-filled eyes.

"I honor you now, Grace Hull, Heir of the Hunters, with the paint of our people and the love in my soul. Forever may you reign."

Her mouth parts, and she grabs the paint tin and tosses it to the side before slamming her body into mine and kissing me with a fire I'm privileged to try to handle. I savor the feel of her lips and the press of her against me, needing her more than ever.

I lift Grace, and her legs lock around my hips, gripping me with everything she has as her hands tangle in my hair and tip my head back from her lips.

"We'll change the world, Kade. We were brought together for a reason."

I smile into her mouth. "Yes. We were," I say and pull her back to my lips.

My magic celebrates, golden raindrops splashing.

Grace moans into my mouth, tongue threading with mine, her hands everywhere, leaving fire in their wake. She writhes against me, clutching me with her entire being, and rips a groan from my throat at the feel of her.

I lift Grace off my hips, our paint blended from our passion, and fall to my knees before her, tugging off her boots and snatching down her pants, throwing them behind me. My fingertips sweep up her legs, and I dip my head to graze my mouth along her inner thigh, touching the soft skin that makes her buck and beg.

"You're perfection," I growl, my lips trailing to her upper thigh, soft skin teasing me toward insanity.

Grace hums, eyes closing as her head tips back, and my fingers find her center—the core that beckons me every waking moment.

A gasp escapes her alluring mouth, my want becoming feral, and I watch her intently as I slide two fingers inside her, curling into her favorite spot.

"You're so ready for me," I say as satisfaction ripples through me.

Her hands grip my shoulders, and the gleam in her eyes makes me throb against the constraint of my trousers.

"It's hard *not* to be ready for you, Kade," she says in a sultry voice that makes my name sound like her own personal gospel. "*Look* at you."

I toss her the boyish grin she loves, with her compliment firing into my heart, and plunge and pulse my fingers, her body bowing over my shoulder with her feminine moan ricocheting around us.

My palm slides up her sternum, pushing her upright, and Grace looks down at me, tooth hooked over her bottom lip. I dive eagerly, needing my starving mouth flush with her.

Breath skittering over sensitive skin, I pull those short exhales from her throat that drive me wild and galvanize my need for this woman. I thrash my tongue against her, swirling and flicking while my hand works mercilessly to melt her knees.

It's my favorite thing, to coax the sounds of pleasure from her mouth and feel her tense and brace herself as arousal teases her surrender.

"Please, Kade," she begs, clawing at me and shaking in my grasp.

I know what she needs, and I need to be inside her just as badly. Desperately.

With one last taste, I rise, dragging my fingers slowly out of her and up her clit. Grace nips at my lips while she rips the tie loose from my pants. She groans when she frees me, her hand grabbing my cock with a greediness that curls my lip.

Satisfaction floods me as I watch the wanton hunger spark in her eyes. "You want that?"

She nods, sliding her hand along me, and I jerk in her grip.

"You *need* that?"

"Yes," she says breathily. "Fuck me like you love me, Hunter."

Her words whisper along my soul.

"Gladly," I growl, spinning her, and she spreads herself for me. "Gods," I whisper, savoring the view before I grip her hips and bury myself deeply into her tight, wet heat, thrusting to the hilt. Her cry and my groan shudder together into the addicting blend of our ravenous devouring of one another.

Sweat rolls down my spine despite the chill as I fuck her fiercely. And Grace takes me, pressing backward and demanding more. I willingly give it for as long as she requires. She's everything to me—all I ever wanted—and I'll worship her with a reverence that the gods envy.

Her hands cover mine, and I pause while she steps away and watch myself slide out of her.

Grace turns, eyes consuming me. "On the ground, Hunter," she commands, and I plant my ass down quickly.

Grace lowers slowly, her perfect tits peaked with her arousal, and she hovers her center above my tip. Her black hair falls forward as she braces her hand on my chest, leaving an imprint of herself in the paint with a hungry grin. Her thighs press into my hips as she takes me inside herself, sliding down my length with a moan that threatens to undo me.

Clenching around me with no mercy, I watch her intently as her back arches with her pleasure. And then Grace takes me to an intoxicating heaven, riding me, and I join her effort, thrust after thrust up into her.

I don't want this to end. I need her beyond this minute, beyond this hour, and this night. There is never enough time with this woman.

Her fingertips rub her clit, and I drink in the sight of her pleasuring herself with my cock inside her.

"Kade!" she screams. "Gods, please don't stop."

I grip her hips and keep our pace with ease.

She knows I'll never stop until she's trembling and quivering with nothing left to give, but she always begs me, and I gladly obey her commands.

Every. *Thrust.*

Single. *Thrust.*

Time. *Thrust.*

Her small nails dig into my chest, leaving little marks I'll be disappointed to cover with my clothes and even more disappointed when they fade.

Grace's eyes latch to mine, her mouth parting as she clenches, and her first release begins.

"More," she gasps through her orgasm, and I drown myself in her soaking-wet heat, pumping into her.

She drips down my length, and potent desire rips through me.

Grace's moans tumble out of her and surround me like they're the only sound in the world.

"What a good little Hunter you are," I praise as her eyes flutter open, and she slams herself down on me. "Are you going to come again for me?"

She nods, leaning down and taking my mouth with hers. Our tongues lash, and I grip the back of her head, threading my hand in her hair, then I tug her back from my lips to stare into those green eyes. I wonder how I ever survived without her as I savor the tooth she pulls over her bottom lip, and her imprisoning smirk brings me dangerously close to flipping her over and pounding mercilessly until I can't breathe.

Grace sits upright, and her words pour over me. "This life is so much better with you in it, Hunter."

And I know we're the same in this way—we believe we're better together, stronger, and embrace the life the gods gave us because it doesn't really mean anything without each other.

Her eyes close, and I feel her pussy tighten around me, and our rhythm ensues as Grace rides me and takes us to our edge, to the place our bodies know, to the sacred ground we walk that is uniquely ours. I memorize the vision of her above me as her climax explodes again, watching her until her shudders subside.

I stand, keeping us connected, and Grace wraps her legs around my hips, consuming my mouth as I stride for the wall, slamming her up against it just hard enough to make her groan. She braces her weight on my shoulders as I pound into her and unleash myself on my wife.

Savoring her shaky breath in my ear, my hands grip under her thighs, and I drill pleasure until we can no longer stand it. Until I *need* to mark her. To feel her take me fully.

We explode together in our ecstasy; I consume Grace's mouth as she kisses me and I pulse into her.

Breath thready, I pump the last of myself into her, giving her everything I have, just like I promised I always would.

# CHAPTER 15

## VEYA

### Present Day

DEL AND I STARE each other down in front of the fire in my bedchamber, and I pray to the gods I won't regret what I'm about to say.

"I'll consider an alliance. More importantly, I'll let you live. *For now.*"

Del rises from his knees. "Queen Veya," he says with a thankful nod of his chin and a red flash of his eyes, crimson blotting plum like spilled ink before he turns away.

"Don't make me fucking regret it, Del."

His face jerks back to me as he stands over me, expression on fire. "I *won't*," he growls, the fire spitting behind him. "I've been trying to find Aurelia a way out of the cellar for over a year. You gave me that. You have my *unending* loyalty for it. I *swear* it."

My brows pinch. "A year? But she's still human. How—"

Del's features darken to something feral. "Nerian keeps them caged until he can't stand to restrain himself."

My insides turn over, anger surging anew over Nerian. And I want to accept all the assistance I can get taking this king out, my impending decision to include Del in our plans becoming more confident by the minute.

His gaze softens. "He kept Christine for five years before you set her free."

"Fuck," I whisper, closing my eyes in memory of Christine, my sorrow for that sweet girl twisting my mouth into a grim frown. One of the most brutal, intimate moments of my life is shared with a girl I will never see again, and the memory threatens to rip me wide open, slicing through me anew.

I gather myself and open my eyes, focus trained on Del as he sinks back in his chair. The more he shares, the more I dare to trust him. I want to. Desperately, for both our sakes.

I'll just take it hour by hour.

"How do we get the girls who don't want to turn out of the castle?"

"I have a plan. Shall we move this to the sitting room to include the others?" he asks, his handsome smile aimed right at me.

"Fine." I uncross my legs to rise, the fabric of my robe shifting, exposing the length of my thigh.

Del's gaze smolders, running down my body, taking in every inch of me and leaving behind a heat I haven't felt in a long time in its wake.

He's not even *trying* to mask his attraction.

With a clear of my throat, I tighten my dressing cloak, its silk brushing against my skin like fingertips I wish were real. But I had love in my life once already, and the ghost of that loss is a pain I'm not sure I can repeat.

"You're bashful, and I can't figure out why," Del says bluntly, striding for the door, and we regard one another in a comfortable silence I wasn't expecting. Del breaks it with a smirk. "And you're absolutely stunning. You don't need to hide yourself, Veya."

My mouth parts, but he exits my bedroom, leaving me with the consolation of not having to reply to his compliment. After a moment to collect myself from a cacophony of jarring emotions, I join the others. The girls are asleep on the sofas and settees.

Charlotte looks up from Aurelia, her fingertips stroking the girl's long, dark strands across her lap, the same espresso black as Del's.

Emmanuel secures the iron shutters as dawn peers across the horizon and stands over his doe again.

"Let's let them rest and sober for a few hours. They have a big decision to make," I tell everyone.

No one argues with me.

"And what decision is that?" Charlotte asks.

"We'll turn them if they request it; otherwise, we're getting them back to their families," I say.

Charlotte's eyes skirt to Del. "And you're fine with that?"

"It was his idea," I say and curse myself for jumping to Del's defense. And then I curse again at the smug look on his face.

"Do you want to know the plan?" Del asks through a devastating smile.

Emmanuel scoffs, and Second crosses his thick arms over his wide chest and narrows his eyes at Del.

"Luckily, your queen's actions with Christine give us the perfect way to hide the girls who don't want to turn," Del says, sauntering to the fireplace and turning his back to the flame. "We can burn a large pyre, thick and deep enough that you can't tell if bodies are there. It'll be both a distraction for us to get them out of castle grounds and the reason we don't have dead girls to show off." Del sighs and meets my eyes. "I'm hoping those who want to turn will secure a layer of trust thick enough to believe we burned the others."

*Never trust a vampire.*

It's a decent plan. And I can't come up with anything better.

"I like it," I agree.

"This has to go well," Emmanuel growls, gazing down at his doe. His eyes don't leave her face, and I'm pretty sure I'm staring at a newfound, breathing weakness for my top assassin.

"We will do everything we can to ensure their safety. She's my family," Del says, gesturing to Aurelia. "We will get them out."

Emmanuel shakes his head. "Not what I meant. The full moon is tomorrow night. If we aren't successful this evening—"

"Shit," Second spits.

With everything that's happened, I'd forgotten about the full moon. We'll all be out of our minds tomorrow night and useless to these women.

"Then we make *sure* we're successful," Del says, and Emmanuel nods at him.

My mind races. If we aren't able to ensure their safety by then, especially if their escape is discovered, Nerian has hundreds of human guards to do his dirty work in the bright light of day, or during a full moon.

"We need to get them *out*."

Del rolls his eyes at me. "I already said we would."

"Watch those pretty eyes, Del. They should never roll in my direction."

He nods at me through a smirk and then fixes his face.

I roll out my neck and shoulders, trying to fight off my emotional and daytime exhaustion. "We need to get them to the *Night Kingdom*. It's too risky to send them to their families in Goreon. We can't ensure their safety, especially with the full moon." I look at Del. "We house them in our territory until we know it's safe to return. Especially given our other pressing goals."

Second glowers at me, and Emmanuel and Charlotte bounce their focus between Del and me.

"Something we need to know from your bedroom dalliance?" Second asks brusquely.

My turn to roll my eyes. "Del has asked for our assistance in taking Nerian's throne."

My people lose an entire shade, alabaster complexions looking back at me now.

Second moves his hand to his hilt. "Just to be clear," he grits. "Are we speaking about Goreon treason with the *second of Goreon* right now?"

"We are," I reply.

Del hits us with a winning grin before he speaks. "I agree we should send the girls to the Night Kingdom. Thank you for your gracious offer," he says.

"The girls will be safe there. I promise you. We'll send a letter with them, my legion at the wall will get them to Prosperity."

Del nods.

"Don't you want to know what Prosperity is before agreeing to it?" Charlotte coos at Del.

He looks down at her, face softening as he watches Charlotte hold Aurelia. "I gave myself a tour of your kingdom decades ago."

"*Godsdamnit,*" Second fumes and marches his ass over to the window like he can stare out of it to cool off.

"Del," I say and he looks at me. "Do you know if any of them will want to turn?"

He gazes at the girls from the cellar, his throat tracking a slow swallow. "Yeah. Sophie will want to turn," he says about my siren. "She has no one left."

He shifts his focus to Emmanuel's doe. "Amelia will turn. She's hated her vulnerability ever since she was locked in that cage. The one with the braid is Samantha," he says, peering down at Second's girls, curled together. "She has human family. She'll go to the Night Kingdom. And the blonde is Hannah. I fear she may not want either option. Death preferred."

"Whatever for?" Second asks, expression stern as he whips his gaze from the steel shutters he can't see through.

"Her unborn child didn't survive her capture."

I tent my fingertips against my forehead, pressing my hands into my face to stave off the curdling scream I'd like to release. "You know all their real names?" I ask softly, dropping my hands.

Del nods, leaning an elbow against the mantle. "I snuck down to the cellar when I could. To talk to them, to keep their spirits up."

"And will we turn Aurelia?" I ask gently.

"She's *sixteen*," Del snarls. "She has too much human life left to toss it away. She's *not* turning."

"Why didn't you just break them out?" Charlotte asks. "You had access."

He pins Charlotte with a look that has me reaching for the blade at my thigh. "I would lose the position of second and my life. The greater purpose, my ultimate mission, had to be more important. It just *had* to be—" His voice breaks, and I wonder if he's still trying to convince himself he made the right decision for so long.

Second rescues him. "We need to take the girls as far as we can toward the Night Kingdom tonight. They'll have to finish the journey during the day, but we have human guards at the border to receive them. So, who stays with the pyre, and who's going toward the wall?"

"Queen Veya needs to stay, and so do I," Del says. "We can't alert Nerian to our absence."

My eyes find Em, and he nods. My assassin will stay by my side.

"If absences are noted by the king, Second leaving for the Night Kingdom wouldn't be frowned upon," I say. "I can tell Nerian there was a stirring to deal with." I look at Second. "And I'm not sending you alone with innocents to defend. Charlotte goes too."

Charlotte strokes Aurelia's hair. "More than happy to."

"Good … that sounds good," Del says, staring into the fire like he's reviewing the plan in his head and searching for holes.

We linger in the parlor for a few hours while the girls sleep. Finally, Aurelia stirs in Charlotte's lap, and Del rushes to her, kneeling down beside them.

"Aurelia," he whispers, and her eyes flutter open.

"Hi," she squeaks, her high-pitched voice chirping through a sob.

"You're out. You never have to go back there. You're safe now," Del comforts, his hand rubbing her arm.

Aurelia sits up, dark hair falling around her shoulders, lilac eyes bright and flitting about the room. Her focus lands on Charlotte beside her.

"Thank you for choosing me," she says.

Charlotte's perfect smile lights up her face with honest joy. "I'm thankful for that, too."

The girls awaken around us. Second's choices, Hannah and Samantha, sit up and huddle against one another, eyes jumping from one vampire to the next, chests puffing in fear.

"You're safe," Del says quickly, and they settle instantly at the sight of him.

Amelia stirs, eyes wild in her sobriety as she takes in a room of vampires, but, like the others, she finds Del and relaxes.

*They trust him.*

"You can trust these vampires," Del says to the girls.

Amelia's gaze lands on Emmanuel as he kneels down next to the settee.

"He's right. You will trust me, Amelia," he says to her.

Her brown eyes latch onto his. "All right," she says firmly.

"Good."

My siren is the last to wake, and I crouch before her. "Sophie," I say as she opens her eyes, and the boldness of emerald gleams so much brighter now. "Welcome back," I tell her.

Her eyes shift to Del, the tension in her shoulders softening, and then her focus homes in on me. "Make me a fucking vampire," she commands.

A small smile plays on my lips. "It's not a life I would have asked for," I tell her. "Are you sure? We can get you to the Night Kingdom if you'd prefer."

"I've had enough humanity. I'm certain."

"I understand."

I turn toward the others. "Make your choices, darlings. Vampire, and you remain here with us. Human, and you leave for the Night Kingdom at sunset."

Amelia shoves her wrist at Emmanuel's mouth. He catches her slender arm with his strong hand and closes his fingers around her with a clear of his throat. Eyes flashing red, he moves her delicate wrist away from his lips.

Del is two for two on his guesses.

"I will go to the Night Kingdom," Samantha says, her smile wide. "I've heard stories about how wonderful it is there."

"It is," I tell her.

"How do you know for certain?" she asks, eyes eager.

"Because I'm her queen, and I built her."

Her mouth falls open, and her cheeks flush rose. "Oh my gods," she whispers.

"Aurelia will join you," Del interjects, and Aurelia scoffs at him.

"I get a say, *too*," she protests, looking at him with teenage indignation.

He raises his eyebrows, and she plants her arms over her chest. The staring contest is one for the ages.

Aurelia finally groans. "*Fine*. Night Kingdom for me."

"And for you, Hannah?" Second asks his blonde girl.

She looks up at him and shakes her head. "I have nothing to live for," she says, voice hollow as her arms wrap around her flat belly.

Second watches her solemnly for a moment and then comes right out with it. "You want to die instead?"

She nods. "I lost my baby."

"I know. Loss gets different with time," he tells her. "But it will never go away."

*Is he trying to talk her into the grave?*

"Who have you lost?" she asks Second.

He swallows. "My best friend. He was my brother in every way the word matters." Second kneels before her. "Let us help you through it. Just give us a few years. If you still want to die, I'll do it myself," he promises her.

*Well, that's one way to go about it.*

Hannah's eyes search his. "Six months."

"One year," he jabs back.

I smirk at the negotiation. Only in the vampire world are we negotiating death sentences.

Hannah sighs. "Fine. One year. And I'd like to spend it as a vampire."

Second looks at her as she extends her wrist. Then he sets it back on her lap. "I'll give that to you if it's what you want. But we're not doing it yet. You need to bask in the sun one more time."

Silence falls heavy.

Second's deep voice filters out with kindness. "And not your wrist. Your bite marks are the last scar you'll ever have. It'll mean something to you. Choose a place you can cover."

She rubs her wrist. "Good to know."

I roll out my neck. It's midday based on how my body is forcing itself to stay awake. "Second is right. Those who are turning should spend some time outside."

Hannah looks back at her rescuer. "Your name is Second?"

He narrows his eyes at her. "It's a good name."

"I didn't say it wasn't."

Second cracks the faintest smile, and my heart wrings.

Del crosses the room with a snort. "I'll gather travel clothes and supplies for Aurelia and Samantha." He points at Second. "I'll be back with a map to show you the best route and where to acquire horses for the rest of their journey without you tomorrow."

Second nods at him. "Good."

"Come with me, ladies. You can spend time on my balcony while I gather things," Del says and strolls out of the suite, with scrambling girls in his wake.

Two hours later, we convene in my suite again. Sunkissed cheeks and hopeful smiles dot the sitting room, ready for their next chapter.

"Who would you like to turn you, Sophie?" I ask as Del and Second review the map of Goreon at the mahogany desk in the corner.

Sophie's upper lip curls in a sly grin. Already an alluring beauty, she'll make an even more stunning vampire, the bite of her confidence sure to keep her alive for centuries.

"The queen, of course," she purrs with a bow, her blazing hair falling forward.

"Where would you like your mark?"

Sophie strips her nightdress, naked before me, and holds her arm above her head. "Ribcage, near my heart."

I smile at her, my fangs elongating.

Confidence. Beauty. Commanding.

*Bold and brave.*

"It's my honor. And what will I call you from this moment forth?"

She looks at me around her arm. "Nix."

"Are you ready, Nix?"

She swallows and nods. "To forever in the dark," she says, and my mouth brushes against her skin, fangs sinking in.

My body races as the taste of blood from the vein hits my mouth, but I hold everything back, forcing myself to release my puncture from Nix without drinking.

The trickle of blood in my mouth is enough to sustain me for days, or so it feels that way.

"What now?" Nix asks.

I step back from her. "It only takes a few minutes," I say kindly. "It'll hurt when your fangs grow in, and your eyes will sting with their first flash of red, and your body will experience pain as you harden into immortality."

A tear slips down Nix's cheek. "Yes, I feel it."

"Welcome to hell, Nix."

She shakes her head. "I've been to hell. This will be my heaven," she says, and my guilt flits away at her words.

Hair that was already fire becomes a brilliant, curling orange as Nix turns. Her cheekbones sharpen, lips plump, and the pigment of her skin lightens into porcelain glowing beneath blazing, lengthening ringlets. Nix draws her fingertips up her arm, her muscles defining, and the scars around her wrists from endless hours in chains fade.

"Oh my gods," she whispers, stepping in front of the mirror in the room and gazing upon herself. "I didn't realize we got prettier."

"You were beautiful as you were," I tell her.

She smirks at me in the glass. "You're kind, but now I'm ... *striking*."

Charlotte giggles from the sofa. "You're going to get any attention you want. We might need to assign a bodyguard for you," she teases.

*It might actually be necessary.*

"I'll just take one of the hundred blades from Uncle Del's chambers."

My eyes dart to Del as he looks up from the map and gives Nix a wink. He downplayed his devotion to these girls, his kindness, his influence in their lives. You don't earn a familiar name like that without effort and love.

Amelia catches my attention as she saunters across the room to Emmanuel.

Leaning against the wall, my assassin watches her with rapt attention.

She stands before him, staring up into his blazing eyes.

*Definitely an unforeseen weakness.*

"Ask for what you want," he says.

She takes a step closer. "Will you turn me?"

"If you make me one promise."

She frowns up at him. "What's the promise?"

"You can never touch me."

Her mouth parts, and her eyes narrow. "But—"

"Never," he says fiercely.

Amelia's expression clouds. "I don't understand—"

"Promise me," he growls.

"Don't growl your words at me, sir," she shoots back, and I hide my grin behind my hand.

He doesn't flinch. "It's Emmanuel, and you will trust me."

"I already said I do."

"Then act like it."

Amelia glowers at my assassin, and then her chin tilts. "Can I touch you before you turn me?"

His eyes blow wide in surprise. I wasn't expecting that question either.

His gaze assesses Amelia, her soft brown hair brushing at her waist as she steps closer to him.

"Careful, I bite," he says through a smirk I've never seen and a smolder that could bring us all to our knees.

She takes another step, her delicate body poised before one of the deadliest males I know. "That wasn't a 'no.'"

"It wasn't," he says tightly.

She reaches her fingertips to his face and draws them along his sharp jawline.

"Cold," she whispers, and her hand travels down the side of his throat as Emmanuel swallows.

My eyes flick to Charlotte gaping at them from the sofa. Glad to know I'm not the only one amazed by what's happening.

Amelia runs her hand along his bicep. "Strong," she says and steps into his space, pressing herself against him, the wall at his back and bravery at his front.

She leans up on her tiptoes and brushes her lips against his. "Soft," she whispers into his mouth.

Emmanuel's hand cups the back of her head as she pulls back just enough to put her wrist to his lips.

"That's a difficult spot to cover," he says, eyes pinned to hers.

"I want to be able to see it every day, whenever I want. Mark me, Emmanuel," she commands.

A snarl rips from his lips, and his fangs dart for her skin.

"You can take more," she tells him, and his eyes flash crimson, never leaving her gaze, but he unlatches himself without drinking and plasters his body against the wall. He breathes heavily, a finger swiping her blood from his lip.

"You can call me Hartley," she says, eyeing her new marks.

"It suits you," Emmanuel says, eyes on fire.

Hartley grins at him, then backs away, a small moan escaping her as the pain sets in.

Turning to me, her eyes flash red. "I look forward to having a ruler worthy of my service," she says with a deep bow, and her fangs release for the first time through her thankful smile.

"And what service would that be?" I ask curiously, loving her confidence as her acorn-brown hair shifts into layers of honey, dark caramel and chocolate.

"Whatever is required. Although, I'm quite skilled with a bow. I hunted for my village before I was captured. Perhaps you can train me to fight for you."

My suppressed smile and raised eyebrows find Emmanuel. "I know just the trainer."

Hartley follows my gaze and spins back to Emmanuel.

"You?" Hartley asks, tilting her head, eyes running up him. "Who are you?"

He spins his blade. "The devil you never see coming."

Del snorts in the corner, fingertip pointed on the map in front of Second. Emmanuel's blade is airborne and pinned in Del's heart before his snort fully forms in my ears.

"*Fuck!*" Del shouts, yanking the knife from his chest.

Emmanuel winks at Hartley.

"*Asshole*," Del spits and throws the blade back at my assassin with perfect aim.

Emmanuel catches it between his fingertips, nose wrinkled at Del's blood soiling the steel.

Del fires a blazing gaze at me, and I shrug. "You'll be fine in two minutes," I offer in response.

He rolls out his shoulder and stabs his finger back on the map. "As I was *saying*," he tells Second, who chuckles softly next to him.

I smile at Hannah, catching her attention.

"Guess I'm last," she whispers from the sofa next to Charlotte.

Second abandons the map and charges across the room to Hannah. "Where do you want it?" he asks abruptly. "And pick a spot that will do for a shit-ton longer than one year."

"Mark me next to my other scar."

"And where is that?"

She opens her thighs for Second, and I wonder what her other scar is from.

He doesn't balk. He gets on his knees, slides open her dressing gown, and finds the mark on her inner thigh. Second sinks his fangs into her flesh, and Hannah lets out a relieved sigh, like she's thankful the journey to her end is beginning.

"What will you call yourself?" he asks as he releases himself from her and swipes her blood away with his finger.

"Ellie."

"Not much of a vampire name," Second teases, backing away from between Ellie's legs.

"It's the name I would've given my daughter."

Her words slice through the air, and Second's eyes flick to mine. I return his gaze with a soft smile.

"Ellie it is, then," he says, standing to inspect the travel packs Del brought.

Across the room, Del is whispering to Aurelia, her tears running and head nodding. She rushes him, hugging tightly before he releases his palms gripping her shoulders.

Del meets my eyes. "Write the letter," he tells me. "It's time. And *we* need to start a very large fire." He grins, plum eyes flashing through his dripping charm.

I pull parchment from the desk drawer in the corner and scrawl the message for Officer Holton at the wall.

Second drags Samantha's and Aurelia's travel packs over his shoulders beside me.

I savor the ink drying on the page before I fold it, the edges of my signature bleeding my promise into permanence.

"Be safe. Be swift," I say, shoving the note into Second's palm.

He looks down at me. "We will be, my queen."

# CHAPTER 16

## KADE

Two Hundred Years Ago – Goreon Kingdom

I SECURE GRACE'S second bracer, pulling the strings taught over her slender forearm. "What can I do to convince you to stay behind?"

She smiles up at me, cheeks still aglow from her arousal. "You married a woman who will sacrifice and defend until her last breath. Get the fuck over it, Kade."

"Those are fighting words, woman."

"Yeah, well, *we're* going to have plenty of that, aren't we?"

I grunt. "I guess *we* are."

"Aye," she says as Riot barrels through the basement door.

"What the hell is taking so long down here?" he demands, eyeing our state of dress.

"Just taking our Captain for the ride of his life before we go play with swords and rescue Sam's ass," Grace says, grinning up at me.

Riot's mouth falls open behind her. He turns on his heel in a huff. "You have no boundaries, Grace," he mutters, disappearing back up the stairwell.

I smirk at my wife as we clothe. "You do that on purpose."

"He's so easily riled by it."

I laugh, securing twin swords at my back, and Grace hands my cream-hilted blade to me before sheathing her own at her thigh. We collect the rest of our weapons and climb the stairs to join the Central outfit in the living room.

Rhett looks like his skin is itching he's so ready, standing closest to the door; Master Hull stands beside him.

"Let's move out," I say and lead my men toward the underground.

The closest access is two streets over, and the Hunters of Central descend quickly, disappearing out of sight.

Goreon is still shrouded in winter's hell, and it's especially unforgiving in the dark, damp tunnels. My breath billows as we march the mile underneath Southend to the meeting location beneath Lou's tavern.

I've planned it so our timing should be perfect, entering the castle as the sun goes down, when vampires on serum will be defenseless in their catatonic, drugged state.

It'll be a slaughter.

And then we take on the dreamwalkers, doing what we do best, what the gods designed us to do.

A vampire in a dreamwalk—physical body turned feral while their mind suffers through a rapture—is a decent opponent. And if the king has assembled an army with talent, we're in for a battle. Yet the opportunity to assassinate the half of our enemy who chose the serum, numbing their pain and human memories, is something we got lucky with tonight.

Sam doesn't have much longer. And even if he did, I can't stand by while he suffers. He belongs to us, he's a Hunter, and we don't leave Hunters behind.

I turn the last corner, edging around earth and rock, and we spill into the circular underground room that connects tunnels throughout the city.

A hundred years ago, the sublevel system was utilized by vampires during the day, but they haven't been down here since all who entered began to disappear, never to return.

That was phase one of the Hunter attack against the Goreon king—eliminate daylight movement.

We filter into the chamber and wait.

Within ten minutes, the thud of boots and clank of weapons sound in the distance. Hunters emerge from the various spokes; Ned and Brachett stalk toward us, their men trailing them. Longton with the Northern outfit is not far behind.

Our magic pulses together, a throbbing heart beating for a single purpose.

"Welcome, Hunters," I say as males fill the room, Grace and Master Hull on either side of me. "These tunnels formerly connected to the castle, but our enemy filled the access with stone decades ago. You'll enter the castle via the bridge at the narrow part of the bay on my signal. We'll swarm up through the dungeons." I gaze upon my legion, their fierce faces and exposed skin covered in black and blue war paint. "The goal is straightforward. We take the castle. We rescue Sam. No vampire left alive. We start anew."

Grace breathes deeply beside me, her smile stretching, and paint creases around her eyes.

"Protect each other; know that chaos and death will work to cloud your focus and judgment." I look into the eyes of the men around me. "*Remember* who you are. *Remember* who you fight for. *Remember* that this is the dawn of the era of the *Hunter*—"

Cheers ring out.

"No one in that castle is innocent of the atrocities in our kingdom."

My magic boils in agreement.

"Let's go kill some *fucking* vampires!" I scream, and the responding roar is a war cry that threatens to rattle tears from my eyes.

We march toward the castle together until we reach my exit.

I swipe a thumb along Grace's jaw. "I'll see you on the bridge."

"See you there," she says, and I bound up the stone stairs to the surface while Riot and Grace guide the legion underground to the nearest exit by the castle.

I emerge onto the streets of Goreon City; the early evening traffic of workers scurrying home before dark is busy and clogged. My armor and weapons draw curious attention as I pick up the pace to the edge of the city. Finally, I leave the last of the cobbled streets and jog around the north side of the bay, pausing to peer through my telescope.

*No human guards.*

It's Hunters versus vampires. Just as it should be.

I creep along the border of the stronghold to the sewer entrance, the sun beginning to set behind the mountains. Riot has my swords, bow, and garrote, but I made sure to keep a few stakes across my chest and daggers at my hips. My heart beats steadily as I keep adrenaline at bay and approach the access point, ensuring the ring of keys is secure on my belt.

The last whisper of pink fades under sparking stars, and the moon crests the ridge.

*Please, gods, help me end this. Let me get Sam out of this hell.*

I freeze my breath and plunge.

Through the sludge, I swim toward our future.

The underwater gate is still broken open, just as I left it earlier, and I pull myself through. My fingertips find the edge of the stone platform, and I surface enough to wipe the shit from my eyes before hauling myself up.

I race along the stone hallway to the wooden door.

It's been hung back in place.

*Not surprising.*

I yank the pins from the hinges and let myself through again. There are no guards; they only work during the day, and they *definitely* don't work on the full moon.

Retracing the path the guard led me down earlier, I pass cell after cell. And then my eyes grow wide as my magic tracks movement and bodies in the darkness. My vision sharpens, and my insides curdle as I take in the sight before me.

The cells are stuffed with humans—a feast for after the full moon packed into cages for safekeeping. Most are alive, some drained, as though the guards who stashed them in here couldn't control their bloodlust. The sound of the humans' pleas boils my anger, and I retrace my steps to the first brimming cage, my magic whirring and muscles transforming.

My magic will remain in the bars of these cages if I use it, but the lives I'm saving make the risk worth it. We don't typically leave traces of ourselves outside of Mortifer—we never want the use of our magic to fall into enemy hands—but this warrants an exception because I don't have time to fiddle with keys and unlock every cell.

So I make my choice.

Gripping the bar of the first cell, I fire my magic down the entire row, and lock after lock flies through the air, clattering against stone.

In seconds, I free hundreds.

My eyes meet a starved man on the other side of the bars, and I swing the cage open. "Follow me," I tell him and move briskly down the corridor.

I jog down the hallway toward the dungeon door, bare feet pattering behind. Thankful whispers and whimpers echo in the stone hallway, and a teenage girl races ahead of me.

We reach the massive iron door, and I unclip the ring of keys.

*Please, gods.*

The girl looks at me, eyeing the keys and then the holes.

"Which one fits?" she asks.

"I don't know," I say, trying the first one and failing.

She bats my hand away and peers into the first keyhole. "Three teeth."

I stare at her, stunned. Shaking myself to attention, I assess the keychain. Five options with three teeth.

"How did you know to check for that?" I ask her as I try the first one.

It doesn't turn.

"Father was a locksmith," she sniffles.

"Was?"

"He's dead in the cell."

*Fuck.*

"Mother?"

"Turned."

I try the next key. Nothing.

"What's your name?" I ask her while I choose the next key.

"Rosy."

"Go to Southend, Rosy. There's a tavern near the old church. Do you know where I'm talking about?"

She nods at me as I try the third key. Nothing.

"Tell them Kade sent you. They'll look after you."

"Thank you," she whispers.

I insert the fourth key, and the lock clicks and turns.

Rosy smiles up at me, and I grin back, quickly unlocking the last two bolts and hauling the heavy iron door open.

I lead a sea of humans across the bridge, the bay glistening around us under the bright moon. And echoing off the water, the telltale sign of such a night—screaming rings in our ears.

Dreamwalking has begun.

At the edge of the tree line beyond, Hunters emerge into the moonlight, hundreds prepared for war.

Riot's and Grace's expressions grow wide and angry as they take in the innocents behind me. Grace steps forward, ushering people past her into the cover of the trees beyond.

Rhett sidles up next to Riot, expression on fire.

"What the fuck," Riot growls.

"Cages were full this time," I tell them.

"Aye," he spits.

Rage from the entire legion races in my veins, and I won't complain about the natural fuel feeding my warriors in the moments before battle.

I wade into the edge of the bay, dunking myself underneath and erupting from the icy water, shit-free and heart on fire. After shaking myself out on the bank, Riot offloads my weapons one at a time to me, and I strap my swords across my back, garrote at my waist, bolt belt over my chest, and crossbow in my grip.

"There's hundreds of them," Rhett says, gazing back at the edge of the woods as Hunters offer clothing from their backs to the rescued humans.

Tonight's attack on this castle is already worth it. So many lives have been saved, and without Sam's capture, they'd all have been dead in the morning.

Grace's brow pinches. "We would've noticed that many disappearances from Southend and Goreon City today."

Rhett looks at his Heir. "Or they brought them in from throughout Goreon."

Riot nods. "That's more likely."

"Aye," Grace agrees. She drags her gaze from the humans to peer up at me, her small frame over a foot below Riot beside her. "I love you, Kade," she whispers, and I pull her into me, kissing her deeply.

"I love you more, my darling," I promise and release her.

She smiles, the moonlight bright across her face. "Swords at our backs."

I cup her jaw, my wet, frozen skin warming against her. "Hearts at our fronts."

Turning away from the legion, I face the bridge with magic flooding me in a gold river. I raise an arm and march forward, leading Hunters across the passage to our future.

# CHAPTER 17

## VEYA

Present Day

W E STAND BEFORE the blazing pyre, mourning Aurelia and Samantha.

Huddled together, Hartley, Nix, and Ellie shed convincing tears and distraught cries for their cellar companions all these years.

Second and Charlotte left with Aurelia and Samantha a few hours ago, slipping into the tree line a mile from castle grounds. And I can barely breathe under the stress of it.

Del is frozen, a statue of striking perfection as his stony gaze refuses to move from the forest beyond.

"Del," I whisper.

"The not knowing is going to rip my fucking heart out," he breathes, just over the sound of the surging pyre and howling wind swirling through our cloaks.

I nod at him, barely able to focus on anything but Second, Charlotte, and the girls. With a few more hours of night left, Second and Charlotte will need to shelter for the day and lock themselves away for the full moon. Which means our girls are on their own at dawn.

"Second and Charlotte will protect them for as long as they have them. I swear it."

Del still doesn't move. "I know," he utters, breath pluming before us.

"Where do you think they are right now?" I ask him, my mind running wild.

"They should be an hour from the stable I sent them to. And their shelter is nearby."

"Good," I say, my voice drowned out by the roar and pop of the bonfire, which reaches into the sky so high I have to crane my neck to see the tips of the flames.

Del's chin dips, his focus in the snow as he inhales deeply and then blows out a slow exhale. Determined, amethyst eyes spark at me through the darkness before he says, "We should continue our conversation regarding our mutual interest."

*Yes. We should.*

"Agreed," I say and stare into the flaming empty grave, the sharp snapping of burnt logs striking nerves down my spine, and I try to muster hope to counter it, to sustain me through the day ahead. I try to find a bearable baseline because Del is going to need one of us with our head straight.

A throat clears from behind us, and Del and I spin to see General Balor scowling at us.

"What is it, Balor?" Del demands in a voice I haven't heard from him, his demeanor flipping from concerned to callous instantly.

Balor hesitates, and I'm thrilled Del sets this male on edge. "The king requests an audience with Queen Veya." Emmanuel steps next to me, and Balor's gaze slides to him. "*Alone*," he clarifies.

"That seems unnecessary," I say. "Surely he can't expect such an intimate conversation so soon?"

Balor sneers at me. "I'm not privy to his intentions, *Queen*. But I'm sure, whatever they may be, are ... *deserved*."

I leash a snarl and glare at Balor.

"Let's get you to the king then," Del says in a chipper voice, striding past all of us toward the castle.

I appreciate Del's unassuming chaperone and keep my face neutral under Balor's focus still pinned to me.

"Girls, go to my suite," I tell them, and they shuffle off together.

"I'm by your side until I can't be," Em says, and we follow Balor, who's turned on his heel.

"You always end up where you need to be. I'm not worried," I say, despite the dread building in my chest.

Emmanuel keeps a pace ahead as I follow the line of males to the looming stronghold, its blackened façade darker than the pitch night it stands in.

Balor struts through the grand doors of the antechamber.

"You'll wait here," he tells Emmanuel, and my assassin steps into shadow and disappears.

I follow Del into the throne room, which is empty of Nerian's court; only guards and the king are present.

Del is an unexpected comfort, drowning my insecurities with his confident stride and intentional presence for this audience with evil.

Nerian is draped over his throne haphazardly, lying on his back and playing absently with his tooth necklace. He traces his fingers along the teeth dangling in front of his face, and I have to work to keep my face neutral.

"My king," Balor calls, trying to wrangle his attention, but Nerian just grins at his necklace dancing in the candlelight.

Del ascends the dais and peers over him.

"King Nerian," he drawls.

Nerian jerks to attention. "Ah! You're herrrrre," he slurs.

"Drunk on blood *and* wine from your cellar, it seems," Del says, his second persona a well-worn mask.

"Did you turn your girlsss—" Nerian slogs his body around to sit up in his throne, drunk eyes raking over me.

I curtsy *slightly*. "We enjoyed them greatly and turned three. The other two are burning outside as we speak. Second lost control."

Nerian's laughter scrapes along my skin. "I knew he was starving. That's just fantassstic." He rolls onto his side, clinging to his throne, and Del steps away right before the king vomits on the dais.

Wine runs down the steps toward me, and I shift to the side to avoid it.

Nerian has destroyed himself.

"We can leave you to your evening, my king," Del says, eyes shifting to mine.

"Yes, good. Fetch me replacements for the cellar to review next week," he says, sobriety claiming him for a moment as his eyes flash in pleasure with talk of his cellar.

It requires all of my control to keep my face blank while my rage is boiling beneath my skin. I refuse to let any more *replacements* end up there.

The king focuses on the teeth dangling in his grasp as Del joins me at the foot of the dais, saying quietly, "He always drinks before the full moon"

"Does he take the serum?" I ask.

Del looks at me. "Surprisingly, no."

I hum in thought. "Evil doesn't sprout from nowhere," I say. "Perhaps he needs to walk amongst whatever fuels it."

Del glances up at Nerian. "He's done for the night. He's piss-drunk."

*A visiting queen isn't even enough motivation to restrain himself.*

I wonder if we could kill him now, but there are a hundred guards surrounding us, and Charlotte and Second are gone.

"Let's get out of here," Del says, leading the way.

Balor waits for us as we approach the antechamber. "Where are you two going?"

Del pauses, his hand gently brushing at my hip to keep me back, which seems dramatic until I notice Balor's hand on his hilt, and I'm surprised there isn't a low growl coming from his throat to go with the look on his face.

"Why is that your business?" Del demands.

Balor scoffs. "The king has made everything my business. And I intend to follow my orders to the letter."

"Which are?" Del asks, raising an eyebrow at the general.

Balor looks at the ceiling to recall the words he memorized. "Keep the queen in line. And if she gives you any trouble—" He dips his chin and looks right at me. "Just kill her already."

"Those aren't your orders," Del laughs.

I'm not so sure Del is correct as I stare into Balor's taunting gaze.

"As of twenty minutes ago, they are."

Del scoffs. "And when have we *ever* taken Nerian's drunk words in the hours before a full moon seriously?"

Balor sneers at us. "There's always a first time."

"Like Queen Veya said, Balor. Don't be a dick." Del's hand finds the small of my back, and he guides me through the chamber, buzzing energy firing through me while I try to tamp my smirk. We snap toward my rooms, Em joining us from nowhere.

"Balor is the fucking worst," I snarl under my breath outside our suite.

Del chuckles. "Try living with him."

Em pauses at our door. "Where's the court? Castle seems pretty empty."

"Full moon. They've all escaped to their estates," Del says.

Em snorts as we enter. The girls are waiting here like I asked, and I'm thankful to find them showered, clothed, and unbothered on the sofa, feet propped up in front of the fire. Charlotte's closet has been put to excellent use.

We need to prepare them for the next twenty-four hours.

"Ladies, your first dreamwalk is in about twelve hours. You'll lose control over your body and mind. Your memories will take over and become your reality. There is nothing you can do," I say.

"We know," Nix says, tying up her fiery hair. "The king often chose the cellar for his dreamwalking. He'd flip off the fire so he didn't burn himself, and we'd practically freeze to death the entire night."

I cringe at the thought of Nerian out of his mind and the girls within his grasp. "I see. I'm sure Del can offer serum if you prefer to be unconscious."

Hartley smiles. "I'll always take the chance I'm thrown into a good memory. No serum for me."

Ellie's sad eyes look up from the fireplace into mine. "I'd rather be unconscious."

"I'll get you some serum," Del says gently.

"For you, Nix?" I ask.

She sighs. "I'll take my chances with the walk. I'd love to see my mother again."

I give her an approving nod. I always take my chances, too.

"Daylight is upon us shortly, and we haven't slept in a while. Let's rest before the full moon," I tell everyone.

Emmanuel secures the shutters as Del rakes back the hair that's flopped into his eyes; all of us are a little unkempt at this point. "I should return to the west wing," he says. "It would be odd for me to remain here for this sleep."

"Of course. We'll be fine," I assure him and gesture to Emmanuel.

Del nods. "Ladies, come with me. I will see you to separate, locked rooms where you can sleep and dreamwalk in private. And I'll get you something to drink."

Ellie wrinkles her nose.

"It's not terrible, and your body needs it," Del says.

"Fine," Ellie sighs and crosses the room to us, Nix following. But Hartley snaps in front of me, inches from my face, and her eyes blow wide.

"Oh my gods, sorry. Too close," she says, stumbling back.

A brief pause extends before Del and I break into hysterical laughter.

"It'll take a while to practice your aim and spacing, Hartley," Del says through his throaty laugh.

My eyes water in my joy of the innocent moment.

Emmanuel approaches her, gaze roaming Hartley up and down. "Snapping on command your first day is very impressive," he praises, and I try to keep my jaw off the ground. I've never heard the male compliment anyone.

"Perhaps your trajectory as an assassin for the Night Kingdom is a wise choice," I say.

Emmanuel's narrowed eyes find mine. "No one said anything about *assassin*," he retorts.

Emmanuel rarely argues with me on anything not to do with my safety. So rare, I think it's been a few decades. "I won't deny talent the position it deserves. We'll see what comes of her."

"Well, I'd at least like a shot at it," Hartley says, tossing her hands on her hips between us as Emmanuel and I stare at one another.

Em finally gives up and walks off.

"You'll get your shot," I promise her, and Hartley bows deeply before following Del, Nix, and Ellie out of my rooms.

As soon as the door snicks shut, Emmanuel is back and pacing—another rarity.

"What is *wrong* with you?"

He halts and faces me. "What if she's my mate?"

I roll my eyes. "Come on, Em. The odds of that are close to zero."

"I can't have my mate as an assassin for the crown. I won't be able to focus."

My eyebrows raise. I'm surprised by his assuredness and his admission to distraction. "You don't know what she is to you."

He starts pacing again. "I'm drawn to her. It's scaring the shit out of me. I can't ignore that and hope for the fucking best."

I splay my hands, desperate to understand how he sees the future. "So what, we're just going to lock her in a tower to keep her safe until you feel up to testing out a bond? Or better yet, if she is your mate, you're going to abandon your life's work and run away together?"

His body stills next to the roaring hearth, but he doesn't respond, which means neither option is off the table.

I try a different tack. "Or, as mates, you'll be unstoppable. Your ability to communicate without speaking, your physical knowledge of each other through the bond. There are numerous advantages."

"You're forgetting the best part, *Veya*," he says, tone rigid as his eyes slide to mine. "My death is her death, and hers is mine."

That's not always the case from what we've learned from other vampires over the centuries, but I won't pick another battle. "Look, I know you don't want a mate in your life," I say. "It complicates things. *Trust me*, I understand that. But we don't know who she is to you yet. Let's worry about this *after* we take Goreon."

His eyes clear of concern at my request. "Fine. Let's get some rest," he says, disappearing through my bedchamber door without another word.

I stare into the crackling fire, my body defeated with exhaustion.

My mind shifts to Aurelia and Samantha as they race on horseback through the day to the Night Kingdom wall, and I send a prayer to the gods to watch over them.

I learned long ago not to fortify faith with false hope; fate will always win in the end. But it won't stop me from groveling to the gods and laying my wishes at their feet.

Heaving my emotions out with a forced exhale, I move to my room and change for bed, Emmanuel already softly snoring on my floor, still dressed and armed.

My bedroom door flies open just before sunset, and guards snap throughout my suite.

"*What is the meaning of this*?" I snarl. Emmanuel, a breath from me, has blades drawn.

General Balor sneers at us. "The king would like you safely stowed for the full moon. He can't have queens wandering where they shouldn't."

I peer at him, confused; every vampire usually locks themselves away for safekeeping during dreamwalk, anyway. "A reasonable request," I bite. "Why the dramatic show in my bedchamber, Balor?"

He shrugs. "I didn't want any trouble with my orders."

I let my gaze run up the male. "Or you're overcompensating."

Balor snarls at me.

"What is wrong with my chambers for the full moon?" I ask.

He tilts his chin and steps toward me, only to be greeted by Emmanuel's hiss. Balor pauses and sighs at us. "Just let me stow you where the king wants so we can all get this night over with. It doesn't fucking matter to me where I put you, but I'm going to follow orders."

As much as I hate to admit it, it's probably wise, given how drunk Nerian is. For all our sakes, I can't imagine what an argument over this could escalate to, and it's not worth the risk to fight them on it with Charlotte and Second gone. We need to keep tensions low and get through the night.

I huff at him. "Well, let's go, General. Stow away."

"You too," Balor yips at Emmanuel and jerks his head for us to follow him. "And where are the other two?"

"Gone to my territory to handle an urgent matter," I say.

Balor grunts and traipses out of the bedroom.

Guards flank us, leading us down to the ground floor and then through a long, gilded hallway to a door into the sublevels.

A dingy smell wafts upward, and plaster turns to stone as we descend to the dungeons.

I sigh, whisking myself down the stairs.

A locked bedroom door or a locked cell door—they're the same, just a frigid stone floor for a seat instead of the comfort of my suite.

It's so *Nerian*.

# CHAPTER 18

## KADE

*Two Hundred Years Ago – Goreon Kingdom*

M Y BOOT CROSSES the threshold into the Goreon dungeon, Riot beside me.

We move in deathly silence through the empty jail, our soft footfalls covered by the chaos above, the shredding screams and moaning, the crying and shouting. The talking.

We follow the sound of dreamwalking.

Riot and I lift an internal door off its hinges, and the legion snakes up the stairwell.

I signal for everyone to halt and edge around the corner, peering down a gilded hallway lit with torches, gold glinting in the light of fire.

The wealth in just this hallway is astounding.

And it's the starving children and desperate parents outside these walls who paid for it.

I shift into the empty hall, Hunters filing out of the stairwell behind me. This is where we part ways and fan out into the castle in our predetermined groups. Our advantage of surprise only works well if we attack and kill as many as possible in the first fucking go, hitting as wide and as fast as we can. We gave ourselves five minutes to identify our initial targets.

"See you on the other side," Uncle Brachett whispers, and then he, Longton, and Ned take off in opposite directions with their men.

Reaching my magic out, I try to connect to Sam.

Nothing.

*Fuck.*

I join my small team, which is purposefully my closest Hunter family, toward the stairwell at the end of the gilded hall. I wouldn't be able to focus if any of them were out of my sight. Master Hull and Grace lead the way, Riot and I in the center, and Rhett behind us.

My father told me bedtime stories that included the anatomy of this castle, writing the skeleton of its rooms into my memory before I ever knew the importance of it.

We climb to the second floor, up a carpeted stairwell as wide as the streets in the city. Paintings hang along the walls: portraits of royals, depictions of infamous drainings, and the brutality that led to the Goreon empire—all on display.

We're halfway up the stairwell when a vampire snaps into existence in front of Grace, screaming, its fangs bared and eyes vacant, and my soul leaves me.

Riot's and my magic whips into a frenzy, gold splashing and sloshing.

Grace slashes her blades through the vampire's neck without hesitation, and the head topples down the stairs. Her reaction time is like nothing I've ever seen from her.

*Trust the talent you know she has, damnit. Calm the fuck down.*

"Too close," Riot whispers beside me, and I glance over at him, knowing my face is as white as it feels.

"Settle down, boys. We're just getting started," Grace chirps, not bothering to look back and climbs the stairs two at a time, ready and eager.

Her confidence wraps around me, and I let it, desperate to calm my racing heart. Grace has always been this way. Independent, fierce, and unpredictable.

"Yes, ma'am," Riot says. There's no sarcasm in his tone, and I feel his magic settle at his Heir's words.

"Two more minutes," I whisper as we head down a hallway, and I pick the lock into the first door. Peering around its edge, I find vampires dressed in their finest, passed out on a bed together.

I guess they partied before taking the serum.

Ducking back into the hallway, I count twenty doors behind our party and say, "Bedrooms. Clear a room and keep moving to the next until we execute the entire wing."

We each choose a door and enter on my signal.

Six unconscious vampires are littered about on plush furniture, and one shifts at the sound of the door closing, a moan escaping its mouth.

I creep silently across the room and shove a stake through its heart.

It gurgles and jerks, eyes trying to pop open, but the serum holds them shut, and a tear slips down its cheek.

I stake the remaining five in seconds and dip back into the hallway, Riot coming out of his room beside me.

Grace is already darting through her next chosen door.

"She's *winning*," Riot whines and races to his next target.

*Gods, I love my people.*

I enter another bedroom, freezing in disgust. Two unconscious humans are chained to the wall with ports jammed into their thighs, a slow drip of blood falling from the attached tubes.

I cross the room and kneel before them, hand skirting to the woman's neck and then the other.

*No pulses.*

I turn, rage simmering. Why even bother with the port if they're going to drain them anyway? I guess the blood lasts longer through the port than a single-serving bite.

Anger fueling every step, I race to the lounge on the far side of the bedroom, stabbing the five vampires draped over furniture, wishing it hurt with the same pain and fear that ran through the tortured humans chained in this room. I tamp down my desire to inflict what these vampires truly deserve because that would require much more time and consciousness.

Master Hull emerges into the hallway as I do, and we run to the end of the corridor, taking the last three rooms. I sense Rhett's magic at the door on my left, so I open the one on the right.

The dreamwalker's face swivels to the open door I'm standing in, eyes vacant.

"Glad you're home, darling," it says to me. "I've missed you terribly. Where have you been?"

Its face blanches even more than it already has, and I haven't moved an inch.

"*You're turned*!" it screams at me, backing away and running into the wall behind it. "My love, how?" it asks, fear and sadness lacing its tone while it scrambles to the side and stumbles over a chair.

I step into the bedroom and close the door.

"Get away from me. Don't do this. Please, honey, it's *me*," it begs no one.

The dreamwalker pulls at my empathy, but I shove the emotion back down. There's no mercy tonight, or ever. Once turned, I can't think about the human life they led— that person died, and a threat was born.

I approach the vampire, its fangs popping, and a snarl rips from its throat, sensing a Hunter threat.

"I don't want to be a vampire. Please, just leave, I beg you! If you ever loved me—"

I raise my crossbow and fire a stake through its heart.

"Wish granted," I whisper. "Rest now."

I stake the remaining four and rejoin my warriors.

"All clear," Riot says, grinning through blood spatter.

"Got a bit messy with it, did you?" Rhett jests.

Riot shrugs. "Had an aggressive dreamwalker. Fucker was strong."

Grace taps his crossbow. "You know you can use that."

Rhett's shoulders bounce beside her, and Riot wipes his brow with his sleeve. "I needed to warm up; the exercise felt great."

"Gods bless, you obnoxious beast," Grace says, eyes rolling along with everyone else's.

"Let's move to the next hall," I say, and we plow through the double doors and into the wing beyond.

I'm thrilled we took down so many in minutes—this is exactly what we needed. I reach out to Sam again, and the smallest blip splashes back at me, like he's barely conscious, but it's all I need.

"Sam is in the throne room," I say to our party.

Grace and Master whip around with hopeful faces.

"His status?" Master asks.

I shake my head. "Not good. Barely conscious."

He nods. "Let's get a move on it, then."

I feel Longton and Brachett above us, their magic whirring. They're fighting hard, overrun with enemy targets and pushing their bodies.

"Stress above. Let's clear this wing quickly and go help," I say, loading my crossbow as my people sprint into action.

We fly in and out of the next wing of rooms and soon put another thirty down.

Our scouting over the years determined there are at least two hundred permanent residents within the castle. And any number could be visiting or staying, especially on a night like tonight. But that's another perk: the opportunity to eradicate a larger population in a single night.

We spiral up the next stairwell, following the screaming and yelling, and jump into chaos. Slain headless vampires lay trampled on the ground, and blades flash throughout the hall as twelve Hunters take on the fifty dreamwalkers still standing.

Grace barrels past me and charges into the fray.

*This woman.*

I fire two bolts before reloading and strapping the crossbow to my back in favor of my blades. My form hardens and my mind hones, and I'm whirling through the hall, my speed untraceable as I slash through one neck and then another. I throw a blade in the air to free a hand and plunge a bolt from my belt into the heart of the vampire charging me from my right. Catching my blade, I swing at the moaning dreamwalker in front of me, taking its head clean off.

My movements are a blur as instinct and training take over. I stake the next on my left and punch another to my right, sending it stumbling before I rip wood from the flesh of the crumpling vampire and plunge it into the heart of the next.

My magic screams in alarm, gold curdling, and I whip around.

Master Hull is moving like he's seen thirty fewer years, his magic pushing him to unnatural limits, and I watch him step in front of a sword aimed for Grace's back. He takes the blade in his shoulder.

Grace spins, her face plastered with shock as the vampire lunges for her father. Before either of them can react, it sinks its fangs into Master's neck.

Something dark and vicious pierces Grace's eyes as she jams a bolt into the vampire's back, and its fangs uproot from her father's skin.

I slash through two vampires approaching me, fighting toward the other end of the hall to get to them. Eyes pinned on my family, I watch Master Hull shove the vampire off, and it flounders and tries to crawl away, but Grace strikes her sword down hard, severing its head.

"*I'm fine!*" Hull shouts and shoos Grace away, but she doesn't leave his side, inspecting her father's wounds.

Her jaw clenches, and I can see the worry in her eyes.

She's not overreacting. I feel Master's magic draining.

He's not *fine*.

Grace unleashes her anger, jumping up to defend her father. She's the embodiment of fury and love, blades slashing as she dances from one vampire to the next, her speed and dexterity mesmerizing, a bird flitting and swooping, uncatchable—and killing everything in its path.

I've never seen something so beautiful and brutal entwine in a single moment.

She's trying to end this so we can tend to her father, and I join her.

We work each end of the hall, killing our way toward one another.

A vampire snaps to my side, and I take the hilt of its sword in my mouth before I can react. My head jolts back, and I touch my tongue to my tooth.

*Chipped. Fantastic.*

Slicing the offending vampire's head off, I refocus down the hall toward Grace.

Dim candlelight dances, steel glints, and blood sprays as an evening storm brews outside, my magic sensing the shift in temperature against my skin as wind sweeps through an open window. Lightning strikes, and the hall illuminates, the red paint of death streaking walls and sloshing under boots. Hunters slash and stab, fierce painted warriors deliver death until only one dreamwalker remains. My stake pierces its heart as Grace rakes her gaze over me.

"We're good at this," she says before running for her father.

*Obviously.*

I chase after her, crouching beside Master Hull.

He's not in good shape, and I need the heroics to end before we're making another funeral procession to Mortifer.

"Time for you to leave," I tell him.

He glares at me, slapping a cloth over his wound. "Tie my belt around it, Captain, and get me the fuck up."

Unfortunately, the Hunter chain of command leaves only two people above me: Grace, and this stubborn man.

I whip his belt off and cinch it under his armpit. "Not much of a patch job," I mutter.

My magic agrees with me; his wound is deep, and his pain is equally terrible.

I reach out to sense the Hunters. No one else is injured, and I exhale in relief.

Uncle Brachett barrels toward us, eyeing his Master.

"The throne room," I tell Brachett, standing and pulling Master up with me. "That's where they're holding Sam."

"Aye," he says, breathing heavily.

I'm fondling the new chip in my tooth again when Riot's face scrunches at me. "What are you doing?"

"Fucker got me in the mouth. Chipped my damn tooth."

Grace rolls her eyes. "You're beautiful; it just makes you more rugged," she tells me, and I flash her a winning, bloody smile. "See? Way more handsome," she encourages.

I huff at my wife and survey the hall.

Blood-covered warriors grin back at me.

"To the throne room, Hunters!" I call and lead the way, eager to get to my brother-in-law and get him the hell out of here.

We weave through halls and descend to the ground floor toward the main entrance of the stronghold.

My magic simmers, celebrating as we gain ground on Sam. The feeling is mutual.

We take down the enemy in our path, hallway after hallway of dreamwalkers, like the king knew we were coming and invited all of Goreon's vampires to defend what's theirs during the full moon. Plowing through the antechamber, we burst through the throne room doors—

*Holy gods.*

# CHAPTER 19

## VEYA

Present Day

I 'M NOT SURE this is an appropriate place to stow a queen," I protest as we pass a row of empty holding cells and head down another corridor.

"It's what the king wants," Balor says blandly. His indifference is odd; I'd think he would be thrilled to throw me down here. Perhaps he's nervous for his own dreamwalk.

"Can we get some pillows or something?" Emmanuel snarks.

Balor approaches a cell and opens the door. "In," he commands and then yanks the cell beside it open for Emmanuel.

A guard juts out his palm for Emmanuel's weapons.

"The only way you're getting any of my steel is if it's embedded in your skull," Em says and strides into his cell fully armed.

I breeze into my cage with my blades strapped to my thighs. "Go ahead, Balor." I nod at the open door. "Let's all get this night behind us, shall we?"

He bolts the barred doors and locks them, and the buzz of magic fires across the bars the moment the locks are in place.

My shocked gaze darts to Balor, whose sneer springs from nowhere.

"What is *Hunter* magic doing on these cell doors?" I snarl.

Balor shrugs. "A Hunter left his mark here. I don't complain about the perk."

*Fuck.*

A locked cell *would have been* the same as a locked door. We could have escaped if needed, vampiric strength being capable of ripping open locks or bars. But we can't break open a cell locked with Hunter magic.

Second is going to kill me.

King Nerian stumbles into view, gripping the bars, and his palms sear against them. He steadies himself and removes his hands, shaking out his charred flesh.

"I love an obedient female," he says and guzzles wine from the bottle his guard hands him.

My eyes narrow on Nerian. "This is an overstep I won't look past, Nerian."

"Are you uncomfortable in there? I'm sorry. You're right," he slurs.

Nerian jerks his chin, and Balor unlocks my cell, which confuses me until two soldiers snap into existence and shove Del into the cell with me.

"There. That's better. Someone to keep you company through the night." Nerian laughs.

The cell locks again and magic buzzes.

"How *dare* you jeopardize a queen like this during dreamwalk!" I snarl, my gut dropping at the vulnerability of Del and me in such proximity when we're out of our minds.

Del's panicked eyes share my concerns.

Nerian laughs and ignores me. "Don't play with my future wife without me, Deleos. Or *do*—I don't really give a fuck." The king tilts his chin at us, and his eyes flash. "Let's make it *interesting*."

*Oh gods.*

The bastard summons our clothing through the bars, and I shield myself, fangs bared in my undergarments.

Emmanuel hisses in the neighboring cell, just as disrobed, and Del chains his gaze to the ground, away from an almost-naked queen.

Skin exposed and fear ratcheting, I stare at Del's muscled flesh and the countless points of contact the gods could use to thread an eternal bond between us.

Nerian just started a war. And I'm inside his cell, wrapped in Hunter magic.

The king sneers at me. "Sweet dreams, my dear."

And then they're gone, snapping into nothing.

Silence extends before Del breaks it. "Nerian doesn't know the meaning of tact or self-control anymore," he says, eyes still pinned to the ground.

"Did he ever?" Em asks.

Del snorts.

I drop my arms, a shiver clanging through me from the chill.

There's nothing I can do about our circumstance, and Del's already been vulnerable in front of me, sharing his human name. What's a little scantily clad skin stacked up next to that?

*Patrick.* His name rings like a church bell in my head, demanding me to honor it.

Del sighs. "I can't believe Nerian did this, though. I wasn't expecting to be in a cell *with* you … or this naked."

"Gods!" Emmanuel barks from the other cell. "It's fucking insanity in this godsforsaken *fucking* place. I'm going to fucking rip his pitiful dick from his groin and stuff it in his shit-eating mouth!"

Del smirks at the ground.

I join him.

"I've never heard you string so many words together, Em," I say.

Emmanuel punches the cell wall, and magic sears him. "Godsdamnit! Fucking hell, godsdamn—" My assassin stops cursing and screams his rage instead. His shredding voice echoes through the dungeon. The male finally settles and looks me in the eyes. His horrified expression stills the breath in my chest. "This is my fault. I *never* should've let you follow Balor down here. I will regret it forever."

"We'll be fine," I tell him, trying to rally my composure and sort through our options before the full moon takes us.

"And I'm still second in Goreon. I have power here," Del tells Emmanuel.

"Are you? Because you're in the damn cell, too," Emmanuel says.

"I'm here on purpose, asshole."

I tamp a flattered smile. "Tell us what happened."

Keeping his gaze averted, he says, "I was privy to the orders to lock you in here."

"You can look at me," I say, finally taking a seat on the cold, miserable stone.

Del drags his gaze across the cell, and the plum of his eyes darkens to a deep purple as they consume every inch of my skin.

My lips part and heat races down my core as he sits down across from me.

"You can look at me, not undress me with your eyes, Del," I scold half-heartedly, although still desperate to subdue the impact of the most striking male I've ever seen.

*Now is* not *the time.*

"You're already practically naked. There's nothing to undress."

And so is he. And he's glorious.

I let my eyes snag on his abdomen flexing with his breath. There's hard muscle everywhere, from his round shoulders down his defined arms, tendons and veins popping like he's built for battle. His masculinity is ridiculously sexy, and his disheveled black hair adds a softened charm that makes me want to fold into his chest with his arms wrapped around me.

Del's turn marks are on his right pec, and I wonder how it happened.

"Nice blades," he says, eyes running up my thighs.

"Oh my gods, why are you in the cell?" Emmanuel interrupts.

Del doesn't take his eyes off me, but his lips quirk in response. "Because I convinced the king it would be fun to rattle Veya by locking me down here with you," he answers, eyes sliding back down my thighs.

"It's *Queen Veya*," Emmanuel corrects him. "And *how* did you convince him?"

Del swallows as his gaze tracks up to my face. "Honestly, it took no effort. Nerian's fucked up, and any suggestion aligning with that is usually taken. Although I didn't think he would put me in the cell *with* you."

I groan and settle my back against the stone floor to stare at the drab, leaking ceiling above me. Emotionally spent, physically on edge, and sexually flustered. Stuck in a cell with the hottest vampire in Goreon, and the Night Kingdom, for that matter.

On a full moon.

"Touch me and I'll fucking kill you, Del. I won't tolerate a mate in my life," I say sharply, swiveling my head to look at him.

Del's eyes jerk to mine. "Don't think I don't *already* know that about you, Veya." He settles onto the floor on the opposite side of the cell, his muscles flexing and quivering as he leans back on his hands. I stare at Del's chiseled chest and then up at his ensnaring smirk above a physique sculpted by the gods.

The lonely, neglected pieces of me wish I could touch him. And that makes the sting of my solitude even more piercing.

"I'll honor your boundary," he says, breath billowing into the chill. "Hells forbid we create a bond we can't run away from."

"Chain yourself," I command.

He huffs at me. "With what? Your panties? Like that's going to hold in a dreamwalk."

Emmanuel tosses two sets of restraints into our cage, and we both turn to gape at him.

"Never without them," he says with a shrug. "Although I haven't used them before. My targets are dead, not captured."

My body senses the setting sun, and I nab my restraints, threading them through the cell bar, Del doing the same.

We secure ourselves around the bars of the cell, relief drenching me. Because if a bond formed between us, I don't know that I could kill Del if it came down to it. I made a rash decision with Fash to protect the desires for my own life and avoid pain I was nowhere near ready to handle.

But now, I can't convince myself to believe that my happiness is worth the price of Del's life.

I sigh, thankful I don't even need to worry about it now, and my mind wanders to the rest of our people as the full moon closes in on us.

"Gods, I hope the girls are surviving out there. They said they knew how to ride. I just hope they hauled hard," I say.

Del huffs, lying down on stone, his ankle chained. "You and I both, Veya."

"They should be nearing the wall by now," Emmanuel adds.

My fingers flex in anticipation of our impending dreamwalk, my desire to escape this cell raging. Hunter magic puts any sane vampire in a state of unease.

"We're taking Goreon when the full moon is over. Nerian crossed a line with this tonight," I say.

"Agreed," Del growls, and Emmanuel groans.

"We have to get out of here *first*," he says.

There are only two ways out of a cell locked with Hunter magic: the key for the lock or a Hunter.

"We'll get out," I assure Em. "Second will get a key. And the male might burn down the castle just for the offense."

"I really hope not. This castle is beautiful; it just needs some cheering up," Del drawls.

"It needs a *full* workover," I retort.

"Is that our first act of Goreon rule? Castle makeover?" Del laughs, as I push at the delirium setting in.

And then it does, and I'm gone.

*Momma braids my hair while we wait for Father to come home. He's been gone for days, and I miss him. We're getting pretty first and then making him dinner.*

*"What should we cook, baby girl?" Momma asks me.*

*I shrug as her fingers pull another section of hair into my braid. "Eggs," I suggest.*

*She laughs. "It's dinner."*

*"But he loves eggs."*

*Momma grabs another section of hair. "True. Eggs it is, then."*

*The rain falls harder outside, like drums on the roof. I love the sound of the rain.*

*She ties off the braid and rubs my arm. "All done. Let's make some eggs."*

*I scurry to the kitchen. I love helping in the kitchen.*

*Momma pulls ingredients from the icebox. "Break the eggs in the bowl while I chop," she says, handing me supplies.*

*I try to count the eggs, but I think I missed a number.*

*"Count the shells again," Momma says. "You can do it."*

*I scrunch my lips and count again.*

*"Well done," Momma praises and scoops the chopped vegetables into the eggs, handing me a spoon.*

*I stir while Momma lights the range. We're a really good team.*

*"Ready to pour?" she asks, and I nod before we lift the bowl together and dump the eggs into the pan.*

*I watch them go into the oven. It's my favorite part, to wait until I smell the food. That's how you know it's almost done.*

*"Let's set the table," Momma says, handing me the plates.*

*I've just finished placing them in their spots when glass crashes onto our floor and a rock skids past me.*

*"Run, baby girl, run!" Momma tells me, but I'm frozen. I can't stop looking at the windows, where the rain is coming into the kitchen. The floor is getting wet.*

*Momma lifts me and shoves me in a cupboard, slamming the door.*

*It's dark in here.*

*The back door bangs open, and I jump at the sound.*

*Boots are stomping around the kitchen.*

*Momma is screaming, "I beg you, don't do this."*

*"King's orders."*

*"I haven't done anything wrong," she yells. I can see her legs through the gap in the wood.*

*"Should have watched the company you keep, then."*

*Momma gurgles, and I see her fall to the floor.*

*I know she doesn't want me to come out, but I want to see if she is hurt.*

*No more boots are stomping.*

*Just the rain pounding in my ears.*

*I push the door open slowly, peeking out to make sure it's safe, and then crawl across the floor to her.*

*Momma is bleeding, a red slice across her neck, and her eyes aren't moving.*

*"Momma," I say, shaking her.*

*When she doesn't respond, I lie next to her, stroking her arm over and over, waiting for Father to get home.*

*The back door bangs in the wind, and I jump again, clutching Momma tighter.*

*The eggs are burning, and I'm shivering.*

*I should close the back door. But I don't want to leave Momma.*

*Hours pass, and my tears won't stop. Father is late, and I'm trying to be strong.*

*The sun rises, and morning light streams into the kitchen. I can't cry anymore, and it's hard to keep my eyes open.*

*Footsteps.*

*I lift my head to the doorway, and Father freezes, staring at us.*

*"No!" he screams, running at us and skidding to his knees. "No, no, no," he cries, pulling Momma into his lap.*

Hours later, I awaken to Del staring at the tears running down my cheeks.

"Not a good one for you, then," he says.

I can barely speak, my throat dry from screaming, like someone poured sand down it.

I swallow. "No," I croak.

Emmanuel stirs, laughter bubbling from his chest.

*At least one of us had a good night.*

"The curse of the vampire," Del whispers and gives me a soft smile. "I'm sorry I can't get us out of here," he says, shifting to sit upright, muscles glistening with sweat despite the chill. "This isn't a place for a queen—"

"I've been in plenty of cages in my life," I tell him. I don't have the energy for his apologies or sympathy after my dreamwalk.

"The fuck have you been through, woman," Del spits.

My gaze meets his, and I note the glisten in his eyes. It wasn't a good dreamwalk for Del, either, it seems.

"My fair share," I say, although it has nothing to do with the cages I've been in.

I curl in on myself to sit up and let my legs extend in front of me, drooping over them with a sigh.

Em tosses us the keys to our restraints, and we unchain ourselves.

"It's daytime. Aurelia and Samantha are in Prosperity by now, or at least sheltered in Death," I whisper.

"Your stronghold names could use a little work," Del says.

I huff, appreciating his attempt to lighten our mood. "I was too busy *ruling* to spend time on frivolous matters," I say, a small smile playing on my lips.

"Well, exactly how are we *ruling* Goreon?" Emmanuel growls from next door, repeatedly throwing his blade at the lock to no avail.

"Once Second and Charlotte are back, we'll take the castle, quickly and quietly," I say.

Del unleashes a grateful smile. "I knew you were the way out of this hell."

I consider the second of Goreon for a moment, an unlikely ally I never saw coming. "You're not the only one who thinks that," I say, heart wringing in desperation to keep my promises and bring peace to Goreon.

Del smirks. "Your people have faith in you, and so do I. And while Nerian sleeps off his hangover and Balor gives his morning orders to the human guards before his rest, I owe you a Goreon secret."

"Will it help us win?" I ask, my eager gaze homed in on his face.

Del's eyes flash. "This one will."

# CHAPTER 20

## KADE

A N ARMY OF HUNDREDS waits for us in the throne room.

A sea of vacant eyes fills the enormous hall, bodies outfitted for war.

My eyes dart to the end of the hall before chaos breaks. The king and queen aren't here, but the dais isn't empty.

Sam is strung up, like a hog for slaughter, head lolling to the side. Dried blood cakes his body, and fresh cuts ooze over his bruised skin. He's been beaten repeatedly, kept unconscious, and my magic heats, sparking like it might catch fire.

"Oh my gods," Grace whispers beside me, eyes locked on her brother.

As one, the vampire army senses our arrival, lips curling into snarls.

With no further hesitation, and with all the rage in my heart, I slice through the closest ones.

"This is going to take all fucking night!" Riot yells over the war cries spouting off around us as we charge down the aisle of the throne room.

"Then let's get to work!" I holler back, and the magic of my Hunters responds to my demands.

An endless supply of vampires funnel into the throne room from the doors on either side of the dais and through the antechamber on the other end. Hunters slaughter our enemy through the first hour with ease, but vampire numbers keep replenishing.

We still haven't been able to get to the dais. The vampires surround Sam in a wall built from bodies.

The king was ready for us, and I have no doubt this is what Sam was warning me of, that he was bait, but it still wouldn't have kept us from making this choice.

Grace and I work our way around the grand room into the third hour, fighting through the night, our fury fueling untamed fire. We've fought together many times before, taking out small covens and defending our towns, but all of it pales alongside this. And we harness everything we know—the rings we've trained in, the weapons we've mastered, and the skill our bodies know to rely on.

We unleash death together.

The Captain and the Heir of the Hunters, husband and wife, destroyer and maker, brawn and beauty, claiming the stone and soil under our boots for our people. For the peace they *deserve*. Side by side, we stake and slice our way toward Sam.

The magic of my warriors thins, exhaustion radiating from everyone as the night wanes. Grace leans against the wall behind me, and I defend her position while she catches her breath, sheathing the blade she can no longer carry and switching to stakes.

Longton and Ned are the first to reach the dais, Master Hull right behind them. They fight with glorious strength and awe-inspiring talent, and my respect for them runs deeper than it ever has.

Ned charges ahead up the stairs, clearing a path for Master Hull to get to his son, while Longton expertly defends their backs.

His broadsword mastery is like no other.

Grace and I move toward the dais, eager to join them, and I'm pissed it's taken as long as it has. We have to get him down.

My thoughts growl, a viciousness festering that ratchets my frustration as I stab hearts and slice throats. But, finally, my boot thuds onto the first marble step of the dais, blood splashing, as Grace ducks underneath my swinging sword, and my target goes down. We don't waste a moment before racing to the top.

Master Hull has Sam's feet untied by the time we get there, our breath heaving, and I reach up to work on the rope around his wrists. Sam's skin is raw and torn, and it takes everything I have to focus, to not be swayed by the anger that clouds my ability to fucking see straight.

The blood-soaked rope loosens, and I unwrap it from the top of the throne it's tied around and catch Sam as his limp body falls into me.

"Sam!" Grace screams, trying to coax him to consciousness, her tears running.

I still can't feel his magic; he's not close to the surface. "Stay with him," I tell her, and she nods as I prop Sam up on the side of the throne. Master Hull crouches beside his son, cupping his face to try to jostle him awake.

Longton, Ned, and I take wave after wave crashing upon the shore we hold.

I survey the grand hall as I fight, Hunters battling fiercely, and Riot is right in the center, commanding a perfect circle around himself. He's midway down the aisle that threads the throne room like a seam, and vampires are going down under fire from his canister in one hand and the stake in his other. Ash and blood rain around him in a brilliant display of Hunter glory.

Rhett joins us on the dais, stabbing his way toward Sam.

"Sam!" he bellows. "Wake the fuck up, you asshole. I *need* you alive, brother."

*Best friends first, stationmates second.*

Rhett skids to his knees, pulling Sam into him. I feel Sam's magic, trickling in a slow drip against mine, and his eyes slide open.

"That's it, Hunter," Rhett says. Grace smiles down at Sam, sweeping his bangs off his sweaty forehead.

And then my magic sears and wails unexpectedly as the first Hunter loses his life.

I gasp for breath, the sting of the loss burning like nothing I've ever experienced, deeper and harsher than Lou, as a station leader goes down in his Hunter form.

My step falters down the top step of the dais, and Grace's face flashes with alarm.

"*Ned is down*!" I yell, slashing through another vampire.

Our focus shifts to the other side of the dais, where Ned lies at Longton's feet.

Master Hull leaves Sam, racing to help Longton as vampires take the opening.

The legion fights harder and moves faster as my magic communicates the loss, and the anger within us boils into fierce action.

And as if the sword went through my own neck, I sense another Hunter from the Eastern outfit die, his magic whispering away in the antechamber, as a tear slides down my cheek, my soul bruised with a wound that feels like it will never heal.

Pain stacked upon pain demands me to carry a profound burden.

Swinging my sword, I take down two vampires running up the stairs, corralling my focus on a single task, begging my heart to hold on.

"*Papa*!" Grace screams over the mayhem.

Another round of agony shoots through my chest, unbearable and ruthless.

My gaze jerks to the sword through Master Hull's heart, searing into my memory.

He smiles at us before he collapses, and his magic leaves this world.

# CHAPTER 21

## VEYA

### Present Day

WELL, WHAT'S the throne-winning secret?" Emmanuel pushes, a chunk of rusted metal flying across his cell from the lock withstanding continued knife practice.

"Nerian is prideful and ruthless, but he's also a coward," Del says, his chest flexing as he leans forward, elbows over his knees.

My eyes catch on his calves and the strength in his thighs, and I beg myself not to be distracted by a long-ignored need.

Emmanuel summons his knife. "That's not a secret."

Del glares at my assassin. "Let me fucking finish, then."

I sigh and shift my attention from this sculpture of a male to the conversation. "Gentlemen, let's use our privacy wisely. I doubt we have much longer."

Del nods at me. "As with any intelligently designed castle that we *won't* be destroying, there are hidden rooms, passageways. Places for a king to hide when he doesn't want to be found." Del pauses to look me in the eye. "And I know his favorite place."

I smile at the king's second. A genuine, thankful grin, because it's impossible to kill a king who can't be found.

"Do tell," I say.

"On one condition," Del says, and my eyes narrow on him.

"I'll entertain it," I reply.

Del clears his throat. "*When* we win this thing, consider letting me remain as second in Goreon." He holds up his hands, muscles flexing under his movement. "*Just* consider it."

My mouth parts. And I respect him for not demanding it as a condition. But still. "Things need to be done my way, held to my standards," I say.

"I understand, and you've proven yourself in that regard. However, you'd be a fool to dismiss that we would be better together, stronger. I know Goreon intimately. I can help you make the choices the people want. I'd be invaluable to you. I swear it."

I nod. I'm not in disagreement, but Second possesses his position in my life for a reason. You can't build that kind of trust in a week.

Del gives me a soft smile. "Just consider it. No need for a decision right now. And in good faith, in love for Goreon and its people, I'll give you everything."

Character has always won me over with the people I let into my life. And Del is striding right up to my door and knocking so loudly it's becoming hard to ignore him. "Tell me, Del."

His eyes pierce mine. "Through the cellar, there's a hidden door behind Aurelia's cage. Inside, follow the passageway to the right. It dead-ends into his lair."

"Thank you," I say, lacing my tone with gratitude.

Emmanuel stands in his cell. "I'm so ready to kill some fucking vampires," he says, fangs popping.

Del and I grin at one another.

"Me too," I say, and Del winks at me.

We wait to be unlocked, resting fitfully through the day and bouncing around ideas for our castle takeover. When the following night begins to tick by, my unease mounts and the boredom eats at us.

"Where the fuck is everyone?" Emmanuel says, breaking the silence.

Del peers down the corridor, trying not to burn his cheek off on the bars, lips pursed. "No clue."

Another hour passes before footsteps ping in the distance and, eventually, Second stalks through the dark at the end of the row of cells, covered in shit.

"Found your way in through the sewer, did you?" I ask. His grimace bubbles laughter I hold in my chest.

Second impales me with a glare. "Almost didn't fit through the damn grate. And how about gratitude for getting your royal ass out of here? I'm so fucking pissed you got yourself locked in here, I can barely see straight."

"Maybe it's just the shit in your eyes," Emmanuel says behind his bars.

Second points a thick finger at Em as he stalks up to our cells, pulling a ring of keys from his belt.

"You three are lucky I've been resourceful since the day I was fucking born," Second spews and unlocks our cell before moving to Emmanuel's.

"Lift some keys off a guard?" Emmanuel asks as Second clips the ring back on his belt.

"Something like that," he says with a sly grin, and then twists to me with his eyebrows in the ceiling. "And where the *hell* are your clothes?"

"Nerian," I growl.

Second wipes the sewage from his face the best he can while we all try not to gag. He breathes deeply once his face is clear enough, gaze settling on me. "Fuck this king. Are we ready to handle what we came here to do?"

"Yes," I say, my mind focusing to a pinpoint as the moment I've been waiting for for so long is finally upon us.

"Considering the massive army under castle grounds, we propose a stealth mission. Swift and efficient before we're completely fucked," Emmanuel says, relaying our most favored option.

Second nods. "We need to eliminate the castle guards and Balor first. Nerian is old and strong; we don't need other distractions."

"Where's Charlotte?" I ask.

"Where do you think?" Second laughs. "She's distracting Nerian so I could swoop in with a heroic rescue."

"And the position of our guards?" I ask.

"With Charlotte."

Del leans against the stone wall, biceps and pecks quivering as he folds his arms over his chest. "The guards won't be far from the king, and it's Nerian, so he's in his throne room, on the dais he loves, with Charlotte at his feet."

I look my people in the eye as I speak. "We move quick, take out everyone before we find Charlotte and the king. I want this place to be a *graveyard.* And then we release everyone out of that farm. Out of the cellar. Out of those barracks that are nothing more than a prison. Out of this *fucking* hell!" I scream.

Del straightens from the wall, abs contracting under his effort. "Let's get some clothes on and kill a king, then."

My eyes drift up his body to his face. "And lots of weapons."

He winks at me.

My heart thumps in my ears, excitement and nerves spinning. "*I'm tired of words,*" I snarl, and with all that I am, I snap toward our rooms, bold and brave and ready to do whatever is necessary to bring this all to an end.

We enter my suite and prepare for battle.

Second rinses the sewer off his body in my washroom and then assists me in strapping my breastplate on while I stomp my feet into boots.

I heave open one of my gown trunks to an arsenal of my favorite weaponry.

We brought everything we would need for this moment.

I strap my daggers to my thighs over the leathers and sling stakes across my chest, where a light of hope blooms unlike it has in years. I sheathe my sword at my back and gather my hairpins and chain, pocketing everything I need to win. The tempo of my heart beats to a drum I haven't felt in a long time as I hoist the crossbow from the trunk and check the trigger, and finally loop the quiver of bolts on my back.

Second arms himself, and we stand breathing heavily at one another, anticipation twirling between us.

"You look glorious," I tell him, twin broadswords across his back, knives and stakes everywhere else.

"As do you, my queen," he says, tugging at my breastplate to ensure it's secured to his satisfaction.

"Are you ready to slaughter our way to a new beginning?"

"With all that I am," he promises me. I smile up at him before spinning toward the footsteps coming through the door.

Del strides into my bedchamber, armed and stunning, leather molded to muscle, and I let my attraction fire through me. I don't try to ignore my arousal this time or push it away. I don't plan on dying in this battle, but if I do, at least I let myself feel something. For once.

"You look ready," I say, nodding at the elegant weaponry he's boasting. I don't recognize the beautiful emblems engraved on his weapons and chest, waves of water with a dagger through them.

His gaze runs up my leathers. "You look—" He smirks before continuing. "We should change the dress code for a queen in Goreon. No more obnoxious gowns. This is better."

My insides hum in response to his approval. "I'll write it into the bylaws."

"Good," he says.

Hartley, Nix, and Ellie peer around the corner, and I nod at them to enter. Emmanuel joins us right behind them, jaw set tight as he stares at Hartley and the leathers she and the others have somehow acquired.

"My darlings, this battle is not for you. I refuse to lose any one of you when we just got you out. But I have another mission for you," I say, and their frustrated expressions shift.

Hartley lifts her chin. "What are your orders, my queen?"

"Get to the dungeon, head to the sewer, and wait. We're going to free your cellar sisters from that hell and send them to you. They'll be weak in their state. You'll need to swim them under the grate and into the bay, cross the bridge and find shelter in the nearest town together before dawn. Do you accept this mission?" I ask. I always give my people a choice.

Ellie releases a snarl, and I love her for it. "We will make *certain* they are safe."

"Good. Hartley and Nix?"

"Of course," Nix says, tying up her fiery hair. "You owe this hair a professional cleansing after this, though."

I smirk at my siren. "I'll bathe you myself if you keep these girls safe."

She bows to me.

Hartley spins a blade in her palm, and I cock my head at her. "Not just arrows then?"

She grins. "Not just arrows, my queen."

Emmanuel looks like he might pounce on her right now, right here, in front of all of us.

"Do you accept this mission, Hartley?"

"I will protect them with my life," she promises, and Emmanuel's eyes blaze behind her.

"Then we'll see you on the other side. Don't bring them back here until you know we've won."

"My queen," Nix says and stalks off into the parlor, trailed by Ellie.

Hartley snaps in front of Emmanuel, a breath away from him. She would make an incredible assassin with the skill she's already demonstrating so quickly.

Em doesn't move an inch, and the corner of his mouth creeps up. "You've been practicing."

"Aye," she says. "I'll see you on the other side, assassin. Don't die."

With a snap, she's gone.

"Gods, she's—"

"Perfect," Emmanuel finishes for me, his face softening, and I've never seen a more relieved male stare back at me. *Thank you*, he mouths at me.

"Can't send her into battle *this* soon," I tell him, and I'm met with a glower for the ages.

Del steps between our gaze, his attention on Emmanuel. "You break her heart, and I'll fucking kill you."

Emmanuel looks him in the eye. "If that day ever comes, I'll gladly let you."

Second sharpens his broadsword against the stone dressing table, pulling all of our attention.

Del spins to him. "You're ruining the furniture."

Second scoffs. "Like that matters."

"It's about to be *our* furniture."

"Eh, looks better with some sharpening marks. This can go in my room."

I snort and look at the men around me, ready to walk into battle at my command and finish this by my side. I couldn't be more grateful for them.

"We have thousands to save below our feet and countless more beyond the grounds of this castle," I say as we move into the parlor, my words spewing with a venom laced from deep within. "I have every belief Charlotte is holding her own in the throne room. We take out whatever guard we can find first, including Balor." I pause. "See you on the other side, my friends."

We exchange our final moment of peace before snapping toward the throne room.

Goreon guards lining the hallway outside the antechamber take one look at our dress and fangs drop.

My fingertips tingle with adrenaline, and I pull a blade from my thigh with one hand and palm a stake in the other.

*This is it.*

Snarls and sneers face us down the length of the wide ebony and gold hallway, and then vampire guards rush us in a horde.

"Come and get it, motherfuckers," Second whispers beside me as our blades clash with our enemy.

I smile into my first slice of Goreon throat, blood spraying as the vampire staggers and Second stakes its heart. *For Christine.*

I stake the next heart running at me. *For the farm.*

And the next. *For the cellar.*

I throw my stake into a guard approaching Second's back and snatch my other dagger.

Spinning in pooled blood, I slice through the neck of the next and swivel, twirling through the foyer outside the antechamber and killing two guards at once, stakes jamming outward at my sides as I lunge and brace for impact. *For the prison barracks.*

No warrior who devotes themselves to the crown deserves a life such as that.

I continue down the hall, Second beside me, and we slaughter our way through the guards who have sneered at us, locked us in their dungeons, and brutalized the people beneath their feet.

Whirling, I see Del and Emmanuel dance together. Del is expertly trained, his technique as exceptional as Emmanuel's, and my curiosity spikes. I knew he could fight by how he won his position as second, but he and my assassin are taking down twenty guards in mere moments, their movements mirroring each other. Their resemblance is so striking, it's uncanny—I was a fool not to be curious before now.

I sheathe my daggers and grab two stakes as a vampire snaps next to me. I stab a stake into his heart without looking.

Del meets my eyes with a smirk, and his head jerks to the left to warn me as a vampire swings his broadsword for my head. I duck and stab a stake into his heart.

Second hurls a headless body at the wall and rips another in half beside me.

An opening to the throne room presents itself, the guard population thinning quickly in the hallway. To my surprise, King Nerian snaps into the antechamber, his eyes catching mine, and he smiles at me like we're about to share a cup of tea at dawn. "Ah, I'm so glad you're willing to fight for what you want, my dear. I'll leave you to it. Let's be sure to meet up later—I have a surprise for you," he drawls, and snaps out of existence.

"The fuck does that mean?!" I scream into the mayhem, eyeing Del, who shrugs at me from the other side of the bloodbath.

Night Kingdom guards pour into the hallway, and Charlotte barrels out behind them, her gown snagging on someone's sword as she tears into a guard's throat with her fucking teeth, then stabs a stake through their heart. My most influential courtier—until she's not. Until she's tired of the games and puts her training to work. My best weapons always hide in plain sight.

Charlotte tears the skirt of her gown from her body, buttons around her waist designed to shed fabric in an instant and reveal her leathers beneath. She yanks out the stakes strapped to her thighs and stabs them into the hearts around her.

Emmanuel snaps through the room, coming up beside Charlotte, and their coordinated brutality thins the guards filling the corridor. They've been training together for decades, and the orchestrated chemistry is breathtaking.

Knuckles kiss my cheek as I spin away from a punch just in time and drive my stake upward into the heart of another guard.

Second curses beside me. "Watch yourself, Veya, before I make you sit this out."

I scoff through the swing of my sword. "Like you could ever *make* me do anything."

He tosses a body out of the way. "If it's your life, I will."

Unfortunately, it's difficult to disown a vampire who's like a brother and has devoted centuries to your protection. So I refocus instead of arguing with him.

"*Behind you!*" Second bellows, and I spin, but I'm too late.

The vampire already has a hand around my throat and a blade aimed at my skull. Its eyes blow wide, and the guard's mouth fills with blood, bones crushing in on themselves, and its hand falls away from me.

I gasp for breath as the vampire crumples at my feet.

Del winks from the other end of the corridor, his stake clattering onto the stone floor before me.

*Thank you*, I mouth across the divide, and he grins through a swing of his sword.

"That was so fucking close," Second spits, staking two vampires beside us.

I twirl around, rejoining Second, and slash my blades into my next opponent.

"I know," I growl, thankful for Del's perfect aim. And his attention.

My focus catches on General Balor climbing the front steps of the castle, his shadowed form outlined by the dim moonlight through the open iron doors.

I snap down the hallway for Balor, Del joining my side, and we block the entrance to the fortress.

I know *I* have my grievances with this male, but I can only imagine how deep they go for Del.

"You won't win this," Balor sneers on the wide landing. "Although I'm sure you *think* you will," he cackles through his mocking tone and draws his broadsword in the falling snow.

The general lunges for me as Del skirts to his other side, but Balor's already snapping around me out of the way before I can react.

He's fast. *Really* fast.

Del flashes past me onto the steps, and I spin, snow flying around me, daggers in each hand, and slice forward, catching Balor's wrist, but nothing else.

He laughs at me, and my anger spikes as Del swings his sword with strength and dexterity for Balor's neck.

Balor ducks with a smile aimed at me. "You're so damn slow. I can take you all night at this pace, Queen." He winks at me, tongue threading his fangs through his insinuation.

I slash for Balor, and he snaps away, spinning from Del's sword again.

Balor's boot slips in the snow as he catches himself.

"Watch your fucking mouth, Balor," Del growls.

Balor's eyes blaze red, his breath billowing in the cold as his lip curls at Del. "Did you have fun with her in that cell, Deleos? Quite the beauty, huh? Those *thighs*."

*This motherfucker.*

Del's eyes flash, crimson burning through amethyst. "You're a dead man."

The general chuckles. "Been dead for centuries."

Del unleashes a fierce snarl, snow crunching under his boot as he lunges for Balor.

Balor snaps behind me.

But I'm already turning, flitting to his right, forcing him to shift his balance. I drag a boot through the snow-covered stone and shove my daggers forward, catching him in the gut.

Balor's hand grabs my throat, squeezing my airway so I can't breathe, while his other wields his sword, clashing with Del's.

I'm tossed down the unforgiving stairs, face scraping on impact.

*Shit.*

I snap behind Balor, one dagger and one stake in hand now as the males fight each other.

Balor shoves Del, and he flies back, slamming against the giant open iron door, its hinges groaning under the force of his body.

The general takes the opening, snapping for me, and I don't hesitate before jamming my dagger into his maw, right where it belongs, before he's even fully formed.

His shocked eyes search mine for mercy he can't beg for.

"We told you to watch your fucking mouth," I spit, yanking my dagger out of flesh and staking his heart before he can speak another word.

Del takes off Balor's head with his sword, and the general's body collapses between us, his blood painting the snow red.

"That was my kill, right?" Del clarifies through the blood spatter across his face, plum eyes vibrant and alive.

I shake my head at him, my stake stabbing out to my side to run through a guard snapping next to me. "It was mine."

Del narrows his gaze, swinging his broadsword to take off another head. "Agree to disagree."

I wink at him and snap back through the entrance and down the hallway to Second. "Balor's dead."

"Good fucking riddance," Second growls as we stab through the next layer of guards, clearing the way further down the hall toward the doorway to the cellar. My eyes find Del as an opening emerges for my escape, and his focus is already on me. "Go! I'll meet you there," he yells, slashing a head off a guard while his eyes remain locked on mine.

I nod, whipping away from him, and Second follows as I race down the stairwell, snapping around the curves. We breach the cellar door—and freeze in our tracks.

Samantha cries out to us, naked and beaten.

My skin crawls. *How is she back in her cage?!*

Second rushes her, ripping the flaming door off its hinges.

"What happened?" he demands.

"They caught us," she cries. "We were so close to the wall, but we didn't make it."

Panic surges through me. "Where's Aurelia?" I ask while Second hands Samantha the shirt off his back.

She shakes her head, tears running, and looks up at us with sad eyes. "The king has her."

Second snaps for the cages, ripping them open as I dart for Aurelia's empty cage and start searching the wall behind it for a latch or a way through.

I peer over my shoulder as Second hands Samantha the dagger from his hip.

"Do you know how to get to the dungeon?" Second asks her.

She nods. "It's where they brought us from when we first arrived, before locking us in here."

"Good. Take the girls to the dungeon—there's an exit to the sewer. The others are waiting to help you. Swim under the gate, and you'll dump into the bay. Take the bridge and run to the nearest village," Second tells Samantha while wrenching open the last cage. "We *will* find you when it's over," he promises. "And if we don't, you know the way to the Night Kingdom now. Try again. Don't *ever* give up. Tell them everything you know."

Samantha nods at him, girls clinging to her. "Thank you, Second," she says and wraps herself around his torso.

"Go!" he demands as my hands find a crevice in the stone.

I press into it, and my heart leaps when the wall groans and slides. I race through the opening, eager to hunt my prey and desperate to find Aurelia.

The passageway is dark and damp, and my boot slips in my haste. I catch myself on the stone wall and regain my balance, my nervous rasp exhaling into the dim corridor.

*I can do this. I have to do this.*

I sprint to the right as Del instructed and come upon a large wooden door that creaks open with ease.

Nerian is hunched over a work table. At the sound of whining hinges, he spins.

My eyes dart around the room, searching for Aurelia.

I try not to be distracted, but the horror in here is the illustration of an insane vampire, a portrait of death and pain and gluttony. The stone walls are lined with canisters and bottles and boxes, filled with bones, jewels, hair. *Trophies*.

I step over the dead girl at my feet, her neck broken at an awful angle, body several days old. And then I step over the next.

They're not Aurelia. *Thank gods, but where is she?!*

A large window on my left is unshuttered, the soft light of dawn beginning to break, and I wonder if Nerian likes to suffer in sunlight, too.

"King Nerian," I address him, kicking an empty wine bottle away with my boot. "I've come to take your throne."

He grins at me. "It's not for sale, dear."

"I wasn't planning on purchasing it from you," I say, spinning my twin blades in my palms, my mind racing with how to approach this. "Seems you've curated quite the collection." My eyes flit around the room, landing on his bloody worktable and then on the large wooden crate in the corner.

"Yes, thank you for noticing."

*Gods, how could anyone not?*

The king threads his bloodstained fingers along the teeth around his neck.

A thousand years of dreamwalking has caught up with this vile male. I can't fathom the mental fatigue of that torture for so long. It has broken him, alongside his bloodlust. The curse of the vampire will take us all someday. And I hope there's someone willing to kill me when I can no longer stand it.

Second approaches behind me, the gait of his boots closing the distance in a few strides.

I hum, taking a short step toward Nerian, buying time to assess my options. I don't see a weapon on the king, but that doesn't mean there isn't one.

"Any favorite pieces?" I ask as Second stands beside me, sword poised.

He taps the teeth he's fingering on his necklace. "My most prized piece! A canine from every Hunter I've killed over the centuries. Beautiful, isn't it?"

# CHAPTER 22

## KADE

*Two Hundred Years Ago – Goreon Kingdom*

A S HUNTERS DIE, so does my soul.

My magic wails at me, and agony pelts, chipping away at me like an axe. The loss of our Master is a weight I don't know how to hold.

*I didn't know it would hurt like this.*

This sorrow is the worst I've ever felt. And an understanding flashes: The choice my father made to save his Hunters all those years ago. I don't think I can blame him so harshly now as my losses threaten my sanity.

We need to end this before we lose anyone else.

This is no longer a mission to kill the king; we need to get out. We've saved hundreds from the dungeon, and Sam is in our grasp. It's time to leave. I won't be foolish enough to go for a glory that wastes more lives.

Brachett races up the dais toward Master Hull.

"Work your way toward the exits! We're leaving!" I command, backing up toward Rhett and Grace to help them with Sam.

Master Hull is slumped next to the throne, eyes vacant, and Brachett hoists him onto his back while I stake through five vampires, my speed untraceable as they attempt to take me down by overwhelming me with their numbers.

*Not a fucking chance.*

Longton lifts Ned onto his back, his burly legs carrying Ned's weight with ease as he rises, eyes on fire, and his magic ricocheting against mine in mourning.

Vampires will come to their senses within the hour, and I need my people close to safety. Close to daylight.

Riot fights further down the aisle, maintaining a wide berth near the antechamber doorway in a brilliant display of Hunter technique and power, his magic whirring and vibrant, his body honed, and his honor threading along his skin as he defends our pathway.

Grace and I force our way down the dais, blood running down the steps as Hunter and vampire life force blend in death for the first time since the Great Divide War. Brachett, Longton, and Rhett carry our people behind us.

My focus darts to the antechamber as I sense the magic of Hunters beyond the door pulse and respond to a vampiric presence.

Dawn breaks, the faintest light funneling in through the entrance hall beyond the antechamber, and vampires begin to come to their senses.

A breath from Riot, the queen snaps into the throne room; she snarls, but he doesn't hesitate to attack. Her fighting skill is decent, holding him off and snapping around his blade. Riot lunges with his broadsword again, but she jumps back, avoiding him with a devilish smile.

Grace and I hurdle over bodies, trying to get to him.

Riot ditches his sword and draws two stakes from his belt in a blink, his Hunter form vibrating with his magic, throwing everything he has into this moment in a flurry of jabs. As she snaps around him, one of Riot's stakes finally hits home into the queen's heart, and the vampire sputters into eternal death.

He spins to find me, a prideful grin plastered wide as I gaze upon his victory and smile back.

*One step closer to ending this rule, one throne down. We'll take that win today.*

Taking the head off a vampire in front of me, we continue to fight our way toward Riot as vampire numbers dwindle around us, either fleeing from us or bending over in pain their bodies wouldn't allow them to experience in dreamwalk.

I hurtle down the aisle, almost to Riot, gripping a stake in each hand, and jab them out to my sides, taking two vampires attacking my flanks. My magic twirls, and I stab stake after stake, with Grace in my wake.

Suddenly, *everyone* freezes in place, and the magic of the Hunters surrounding me screams so loud I choke on my own breath in pain.

I spin around to my worst nightmare.

The king of Goreon has snapped into the hall, and his large hand is clasped around Gracie's delicate neck, pinning her in place. Pale Hunters and hissing vampires focus on the king.

Her face is etched with terror, and gold threads morph into pitch black within me—panic, warning, despair.

My magic's fear is potent and harrowing as the king clutches the Heir, his sneer aimed at her throat.

"She's unbitten. I *beg* you," I snarl, and my soul prays to the gods.

"I'm so glad you're still here," the king drawls. "I was afraid I'd wake up to a mess to clean, but what a pleasant surprise this is." His red eyes flick to mine, and the yards between us are maddening.

"I can't believe you brought a human warrior with you," he continues into her neck, lips grazing my wife, and I want to rip his fucking head off watching him touch her. "Such a sweet-smelling one at that," he says, fingers trailing down Grace's neck.

I take a step toward them, furious, and on the edge of releasing every dark, merciless part of me.

Rhett is behind them, the same distance as I am, with Sam's arm slung over his shoulders. Eyes clear and mind lucid, Sam's focus is now on his sister, his magic pushing him to protect the Heir, just like all of us.

"Unhand her," Sam growls, and the king's attention swivels.

"*You* are supposed to be mine. I sent a note and everything," he says haughtily.

*This vampire is fucking insane.*

The king sighs, rolling out his neck as he drags Grace to his front, wrapping an arm around her chest.

"No matter, you were about used up, weren't you?" the king says, eyeing Sam.

In the next blink, Sam is on the ground, throat slashed and eyes empty, and the king grips Grace by the neck again, her body bent over in front of him.

My rage burns, and everything hurts under the weight of death and desperation. I can't shift my focus from Sam, locked in disbelief, heart—empty.

His life just … gone.

Chaos brims like a raging monster gnawing through the chains that hold it.

Grace whimpers as she stares at her dead brother, gasping in shock.

Rhett drops to his knees, shaking his best friend.

And I force myself to focus on the *one* thing I have left.

*My Gracie.*

I won't risk her life with bloodshed against a king who's faster than I can track or a negotiation with anything less than what she's worth. I drop my stakes, splaying my hands wide. "Spare her, and you can kill me," I growl, my soul and magic spinning with desperation. "A life for a life."

"*No!*" Grace screams, trying to wrench away from the king. "This was *my* choice, Kade!"

I catch her eyes with mine, pouring every ounce of adoration I possess into my look. "There are no conditions to my love, Grace. Including death."

"Ah, I see," the king says through a grin, then tsks at me. "But your *life*, Hunter? For your *woman*?" He scoffs, tipping Grace's head back and assessing her like a prized mare. "Not very becoming of a Hunter to choose his woman over his sworn duty."

My eyes narrow. *This king has no idea who Grace Hull is.*

"I agree to your terms, Hunter. With *one* amendment." The Goreon King points a taunting smile at me, and my muscles tremble with restraint.

But instead of speaking, the bastard sinks his fangs into Gracie's perfect skin.

Her scream slices through me like a blade.

Every fiber of my being wills me to move, to act, to protect what's mine, but my magic freezes me in place, preventing rash action that could result in her untimely death.

The king rips his fangs from Grace's skin, and my soul spears with her pain. Her eyes fill with sorrow, knowing her choices now.

There are only two—death or vampire.

Grace's blood drips down his chin, and she fights his grip, only to be greeted by the king's hiss, red droplets spraying on her face.

Her eyes search mine, yearning and fearful.

A tear slides down my cheek. My jaw is crushing in on itself as my destiny is rewritten before my eyes.

My wife is lost.

My life is lost.

And that hard line I've drawn my entire life between human and vampire is blurring before me. She *can't* die. She's too wonderful, she's too precious to this world. She's the *fucking* Heir!

She *deserves* a future.

"How about a gut wound so you bleed out slow enough to watch your female turn?" the king jeers.

A sword stabs through my belly from behind, and the king's general snaps away with a cackle before I can do anything about it.

The pain is brutal, but I'm so numb at this point, I savor the way it snaps me to attention and races adrenaline through me anew. "*Curse you*," I spit at the king, gripping my stomach.

"I'll leave you to your goodbyes. It's been so fun this time around," the king says and shoves Grace toward me before snapping into nothingness.

"Get into the daylight!" I yell to my Hunters as Grace stumbles, clutching her neck with wild eyes.

Disbelief dances between Grace and me as Rhett tries to revive Sam.

"He's gone, Rhett," I tell him, my gut burning and my soul pining for Sam's magic.

"*Fuck*!" Rhett screams, shaking Sam's shoulders again like he might wake up. "We were supposed to be stationmates until our beards were gray," he cries as Grace kneels beside him and brushes the hair from her brother's eyes.

"Get him outside with us," I say as Riot hoists my arm over his shoulder and Hunters kill the remaining vampires with a death wish.

Rhett lifts Sam onto his back, and we race for the castle doors, Grace beside us.

We sprint into the moment before sunrise, when the horizon still holds a faint light. I sense my Hunters filtering out of the castle, almost safe in the comfort of streaming sunshine, their magic calling to mine in a mournful lullaby.

Uncle Brachett barrels ahead, Master Hull on his back. I have no son, so my Captainhood will fall to my closest relative, Brachett.

Riot lowers me to the ground, snow crunching underneath me, and keeps pressure on my gushing wound. My magic wraps around my physical agony, softening the severity as Grace plasters herself to my side.

I cradle her face as she tries to promise me, "I won't leave you."

The love I have for her burns so painfully I can barely see straight. "You will. You need to leave before the sun takes you."

She shakes her head at me, eyes pleading. "No, Kade. Not a chance in hell."

I chuckle through gurgling blood. "You're already in hell, my love."

Her cries shudder into delirious laughter before misery contorts her face again. "It can't be over. We need more time. I need more time with you," she sobs.

I smile at the love of my life, the woman I can't breathe without. "I know. Me too, Gracie."

She nods at me, her tears running as her fingertips trail my jawline, and her grieving gaze buries me under a cruel desperation to change our circumstance.

"You have to keep going. You have to change Goreon, just like we've always dreamed. You've got all the time in the world now to do it."

Her breath shudders; we only have a few more moments, and I force myself to find my voice again. "I want you to be happy. And you better fucking do it, Gracie."

Her face crumples. "I don't want a future without you."

"Promise me you will finish this. *Promise me.*"

She nods at me through her tears.

The *havoc* Grace could wreak on this world unleashed as a vampire, to skillfully infiltrate them, to take them down from within—

*Yes.* This is better than her death. My magic simmers like a burning sun in agreement and I blanch, the path so clear before me and I never knew to listen to it.

A river of power pushes me toward this decision like a road laid in gold.

Grace Hull is the Hunter who will bring peace to Goreon. We were her way in, her destined protectors until fate threw us into a perfect storm that culminates with her rise.

"What will you call yourself?" I ask, desperate to know the vampire name that will live in our histories.

She buries her head in my neck, nuzzling into me while she considers. "The name we would've given our daughter," she whispers into my skin.

"Veya," I whisper back, tilting my head to hers, humming in approval as my eyes blur with tears. "Change the world, Veya. Make it right, rule the evil, become a queen. *Take* Goreon."

Grace lifts her head from my neck and looks at me, her gaze flashing red and expression stern. A decision written in her eyes. "I *will* finish what we started, Kade. No matter how long it takes, Goreon will see peace. I swear it to you," she snarls, and her promise wraps around my dying soul.

And then Gracie kisses me. Her tongue finds mine, and I savor every second before she pulls away.

"I'll rule them kindly and give life to the people, Kade. I will find a way. *With all that I am.*"

I smile at her through my pain.

My love.

My darling.

My Gracie.

My *Veya*.

"I love you, my *queen*," I whisper, lucky to be the first to utter the word she will hear someday from someone else.

I'm glad to know her name, the woman who will define the future and shape the world around her into our vision, flitting from threat to threat, slaughtering through eternity in her own brutal dance.

Her body steams under the rising sun.

"Go! You *must* go," I urge as she clings to me, her fingers digging into my biceps with a dangerous bite.

Her fangs pop from between her lips, and her green eyes dart to mine, full of alarm and unimaginable sadness.

I yank the chain from my neck, pressing the Hunter crest in Gracie's palm. "You are the bridge between worlds, you are the way this ends, my love. Be *bold*. Be *brave*."

She pockets my necklace, nodding at me through her tears.

"I will always be with you, Grace," I promise her. "Forever may you reign."

"I love you, Kade. In this life and the one after that," she cries.

"Bold and brave, Gracie," I whisper, thumb-swiping a tear from her cheek. She kisses me and then rips herself away before it's too late. Grace snatches our twin blades from the ground before she disappears from my sight for shelter, but the vision of her remains, brilliant and beautiful in my mind, and I hold onto everything we are.

Riot kneels next to me, his hand gripping mine.

The world spins as I try to focus on him. "Protect her. Help her. *Finish* what we started."

"With my life, brother. I will be by her side— *always*," he growls.

I nod. Knowing *exactly* what he means by that. Riot will turn, for her. For us. For the dream.

If I could join them, I would.

"Forever may you rest," Riot says, and I give him the biggest smile I can manage.

Because Grace *will* end this. And I believe in her to do it right, to do it well. And most importantly, to fucking do it.

I slip into unconsciousness, love and hope shrouding me as I surrender to an early grave and leave our life behind and the future to Grace.

*To Queen Veya.*

# CHAPTER 23

## VEYA

Present Day

**N**ERIAN'S WORDS *shatter* me.

Staring at the necklace of teeth draped around the king's neck, my rage becomes feral as I notice the canine, the one in the center. The *chipped* one.

A monster I can't control screams within me staring at Kade's tooth. A wife *desperate* for revenge cries with deep sorrow.

Tears prick my eyes.

And I cling to Kade's dying words, the words that got me through *decades* of grief when I wanted to shrivel into nothing and join him in the afterlife of the gods. But his sacrifice was one I would never waste.

*I am bold. And I am brave.*

Nerian tilts his head, assessing me. "I wanted to ask you, Veya. How was your dreamwalk?"

I hesitate at the random question, trying to leash my rage for Aurelia's sake. "I've had better."

Nerian sighs. "Me too. But I awoke into another nightmare." His casual tone sets me on edge. "Imagine my surprise when my human guards found two girls racing on horseback to the south in the early hours of dawn. And upon inspection," he tsks, "the damning letter they carried. Well—"

My insides spin as he clicks his tongue and slips a piece of parchment from his pocket. Nerian unfolds it slowly, the crinkle of paper grating along my skin as he turns the letter.

"What *confounds* me," the king snarls, "is that a queen would risk our alliance, my respect, and her own safety. For what?"

I feel my fear in my bones and force myself to remain neutral.

He spits. "Two *human* girls." He drags a wine bottle from the table beside him and swigs from it before hurling it at the wall. Glass explodes into the room, slicing exposed skin, and tiny cuts shred my face.

Blood trickles down my cheeks and chin, and I pretend the trails of blood are the tears I can't shed as Nerian continues.

"I couldn't figure out what could possibly be so important about these women. Perhaps your heart is so weak that you would willingly risk your life to send two lives to your kingdom. But then I thought, maybe you knew one of them?" Nerian glares at me. "But you don't have ties to

Goreon, especially not human ones." His lips quirk. "But one of you does."

Del snaps into the lair beside me, and Nerian's face lights up with his evil grin. "Ah! Just in time, Deleos!"

Del's eyes dart to mine. He has no idea about Aurelia. And my heart cries.

Del's focus shifts to the king. "What's going on?" he demands in a hoarse whisper, eyes pinned to the parchment.

"Queen Veya didn't follow my orders," Nerian says as the letter floats to the ground amongst the glass and dead girls.

"Surely we can allow the slip in judgment, my king," Del says, eyes on Nerian, his knuckles turning white around the hilt of his sword.

"Surely, we cannot, *Deleos*," Nerian barks at him, and Del's chin jerks back. The king points at Del, finger shaking with rage. "I thought about my precious Violet and those eyes that always captured me. And I remembered the day I brought her here to surprise us. You looked disgusted by her." Nerian's eyes flick to the crate in the corner. "Which I found odd because your eyes were so similar. I hoped you would find her beautiful, just like yourself, Deleos." He cackles, a sound that bounces off the walls and rains shards of panic, shredding me from within.

His demeanor flips, the king's face darkening with cruel intention. "It's not just violet eyes that you share, is it, Deleos?!" he screams.

"A coincidence, I assure you," Del says blandly.

"Of course. We can make this quick and move on then," Nerian says. "We have kingdoms to discuss, and a war to wage."

My chest squeezes so painfully I'm afraid my ribs might crack. Sending the girls to the Night Kingdom was my idea. There was risk in any choice we made, but my guilt will be unbearable if we lose Aurelia.

If we haven't already.

Nerian snaps to the crate in the corner so quickly I don't see him move. He rips off the lid, throwing it at the stone ceiling, and splinters fly as we turn away to shield ourselves.

My nerves slide along my skin at Nerian's strength and speed. We weren't able to compete with it two hundred years ago, and I'm not so certain our odds have improved.

At all.

Spinning back, we watch Nerian yank Aurelia from the box, her panicked eyes and bruised face staring back at us.

She's alive, and I take a breath.

The king drags her by the arm, his cruel strength digging into her skin as he wrenches her to his side.

Her chest puffs rapidly with her fear, but she locks onto my gaze instead of Del's.

*Good girl.*

"King Nerian, I'm sorry for my bold choice," I begin, taking a step toward them. "This girl was intended for me to enjoy later."

Nerian narrows his eyes at me. "Nice try."

Aurelia spins her focus up at Nerian. "Please, my king, I never wanted to go to the Night Kingdom. I *wanted* to be a vampire like the others."

Gods, this girl can talk her way through anything, just like Del.

"It's true, Nerian. This was my selfish choice," I add. "The girl from the dining room our first night whet an appetite I didn't know I had."

Nerian sneers at me, and then his eyes flick to Del, who is mastering a bored gaze. "Well, then, let's enjoy the meal you were so keen to have together," the king growls, and his fangs sink into Aurelia's wrist.

She cries out, and human life drains before my eyes.

My past haunts me as I stare at Nerian with his fangs in human flesh, Del and Aurelia at his mercy. My throat has been under those fangs. But I got to live—I got to walk away because Kade sacrificed himself for me, because we had something the king wanted more than my death.

A Hunter Captain's life.

Del is tense beside me, frozen and maintaining control.

The Goreon King's eyes grow wide as he drinks, then rips himself from Aurelia. "She tastes as beautiful as I thought she would. *My* Violet."

I hum at him. "She'll make a lovely vampire," I admire, nausea swirling as I try to hold the line between this negotiation and my revenge.

I don't know how we can get to her without Nerian snapping her neck. Second shifts beside me, just as eager and powerless.

Nerian laughs around his tongue flicking outward, licking blood from Aurelia's arm. "No, she won't. We aren't wasting a drop of this. Would you like a taste before I drain her?"

Aurelia cries at the king's damning words and tries to reach for Del.

The king chuckles. "As I suspected: *not* a coincidence," he sneers, and sinks his fangs back into Aurelia, red eyes gleaming. She whimpers, fierce plum eyes fighting for strength as the king brutally feeds on her life force.

Del screams, a guttural rage that slices my heart open and sets my insides on fire, and he loses it, snapping across the lair to them. The king doesn't even flinch; his palm juts out, connecting with Del's chest. His body crunches under the impact and flies across the room, landing with a thud against the wall.

"You defeated my noblemen, Deleos. But there is nothing you can do to me."

Del's blood-red gaze centers on Nerian as he rights himself. "I disagree," he snarls.

Nerian snorts. "You disagree constantly. It's nothing new."

Del draws his daggers from his hips. "Release her, or die."

"Ah! A heroic fight to the death. It's so *you*, Deleos." The king's eyes become crazed. "*I love it.*" Nerian flings a half-conscious Aurelia at the wall. "I'll finish her later. A little *victory* drink."

Second snaps to Aurelia, but Nerian is already there before we see him move, grabbing Second by the throat and throwing him into Del as he snaps into existence beside them.

"*No one touches my Violet!*" Nerian screams as she crawls away from him, and the males stumble backward.

I palm my blades.

Nerian won't let us walk out of here. I just pray Charlotte and Emmanuel get out if we don't.

The thought of my people fuels me. Just like they always have. I am a *Hunter*, and I always will be. No matter what this king made me become. I'll never give up on my promises, and I'll always be willing to die protecting human life.

I can hear Kade's voice in my head, like he's right here with me.

*Be bold. Be brave.*

The three of us attack, blades swiping as Nerian snaps around us in a blur, his laughter enveloping us and ratcheting my anger as my target keeps moving.

Second nicks Nerian with his blade, and the king slaps him across the face.

Second's cheek splits open, bone exposed. "Fuck you," he snarls, his massive form shaking with fury.

"Rude," Nerian spits as Del and I lunge for him.

The king sighs, flitting out of our reach. "Why don't you take a break while I play with your new friends?" Nerian drawls and flashes past me, wrapping his hand around Del's neck and snapping it between his fingers before flinging Goreon's second into the corner.

I stare dumbfounded at Del's unconscious form, our odds of success plummeting.

Nerian rushes me in a blur, the strength of his ancient force blowing me back against the wall, and it crumbles around me as my spine breaks over the stone.

"Veya!" Second bellows, snapping to Nerian, but the king slams Second's enormous body into the ground with a force that rattles the room.

Second tries to get up, groaning, but Nerian stomps on his leg. The snap of his bone echoes alongside his screams.

Del is motionless in the corner, and Aurelia is shaking him.

*Wake up, Del. We need your help.*

Nerian hovers over Second, producing a stake from his coat pocket, but I can't fucking move.

"No!" I scream, tears running. My breath heaves out of my chest, my boot skidding forward as I attempt to right myself with a broken spine supported by the curse of eternal life. The pain is beyond anything I've ever experienced as I cough blood, and I'm held in the balance between life and death.

I curse my immobility, my heart crying. I can't lose another person in my life. And Second doesn't deserve this end.

Nerian looks at me with an amused purse of his lips as he kneels next to my best friend, his knee pressing into Second's throat, and he wheezes beneath the king.

"I'm going to make you watch while I kill all of your people, Veya," he says, smiling. "Starting with this one." Nerian's knee presses in harder, and Second's gurgles stop, his face going pale. "And then I'm going to invade your kingdom and ravage it until there's *nothing* left!" the king screams, spittle flying as he poises the tip of the stake above Second's heart.

*No!*

Rage takes over, dipping into my soul and scraping something loose, something feral and foreign, brutal and unforgiving. A predator claws to the surface, and my body jerks against a blast so intense my eyes slam shut.

Like a river of gold rushing through my veins, my insides are alight with pure energy. I feel more alive than when I was human, and power wraps around my flesh and consumes an old emptiness. My body hones, muscles throbbing and skin tensing, just the way Kade always described his Hunter magic. Something gods-sent embraces my spine, and my boot finds purchase on the stone as I begin to rise.

I feel like I could fight for *days.*

My eyes fly open.

Nerian's devilish grin wilts watching my body warp.

I snap across the room so fast I surprise myself and the king, speed untraceable.

*A Hunter's speed.*

I plunge Kade's cream-hilted dagger into Nerian's chest, and his shocked eyes pierce mine.

I sneer at the king as gold simmers in my veins with power so pure and poignant, my confidence blooms.

"Who the fuck are you?" Nerian demands, rage written in his eyes.

I laugh at him. "You birthed a ruthless warrior from the life you destroyed. The pain you were so eager to throw upon me two hundred years ago became the fire that forged my kingdom and takes yours from you now."

"That doesn't answer my question, *Veya*," he sneers. "I've destroyed many lives over the years."

My Hunter and vampiric strength restrains Nerian, an ancient male bowing to my magic. Uncertainty flashes over him as he realizes his decreased odds, blood spilling down his front. His hand darts upward, knocking my blade free, and he lunges for me, but I snap across the room, drawing him away from Second.

Nerian tosses a blade pulled from his belt across the room, and it sinks into my thigh before I can move again. I push through my agony, Hunter magic spinning and healing, threads of gold wrapping around me with the strength of the gods.

My words snarl out of me. "I will turn Goreon into everything you hate. I will *destroy* what you have built and ensure peace and prosperity for *everyone*. And death to those who don't deserve either. Just like you took everything I *ever* wanted from me. You stole the love of my life, my future children, my brother, my father, my *entire* world." I hurl a stake at Nerian, and it pierces his shoulder. I then grip my daggers, ready to end this.

Nerian rips the wood from his flesh, panting through his effort.

With a curling smile, I give the king exactly what he wants: "I am Grace Hull, daughter of a Master, wife of a Captain, and Heir of the Hunters."

*The Hunter no one saw coming.*

Nerian's eyes blaze with recognition, and I use everything I have left to snap as quickly as I can and force Nerian against the wall.

With all that I am, I stab Kade's blade into his throat and mine into his chest, holding the king in place with my husband's favorite move while I sneer into his wide eyes. "This is for *Kade*. For all those we have lost."

"*Abomination*," he spits through a blood-soaked cough, struggling beneath me.

I grin at Nerian. "No, my king. A *new* breed."

His red eyes bulge as I twist Kade's blade in his throat, and the words that have lived in my hopeful dreams scream out of me through my tears: "*Forever may they rest, and forever may we reign!*" I rip our blades from him and slice our twin daggers through his cold flesh, taking the head off the king.

It hits the ground, Nerian's eyes wide and staring.

Centuries of planning, centuries of hoping—it's done. It's *finally* done.

The destroyed part of me who would never live again became something else, a starving beast for revenge, desperate to heal what is so fucking broken within me. Grace hardened to the warrior I have to be, and I am both now. I am good for those who deserve it and evil to those who don't.

I am the balance embodied.

Kade gave his life so I could change the world. And I've honored that every day of my immortal existence.

*With all that I am. Bold and brave.*

A whisper floats out of me as I stare at the dead king: "Forever may we reign."

Second limps to my side and grips my shoulder as Del groans awake behind us, eyes wide with surprise.

I spin, tears running down my cheeks and blood dripping from my blades. I toss my weapons, collapsing under emotion I can no longer hold.

Second kneels as my sobs turn into a silent scream threatening to stomp me out of existence. The wash of pain and relief is equal in measure. My mission has held me close to Kade, fueling me, reminding me of him and the life I loved, and now it's like he's leaving, whispering away. As though his magic has been twining with mine, now, something untangles from me.

I always took the chance of dreamwalking. Even if it was just once a year that the gods let me spend a night with Kade, it was always worth it. The brush of his fingertips, the adoration in his sparking blue eyes, the feel of his mouth on my skin, lying in his lap while he twirled my hair with his strong hands or in a cage with our blades clashing. It was *always* worth it. And I tried not to let the yearning drive me mad when I awoke alone and suffered in a despair so cruel I didn't want to take my next breath.

We almost didn't make it here. After the sixth consecutive dreamwalk reliving Kade's death, I begged Second to kill me. And then I begged Charlotte when he wouldn't. I knew I couldn't have taken another full moon in the same memory.

But the gods gave me the gift of reprieve, and I found my way back in the arms of my husband the following month. And the cruel desperation began all over again.

*The curse of the vampire.*

I haven't let myself love anyone else with unfulfilled promises and his memory still so alive. A constant ache has been my companion, and we've carried one another for a long time.

"It's over," Second comforts, his palm spread on my back. "You did it, and I'm so proud of you."

I'm proud of us, too.

Second darts from me, escaping the sunrise from the unshuttered window beside us as light spills into Nerian's lair.

Del, Aurelia, and Second don't move from the shadow they stand in, frozen and staring.

And then I feel it.

Warmth streams through the window, sunshine beaming on me.

But I don't burn. There's no pain.

I bask in the memory of my humanity as my Hunter magic twirls and spins. A glowing warmth from within warbles the sweetest summons—the call of the Hunter cascades through me in a consuming caress.

*A new breed, indeed. A vampire Huntress.*

"What the fuck is happening?" Del asks, slowly dragging himself to standing. Aurelia folds into his side underneath his arm, her eyes flashing red.

"I don't know," I whisper, staring back at my hands in the sunshine.

He snorts at me. "We should begin your rule with *honesty*, Veya."

I drag my gaze to Del, sun blinding me for the first time in two centuries, and fresh tears slide down my cheeks through a growing smile.

"Agreed, Patrick," I say to him.

Del's kind, piercing eyes widen at the sound of his human name.

Out of the reach of the sun, Second offers his hand and pulls me to standing, tears in his own eyes.

Relief floods me, and I look up at my Hunter brother. "This is Riot," I tell Del, my voice quivering.

Second unleashes his toothy grin at Del, Riot's humanity flashing into existence for the shortest moment.

I pull the chain that I *always* hold in my pocket.

"Thank you for everything, Riot. Thank you *both*, Veya," Del says, approaching us, his sword slackened at his side, still dripping with the blood of our enemy.

Second nods, his duty encasing him again.

I clasp the Hunter crest around my neck for the first time in two hundred years.

"What is that?" Del asks.

"A piece of me."

He smiles, and something genuine and honest settles between us. "I look forward to learning your story, Veya. *All* of it."

I nod. "I'll tell you, and I need to hear yours. And Patrick—"

Del steps into my space. "Yes, your Highness?" he asks, gaze flitting from the headless king to his new queen.

Through my tears, I offer him a soft smile and lock into his beautiful, earnest eyes. "You can call me Grace."

# CHAPTER 24

## VEYA

Present Day – One Week Later

D EL AND I STEP onto the balcony in the underground Goreon barracks. Blood stores from the Night Kingdom finally arrived today, enough to satisfy the hunger of thousands of trapped, starving warriors.

Males stare up at us.

"*Hail your queen!*" Del announces.

Silence hangs in the air, and then deafening cheers and celebration rattle the railing beneath my hands. I smile at the throbbing mass of warriors.

Del raises his hand, and silence restores itself.

"If you choose to serve me," I begin, "I'll reward you with a life worth living. No more pain, no more pointless killing. You'll never step foot in this prison again. If you prefer to return home to a family or start a new life, please do so. There will be no shame upon you, but you *will* follow the new laws in this land. And if you choose to fight for the crown, you will protect those laws with your life. We'll usher in an era we can all be proud of. But if you don't want this life or don't follow our rules, I'll give you the honor of killing you myself." I stare down at the army that could slaughter their way through any kingdom. "I look forward to releasing you from this horrible place. Blood will be brought to you shortly. Please drink your fill, and then you are free to leave and live your life. Otherwise, please make yourselves comfortable *upstairs*."

One by one, the warriors take a knee before me.

"Thank you in advance for your cooperation. And for those who choose it, thank you for your service."

Doors open below as Night Kingdom guards haul crates of blood stores into the barracks and Goreon soldiers rise from their knees.

I turn to the exit, climbing the stairwell, Del just behind me.

We already eliminated the soldiers Del confirmed participated in unspeakable acts under Nerian and Balor. After the first several offenses came to light, supported by testimony from fellow soldiers, I didn't need to hear any more. Those who remain are at least without transgressions. How they choose to live from this moment on is up to them.

The farm was our first act once Nerian was dead. We removed the ports, and every kitchen and every household in the nearest villages have sent broth and food, blankets and clothing. The humanity of Goreon is now just as it once was, a community, once we nursed it back to life. Families were reunited, and the beginning of a new foundation was formed between vampires and humans in Goreon.

We breach the threshold of the stairwell and stroll into the evening outside toward the castle.

"I need your help destroying something later tonight," I tell Del.

"I thought we agreed *not* to destroy the pretty castle," Del says, shoving his hands in his pockets against the nip in the air.

A rueful laugh escapes my lips. "Just the cellar."

His eyes spark against the night. "I will gladly help you destroy that."

"I thought so."

A soft smile whispers across his face under flickering torches, and thankfulness warms my chest. Del is the one who convinced the king to invite me here. Del handed me the secret to find and kill the king. He fought by our side and trusted us to finish what we started. He was the catalyst for everything, and it culminated in Hunter magic dancing in my veins and me walking in the sun again.

And my promises fulfilled. I am in his debt.

"I can't believe Raven is a vampire," Del whispers, Aurelia's vampire name sliding off his tongue like he can barely stand to say it.

I peer up at him as we walk. "I'm sorry. I know you didn't want that for her."

"Don't be. She'd still be in that cage, death imminent, if it wasn't for you."

"Good thing I accepted that invitation from Nerian."

He smirks. "Good thing."

"We're going to be late," Del says as we reach the castle's entrance.

I laugh. "It's not like they can start without us."

His smile is devastating when I turn to face him. "True," he says.

"Are you ready for an official change in leadership?"

"Yes," he says without hesitation.

We climb the steps into the fortress and make for the antechamber.

Hartley stands a breath from Emmanuel, not touching, as instructed, but close enough that I suppress a smile. The fabric of her gown is draped over the edge of his boots, and the male stares down at her, eyes locked on his doe.

Emmanuel's gaze flicks to me as Del and I approach. "Nice dress," he says to me, and Hartley nods eagerly in agreement with a curtsy.

I laugh. "Hopefully the last gown I'll wear for a long time. And thank you for your service, Em. For helping us get this far to see this day."

"Our work is just beginning," he says.

I nod. "I keep my promises. We'll go to the Southern Continent next, I swear it."

"My queen," Emmanuel says with a dip of his head.

Hartley swivels her joyful face to him. "What's in the Southern Continent?" she asks.

Emmanuel looks down at her. "My homeland."

"Aye," she says. "I'd love to see it."

"Not until it's safe," he says.

She scowls at him. "I'll train. I'll be ready to go with you."

"It'll be a decade before I even consider that as an option."

She dismisses my assassin with a wave. "We'll talk about it."

"We won't," he assures her, and I turn away to hide my smirk.

Nix, Ellie, and Samantha, accompanied by Charlotte and Second, wait by the door to the throne room, and Raven rushes to Del's side. He tucks her under his arm.

"You ready for this?" Charlotte asks with a prideful smile.

I nod, and movement catches my attention as Officer Cave steps out of the shadows.

"You came," I say, voice breaking and tears filling my eyes.

The vampire leans into me. "Your father and brother are bursting with pride. I know it in my *bones*," he whispers.

I glance up at the male who has stood by me for two hundred years, never faltering. "Thank you, Rhett," I whisper back, bursting with gratefulness. "Thank you for being here."

"Wouldn't have missed it for the world, Grace."

I fight back my tears, and my heart warms with my appreciation for Rhett all these years. He joined Riot and me in our mission, twenty years after our first siege on Goreon Castle, knowing he would lose his magic, too. Because the gods stripped Riot of his magic when I turned him. Still, Rhett followed him into that hell.

That will never be a price I ask any Hunter to pay.

Rhett's wife, Rosy, understood his choice to follow us and uphold our promises to Kade. After all, Rosy had a life because Kade rescued her from the dungeons below us and sent her to Lou's when she had nowhere to go, and that's where she found Rhett. They fell in love in a way I know better than most. But then Rhett turned, joining us, and watched Rosy and their children age and die. They're now buried in Lilygate. Rhett is still suffering in that pain.

It's a *cruel* thing, a Hunter losing their magic if they choose to turn. You become everything you hated and lose all that you loved. Riot was the first to ever do that, and the loss of his magic almost killed him. He lost the man he was. A Hunter died, but the gods forced his heart to keep beating.

Immortality for the price of his magic.

I can't imagine losing what runs through my veins now. Yet I'm still unsure what balance will be demanded from me; I'm a vampire and Hunter magic simmers and twirls within me.

"Are you ready?" Del asks, eyes skirting to mine.

I smile at him. "Yes."

He summons the doors open, and we emerge into the crowded hall.

Night Kingdom warriors line the aisle wearing armor and proud faces. We've *all* been waiting for this moment.

Del and I drift down the center, moving with unburdened hearts, side by side, with our populace surrounding us and Second behind us. The throne room brims with Goreon citizens, humans, and vampires waiting to witness the crowning of their new queen. It turns out, most of Nerian's court *hated* life here; their fear kept them in line and in debt to Nerian. I forgave those debts, but it's going to be a long journey as we deal with bloodlust addiction and wealth that needs to be dispersed to the people.

"How do we kill a thousand years of belief and poisoned ideology?" Del asks as we approach the dais.

"I have a plan."

He scoffs. "Of course you do."

"There is always a way," I tell him and glance at my crown resting on the throne before us. "You know, I've thought more about the appointment of the Goreon second."

His responding smolder coaxes an eye roll from me.

"Don't roll those stunning emerald eyes at me, my queen."

I unleash a smile, my heart stuttering unexpectedly at the compliment.

I'm ready for the next chapter. For the next life. My humanity avenged, my kingdom on the brink of peace, my promises fulfilled.

I finger the Hunter pendant at my chest, starving to insert the crest in its intended place and lay eyes on Mortifer once again.

And a visit to Castle Ruthlessness is due. My kinsfolk wait for me.

Del, Second, and I climb the first riser to the dais.

"Did you come to a decision?" Del asks as Second approaches the thrones, lifting my crown, and steps up next to me.

"We'll talk about it afterward," I say as the officiant speaks the inaugural words of Goreon rule, with *several* amendments we made over the past few days.

Del shakes his head at me and my delay in his appointment, but his smile is relentless underneath the joy in his eyes.

"Congratulations, Grace. Forever may you reign," Second whispers as he places the crown on my head.

"Thank you for everything, Riot."

"Until my last breath, in this life and the one after that," he says, sweeping a thumb across my cheek as he secures the crown. "Swords at our backs."

I shudder a breath. "Hearts at our fronts."

"*Aye*," he whispers hoarsely.

And then Riot disappears within himself, and Second steps aside.

I turn to face my people as the Queen of Goreon and claim the crown that will herald the era of the Hunter.

Suddenly, a Night Kingdom soldier bursts through the doors, eyes red and wild, breath heaving, and collapses, his summoned wings limp around him.

*He flew here.*

I snap to him, kneeling next to the warrior as Second and Del drop down beside me a moment later.

Officer Cave lifts his head. "Warrior," he says, jostling him.

The vampire's eyelids slide open. "The Southern Continent has attacked—" he whispers hoarsely.

"Where?" I demand, my guilt surging.

*How did they get past the warriors we sent?*

His cracked lips part, gaze pinned to mine. "Lilygate has fallen."

I shake my head in disbelief, and my breath leaves me.

Our humans. The lives I swore to protect.

All I can do is desperately hope Ben and Victoria and the rest of Lilygate made it to Ruthlessness in time.

Cave curses, and my eyes dart to Second. "We must go. Right now."

"Aye," Second snarls, then screams, "*Horses, now!*" The Night Kingdom soldiers snap to action.

I'll be able to get there first, traveling in daylight. I can make it in less than two days if I don't stop. My heart and adrenaline race, and if I weren't the one everyone was looking to for poise and purpose, I would scream at the top of my lungs and let my tears fall.

But I am queen, and I wrap myself in my duty instead.

I look away from the chaos, turning sharply to Del crouched beside me. "Decision made—you're second of Goreon," I command, and then my voice catches in my throat, worry freezing me, and my thoughts spin as fear for Lilygate attempts to blot out my ability to think. "I'll send word," I finally manage. "We may need your aid before it's over—"

He smiles kindly as my voice breaks. "You're going to want my aid now, *Grace*."

My chest tightens with my human name on Del's lips, but my gaze narrows. "What do you mean?"

Del's plum eyes darken as we rise. "You'll need me, and my brother, to finally take the Southern Continent."

I shake my head, bewildered.

He smirks. "You wanted to know my story. I hail from below the Southern Continent, and I am *Prince* Deleos of Farson."

My eyes blow wide. "I—I don't know what to say. But I need to leave *now*, and I can't stop until I get to Lilygate."

Del's charming smile curls. "Lucky for you, my queen, daylight has never been a problem for me."

With no warning, thick streaks of shadow blast into the air around us, and my magic surges in my veins, rejoicing as Del's power envelops us in darkness.

# ACKNOWLEDGMENTS

I thought long and hard about which manuscript to release as my debut. It's difficult to describe the emotions leading up to putting your first work into the world. Exciting, nauseating, daunting, riddled with uncertainty—but most of all, it's rewarding, and my heart is full. I gave it everything I had. And I couldn't be happier for the creative journey it led me down.

I wrote this book in twenty-five days, which is … insanity. And I felt a certain sort of insane, too. Of course, editing took another month from there, but this was my most whirlwind creation yet, and I'm bursting at the seams for the rest of the series to come out!

Many manuscripts wait in the wings, and I'm just as eager to share them, but this story poured out of me, and I loved it from the moment I put Veya and Kade on paper. And don't get me started on Del and Emmanuel. This book had to come first.

To YOU, my readers, thank you for the privilege of your time. It's such a precious thing. I can't wait for you to get your hands on the rest of this series. We've only just begun. As an indie author tackling all of the publishing tasks myself, your support is *magic*. Along with your posts, reviews, and encouraging messages ... thank you for reading the stories I can't live without telling.

To my very first readers, my mother, Debranne, and my sister-in-law, Kellie: Thank you for trudging through first drafts of all my manuscripts as alpha readers over the past five years, pouring over edited drafts as betas, and now celebrating this final product with me. You believed in me from the start, and I will be forever grateful for that. These pages are for you.

To my father, Marty: You're my biggest cheerleader. The pride you have for your daughter makes my heart sing and my worries disappear.

To my brother, Michael: My steadfast sounding board: Your opinion will always matter to me, and I can't imagine making big life decisions without it.

To Melissa: You answered countless texts with all of my doubts, escaped on writing retreats with me, and *believed* in me without hesitation. Thank you, bb.

To my fellow authors, Brandee and Brooklynn: Thank you for always being there when imposter syndrome kicked in. Your support was crucial, and I will *never* forget it.

To Libby, for keeping me sane.

To Bryn: You listened to this story in its infancy on a road trip to Romantasy Con. The rest is history, and your continued support has been *everything*.

To Justine: You heard the first page I ever wrote of this manuscript, which would end up closing Kade's chapters. Your tear-filled eyes inspired me to get this book written.

To Chanel: It takes a village to get a book into the world, and I'm glad you're a part of it. I'm so thankful for your steady presence, encouragement, and all of your help.

To Danny: You've always supported me, and you never wavered with my author dream. Thank you for encouraging me to step into the light and own the center stage I don't like to stand in.

To Dan and Ali, my photographer and graphic designer: You're both so talented, and I can't wait for the art we get to create together beyond this release.

To my editors, Parisa Zolfaghari and Kelly Helmick: Thank you for your commitment to this project and your valuable advice.

To the staff at Cafe Roze, Schulman's, and Village Pub: Thank you for all the hours on your barstools and witnessing and supporting the journey as it happened.

To Jenna and Caitlin: You set enviable standards and gave me an opportunity that pushed this book into the world with a bang I never dared to hope for: *Thank you* for your support.

To Mackenzie: You've been strapping me into ballgowns and supporting me from the moment I moved to Nashville, thank you.

To Kirsten: You're a last minute life-saver and forever cheerleader, thank you.

To Joshua: This dream made our time together limited and lives busy while I worked both jobs for years …

but here we are, on the other side of the grind to turn the stories living inside me into reality on the page. Thank you for remembering to look beyond the day to the horizon ahead. I love you.

To the authors who have inspired me with their perseverance, talent, and kindness. I'm staring at all of your books on my beloved bookshelf right now, and I can't wait to place this one beside them. Thank you for laying the path for the rest of us.

I'm grateful for the journey this book took me on. Here's to many, many more!

It's time to go write book two of *The Curse of the Vampire Series.*

Until next time,
Kathryn

# KATHRYN KNAPP

## ABOUT THE AUTHOR

Author Kathryn Knapp writes love stories with characters we root for, high stakes that keep us turning pages, and plot twists sure to make us kick our feet ... or throw the book at the wall.

Kathryn currently lives in Tennessee and runs on caffeine, lifting weights, and the love from her community.

You can connect with Kathryn on social media platforms, @katknappwrites, and via her website, www.katknappwrites.com

She would *love* to hear from you.

*THE CURSE OF THE VAMPIRE SERIES*

*BOOK TWO*

*COMING SOON!*

UPDATES AVAILABLE ON
WWW.KATKNAPPWRITES.COM